She rose and made for the cur-tained doorway.

But, with a hand upon her shoulder, Alain turned her gently but firmly to face him.

'Am I not entitled to the customary kiss to seal our betrothal?'

He drew her close, his arms reaching up behind her waist, pressing her to him. Gisela had expected him to kiss her brow or cheek formally, but his lips suddenly closed upon hers, gently at first, then demandingly, so that she was forced to open her own and respond.

'You must not be afraid of me.'

'I am not,' she said huskily. 'I—'

'Good. I shall not expect too much of you—at first.'

Joanna Makepeace taught as head of English in a comprehensive school, before leaving full-time work to write. She lives in Leicester with her mother and a Jack Russell terrier called Jeffrey, and has written over thirty books under different pseudonyms. She loves the old romantic historical films, which she finds more exciting and relaxing than the newer ones.

Recent titles by the same author:

STOLEN HEIRESS
KING'S PAWN
THE DEVIL'S MARK
CROWN HOSTAGE

THE BARON'S BRIDE

Joanna Makepeace

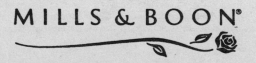

MILLS & BOON®

*First published in Great Britain 1998
Harlequin Mills & Boon Limited,
Eton House, 18-24 Paradise Road, Richmond, Surrey TW9 1SR*

© Joanna Makepeace 1997

ISBN 0 263 80502 6

*Set in Times 10 on 11 pt. by
Rowland Phototypesetting Limited
Bury St Edmunds, Suffolk*

04-9801-79811

*Printed and bound in Great Britain by
Caledonian International Book Manufacturing Ltd, Glasgow*

Chapter One

1152

Gisela could hear the sound of angry voices as she rode through the forest towards Aldith's assart cottage. She glanced worriedly towards Oswin who was riding with her. In this troubled year of 1152, when every man feared attacks upon his property from both known enemies and suspected ones, Walter of Brinkhurst had always insisted that Gisela ride accompanied. Her father's reeve had been inspecting the autumn work on the field strips and was now escorting her on a visit to her former nurse.

Aldith's husband had cut the small assart clearing, but he had died two years ago and Aldith had continued to live in the snug little cottage he'd built for her with her fifteen-year-old-son, Sigurd. Her older son, who had died within the first month of his life, had provided her with the milk to feed Gisela, whose own mother had died soon after the birth, and Aldith had given all of her hungry love for her dead child to her master's daughter.

Though she no longer lived at Brinkhurst Manor, there was still deep affection between them and Gisela visited her nurse frequently.

Gisela put spurs to her palfrey and urged on Oswin, whose usual speed was slow and dignified.

'That sounds as if it is coming from Aldith's cottage. She has always insisted that she is safe there, but Father has been urging her to come to live at Brinkhurst for some time now.'

Within minutes Gisela and her mount burst into the clearing to find Aldith at the gate of her rough wattle fence, facing two men-at-arms and struggling to hold back Sigurd, who was intent on doing one of them some mischief.

Gisela saw by the blue chevron device on their boiled leather coats they were Allestone men. She kicked her feet free of the stirrups, leaped down easily without Oswin's assistance and hastened to reach her frightened nurse, with Oswin puffing more slowly in her wake.

'What is it, Aldith?' she said breathlessly. 'What has Sigurd done?'

She was aware that some of the villeins and serfs frequently broke the forest laws in their pursuit of game. Old Godfrey of Allestone had, like her father, usually turned a blind eye to these proceedings, yet he had, on one or two occasions, delivered judgement on the miscreant at the manor court, though always tempered with mercy.

Now that Godfrey had been killed in a recent skirmish between royal and rebel troops near Gloucester and had had no living heir—his son having died three years before in the war,—the castle and desmesne had been granted to Baron Alain de Treville, by King Stephen.

Gisela knew little about the baron, having seen him only once from a distance in the nearby town of Oakham. He had looked, to her eyes, to be a tall, forbidding figure; she was now afraid that Sigurd might be in trouble and that this man would have little mercy for his misdemeanours.

'He has done nothing, Demoiselle Gisela,' Aldith said, hastily cutting short Sigurd's excited attempt to explain, 'but these fellows say we must leave our cottage before Sunday next. I keep trying to tell them that we have nowhere else to go but this sergeant says. . .' She broke down, tears streaming down her brown, workworn cheeks.

Gisela put a comforting arm round her nurse's shoulders and turned to the intruders.

'I am Gisela of Brinkhurst, the neighbouring manor,' she said peremptorily. 'Aldith is my former nurse. She is very dear to me. What is all this about?'

The older of the two men, a grizzled veteran of about forty, cleared his throat, obviously embarrassed.

'Begging your pardon, demoiselle, I understand your concern, but this is Allestone land and, as you know, to cut an assart in the wood is strictly unlawful.'

'We are all aware of that,' Gisela snapped, 'but there are many such cottages hereabouts. Rolf, Aldith's late husband, worked for Godfrey of Allestone as a skilled forester, a free man, and his assart was tolerated by his master.'

'Aye, demoiselle, but the desmesne now belongs to Baron Alain de Treville and he has ordered me to clear this woodland to a depth of half a mile from Allestone Castle, and, as you can see for yourself, this cottage must be destroyed to allow for the total clearance.'

Aldith burst into tears and Sigurd renewed his attempts to fly at the sergeant.

'Surely some allowance could be made for this cottage. Aldith has lived here for some years and. . .'

'That is quite impossible.' A cold voice broke into Gisela's pleading and she turned hastily to see that a mailed rider had come into the clearing. She had been so intent on Aldith's distress that she had failed to notice the jingle of harness or the soft sound of his courser's progress over the fallen leaves of the forest floor.

She presumed the newcomer was Baron Alain de

Treville from the immediate deference shown to him by
the two men-at-arms. He sat tall in the saddle and she
could discern little of his features under the shadow of
his conical helmet with its jutting nose guard and mailed
coif for, like all men going abroad in these troubled times,
he rode fully armed in mailed hauberk. He gently urged
his mount closer to the opposing parties.

He saw a woman clad in an enveloping mantle of dark
blue wool, caught upon the right shoulder by a heavy
gold clasp which told him she was of knightly class.
Even if it had not done so, the very regal stance and the
haughty poise of her head would have informed him.

Her hair was mainly hidden beneath her head veil of
fine linen and held in place by a simple fillet, covered
in the same blue wool as her mantle, but he could just
see, by an escaping strand from one braid, that she was
fair. He had little chance to judge the stature of her figure,
but the rigidity of her form as she stood proud and erect
made him sure she was slim and very young.

His brown eyes flashed as he recognised a like spirit
to his own. He had heard her high, imperious tones as
he had ridden through the wood and he knew this to be
a woman to match him in stubborn determination. His
long lips twitched slightly as he bowed his head in courteous acknowledgement of her rank. He dismounted and
handed his reins to the younger of his two men and came
striding unhurriedly towards her.

'Demoiselle, I must reiterate that what you ask is
impossible. I regret it must be so, but there it is. I am
Alain de Treville, and you, I surmise, are the daughter
of my near neighbour, Walter of Brinkhurst.'

He shrugged slightly in the Gallic fashion and the
unusual intonation of his Norman French told her he had
probably come originally from the dukedom overseas
and had only lived in England for a few years.

Her lips trembled mutinously. 'Yes, I am Gisela of

Brinkhurst and, as I was explaining to your sergeant here, Aldith, whose cottage this is, is my former nurse and we are very fond of her and anxious to ensure her welfare. She cannot be cast from her home with so little consideration.'

'Believe me, demoiselle, I have given this matter every consideration. This woodland must be cut back to give my garrison a clear view of any approaching enemy force. Your father will explain that it is a very usual tactic. King Stephen has commanded me to improve Allestone's defences, which have been neglected sorely of late.

'Your father will also agree with me that there have been frequent attacks on property in this district by unscrupulous mercenaries. He must be well aware of the need for defensive measures himself.'

His eyes dwelt momentarily upon Gisela's still-indignant form and then travelled to Oswin, whose portly figure and frowning expression revealing alarm at this unfortunate encounter, hovered anxiously some little distance behind his young mistress.

'I see you *do* have an escort, but I consider one man is hardly sufficient to protect you should you be ambushed. I would have thought at least two sturdy men-at-arms would be necessary to accompany you when you leave the boundaries of your father's land.'

'Oswin is perfectly trustworthy,' Gisela snapped irritably. Her father had, indeed, often remonstrated with her recently over such rash behaviour for she had sometimes ventured from the manor lands alone and, as a result of her father's anger, had suffered curtailment of the freedom she had formerly enjoyed since childhood.

'I am sure he is,' the Baron replied mildly as if to a fractious child, 'but it is possible to be too reckless of one's own safety these days and, if you were my daughter, I would insist on more stringent precautions.'

'Quite likely you would,' Gisela returned drily, 'but I am no kin of yours. Now, can we return to the matter in hand? Surely you can make an exception in the case of this one small building?'

He stood facing her, feet astride, one hand upon the serviceable hilt of his longsword. She was annoyed that he continued to smile as if he were reasoning with a child who did not understand the point at issue.

'Demoiselle, you must see that such an exception would defeat the object of the exercise. Your nurse is vulnerable here. The improved defences of Allestone Castle are for her advantage and the rest of the serfs and villeins nearby, as well as for your father and his neighbours, for the castle garrison is at his service should he need to call on it.'

'I hardly think that will be necessary.' Gisela knew her shrillness of tone could be deemed rude and somewhat ungracious for such an offer but she was so incensed by his lordliness that she could not prevent herself from blurting it out.

'I hope your father is of the same opinion,' de Treville commented pithily and she blushed hotly.

'My father has defended his own manor and been ready to answer the King's call and to go to the assistance of his neighbours,' she retorted.

He made no answer and his very silence added to her feeling that her behaviour was both callow and boorish.

'It is not to be borne,' she said angrily. 'Why should Aldith be made homeless simply for a whim of the new master of Allestone?'

'I am prepared to offer your nurse accommodation within the castle precincts where she and her son will be adequately protected,' he replied smoothly, which rather took the wind from her sails and made her draw in breath quickly.

'But there is the question of her vegetable plot. How

will she survive the winter when that is destroyed?'

'Again, I am perfectly prepared to provide for her and the boy. She can take service within the castle.'

Aldith clutched agitatedly at Gisela's arm and she turned to face her. It was evident from her expression and the meaningful glances she directed at first her son, and then the Baron, that she feared for Sigurd within the castle enclosure.

The boy would not bow down easily to discipline. Since his father's death he had roved the forest fearlessly at will, and, doubtless, acquired food for the pot both from the woodland and possibly from the Baron's own private preserves of stew ponds and rabbit warrens.

Gisela said hastily, 'That will not be necessary. Aldith and Sigurd must come to Brinkhurst. I know my father will receive them. I will make arrangements for her belongings to be fetched tomorrow.'

She heard Aldith sigh with relief behind her.

The Baron bowed in answer. 'As you wish, demoiselle,' he said quietly, 'but should your father not wish to accept them, they must come immediately to Allestone.'

He turned as if to move back to his courser, having decided that the matter had been settled satisfactorily. Gisela gave her attention to Aldith and neither of them was aware of what happened next until it was too late. Sigurd gave a great snarl of fury and, leaping the wattle fence, made for his tormentor, whose defenceless back was turned towards him. Gisela heard the boy shout something she could not catch and then came a sudden oath in French from de Treville.

She turned horrified eyes to see the flash of a blade in the November sunlight and to discover that the boy and de Treville were struggling together. Gisela caught Aldith's arm to prevent her rushing to her son's assistance and could only watch helplessly with the two men, who had also been taken completely by surprise.

De Treville must have had ears like a lynx for he had discerned before any of them footsteps coming towards him across the fallen leaves. He had swung round in an instant and wrestled with the boy's arm and now held his wrist in a cruel grasp which made Sigurd give a sudden animal cry of pain.

Gisela saw the hunting knife fall from the boy's hand on to the leaves below and the older of the men-at-arms rushed forward to secure it. He bawled a quick command to his companion, who rushed to the Baron's side, ready to give immediate assistance.

Still de Treville held on to Sigurd's wrist and Gisela saw the boy's face contort in pain and the colour drain from it. Aldith cried out in fear for her son and alarm for the Baron's safety. Gisela thought de Treville would break the boy's wrist as, inexorably, he forced the arm back and back until he released his hold abruptly and Sigurd gave another hoarse half-scream and fell back into the brawny arms of the man-at-arms behind him.

Then, and then only, did de Treville speak. 'Secure him and bring him to Allestone.' The voice was deadly calm and ice cold.

'No, no, oh please——' Aldith burst through the gate and ran towards the Norman baron. '——please, please do not hurt him any more. He was mad with fury. He is just a boy and meant no real harm.'

'Indeed?' De Treville raised two dark eyebrows that Gisela could just discern beneath the rim of his iron helmet and placed his right arm across the mailed sleeve of his left. To Gisela's amazement and deepening alarm, she saw that blood was welling between the rings of the hauberk. She would not have believed that Sigurd's knife could have done such damage and in so short a time.

'You are hurt,' she blurted out, somewhat foolishly she realised later.

His reply was typically ironic. 'So you have noticed, demoiselle.' He waved away his sergeant, who had been overseeing the pinioning of Sigurd's arms behind his back by his younger companion with a coil of rope taken from one of the saddle bags and who was now advancing upon his lord to offer help.

'No, no, man, it is but a scratch, but could have been worse. The knife might well have been buried in my back had I not turned in time.' He regarded the little scene, unsmiling, while Aldith, sobbing, tore a strip from her voluminous skirt and proffered it to him with trembling hands. He thanked her coldly and, using teeth and his uninjured hand, bound it about the wound.

Gisela now regained her wits and came hurriedly towards him. 'My lord,' she said huskily, 'I am sure Aldith is right. The boy is beside himself and did not know what he was about. I beg you to take that into consideration when he is brought before you in the manor court. I'm sure my father will speak for him and. . .'

Again de Treville regarded her sardonically. 'I dread to think what he might have attempted, demoiselle, had he *really* meant me harm. However, we will give ourselves time to think this affair over when we all have cooler heads. In the meantime, your young protégé can cool his within the depths of my gatehouse guardroom.'

The sergeant had secured the rope pinioning Sigurd's arms to the back of his horse and clearly intended to drag the boy behind him on the short ride to Allestone Castle. The Baron nodded to Gisela and Aldith coolly and moved once more to his own horse. Gisela saw he had some difficulty in mounting and was further distressed. Obviously the arm pained him more than he would admit.

If the injury proved serious, Sigurd could pay for his reckless boy's temper with his life. Even if it were not to prove so, many lords would not be inclined to mercy, she knew. She was impelled to plead for the boy again.

'My lord, I beg of you. . .'

He turned just once in the saddle. 'I see, demoiselle, that you are far more concerned for the boy's fate than for mine.' He sighed and she thought, with rising temper, that it was an exaggerated sigh, made merely to cause her concern and possibly to taunt her to further outbursts. She controlled her rising irritation with an effort.

'Naturally, my lord, I am deeply sorry that you are hurt, but you said yourself it is merely a scratch. I beg you to consider that when giving judgement.'

His good hand caught at the bridle rein. 'Usually, demoiselle, I am more concerned to discover what was intended rather than the result and, in this case, you must agree, I would be right to infer that the boy intended to deliver a death blow.'

Before she could make any reply—indeed, she could not really think of a suitable one—he had bowed again in the saddle and urged his men to mount up and ride from the clearing. The two stricken women and Oswin were left to stare helplessly as the three mounted soldiers rode from their sight, the sergeant relentlessly pulling the gasping, stumbling form of Aldith's son behind him.

Only then did the reeve venture a comment. 'Demoiselle Gisela, I think you would be very unwise to make any move to anger the Baron de Treville further. I am sure your father, Sir Walter, would be concerned. Indeed, he might infer from what has occurred that we were instrumental in causing this injury. . .'

'Do you suggest that I encouraged Sigurd to do that?' Gisela demanded furiously and the old man stepped hastily backwards, knowing the intensity of his mistress's feelings when she took it into her head to champion the cause of one or other of the serfs upon the manor.

'Certainly not, demoiselle,' he said hastily, 'but—but

had we not been here, the soldiers would have managed and—and. . .'

Gisela swallowed the sharp bile rising in her throat. She was beginning to believe that, to some extent, Oswin could be right; yet Sigurd had already been furiously angry when they arrived on the scene. She drew a deep breath. She was going to have a very hard job to save the impetuous young fool. She put a comforting arm round Aldith's shoulders.

'Come into the cottage. You can do nothing for the moment. I promise you, Aldith, both I and Father will do our best for Sigurd, whatever Oswin says.' Her blue eyes flashed fire at the hapless reeve, who quailed inwardly and then gave way and prepared to wait outside the cottage stolidly until his mistress was ready to ride back to Brinkhurst.

Gisela persuaded Aldith that she must come at once to Brinkhurst. She could not leave the distraught woman here alone in this cottage.

It would not be beyond the bounds of possibility for Baron Alain de Treville to send men immediately to oust her and destroy the cottage immediately. Punishment must be fast and severe if discipline was to be maintained on his desmesne and, from what she had seen of him, he would rule with an iron hand and not encased in a soft leather glove, either!

Aldith, still weeping, gathered up a bundle of her own clothing and Sigurd's and one or two items she specially prized as being of her husband Rolf's fashioning, and Gisela briskly promised that she would send two men with a cart later to convey the one or two pieces of crudely fashioned furniture the two possessed.

Neither woman dared give voice to the fear that Sigurd would not live to require his belongings. Oswin took up the former nurse pillion behind him and they rode back to Brinkhurst in sombre mood.

Both disturbed and angered by her encounter in Allestone wood, Gisela rode into the courtyard of the Brinkhurst manor, dismounted hurriedly and handed her reins to a young groom who hastened to serve her.

She instructed Oswin to see to it that Aldith and her bundles were conveyed to the kitchen quarters, where she must be fed and cosseted until Gisela had had opportunity to explain what had occurred to her father and make arrangements for Aldith's reception into the household.

She hastened up the steps before the undercroft and into the hall. Her father was seated by the fire, for the November day was chill and raw, and a man seated opposite rose instantly and came towards her with a delighted cry. She almost ran to meet him, her own anxious expression lighting up with unexpected pleasure.

'Kenrick, how good it is to see you. I didn't know you were expected or I would not have gone out this morning to see Aldith.'

'And how is she?' Her father smiled his welcome as his daughter divested herself of her mantle and came to his side near the fire.

Kenrick of Arcote, their nearest neighbour, only a few years older than Gisela and her friend from babyhood, caught his breath, as he always did at sight of her these days. Gisela of Brinkhurst was now on the brink of womanhood.

She was not over-tall for a woman, but stately of poise and already her youthful, budding breasts were thrusting tight against the cloth of her blue woollen gown. He was sure he could have encircled her waist, cinched in tightly with her ornamental leather belt, with one hand, so slight of form was she. Her luxuriant tawny braids caught golden lights from the fire as she moved nearer to her father.

He thought her heart-shaped face with its small, slightly tip-tilted nose, her luminous blue eyes and generous, sensuous mouth with its slightly fuller lower lip, even the remains of the summer freckling on nose and cheeks—for Gisela rode out in all weathers despite her former nurse's warnings about the ruination of her fair complexion—quite enchanting. Now he saw, as her father had already noted, that something had disturbed her badly.

Sir Walter urged her down upon a stool beside him and placed a gentle hand upon her bowed head.

'What is it, Gisela?' His heart thudded against his ribcage as he thought she might well have been accosted, even molested, on this ride into Allestone wood. 'You have not encountered masterless men abroad and had to ride hard to safety?'

'No, nothing like that,' she assured him hastily and turned, a little uncertain smile parting her lips, to face the anxious frown she could see gathering on Kenrick's brow.

'No, I have been in no danger. It is Sigurd, Father. He—he attacked the Lord Baron of Allestone Castle and—and he has been arrested and imprisoned there. It is very serious. Aldith is terribly upset and I have brought her here to Brinkhurst. You will give her shelter?'

'Of course, child. You know we owe so much to Aldith we can never repay her adequately. You say Sigurd dared to attack Alain de Treville? How in the world could that happen with the Baron well guarded? Is he seriously hurt?'

Gisela choked back tears as she tried to marshal her thoughts to tell of the encounter coherently. She explained the Baron's determination to oust Aldith and her son from their home and his reason for clearing the land and her own objections and attempts to dissuade him.

Her eyes clouded with tears as she burst out, 'Then—then he refused point blank to reconsider and made to move away. Sigurd—he—sprang at him with a knife—and—and the Baron's arm was injured. Fortunately he had the presence of mind to turn in time or—or—he might have been killed.'

She read the dawning horror in both her listeners' eyes and added, tearfully, 'I—I blame myself for what—what happened. I should not have interfered. I think—poor Sigurd took that as encouragement for his cause and—and he lost all control.' She stopped and turned away.

'Father, I know how terrible a crime this is, to attempt to kill your lord. In spite of everything, Sigurd is still just a boy and—and you *will* try to save him, won't you, for Aldith's sake?'

Walter of Brinkhurst let out an explosion of breath and leaned back in his chair, considering for a moment.

'Gisela, as you've said, this is a very serious matter indeed. Sigurd may well hang for this, or be maimed, at the very least. The boy is getting past control. I've said as much to Aldith many a time recently. Now, child, stop weeping, you will make yourself ill. You cannot blame yourself. The boy could well have done this whether or no you were present.'

Kenrick gave a hasty nod of agreement to this last statement.

Walter went on, 'Though, I have to say, you were unwise to come to odds with Lord Alain over this. He is quite within his rights to clear his own land for defensive purposes and Aldith's assart was cut by Rolf unlawfully. It is to be hoped that your disagreement with the Baron has not further prejudiced him against the boy. Such a man is unlikely to countenance any criticism of his orders, especially before his men.

'I cannot say how I would have reacted to that myself. However,' he added hastily, as he saw his daughter's eyes begin to brim with tears again, 'what's done is done and we must make the best of it we can. Certainly I will plead for the lad at the manor court, but I have to warn you that my intercession is unlikely to be received well by my neighbour. From what I hear of the man, he makes his own decisions, consulting with no one, and likes to keep himself to himself.'

Gisela reached up to hug her father. She loved him dearly, this broad-built, heavily muscled, still-active and attractive man, whose brown hair was beginning to recede now from his brow. His round, blunt-featured face with the brown eyes that were often disposed to twinkle whenever he gazed on his lovely daughter, the apple of his eye, but which now had darkened with concern for her distress and the reason for it, began to take on an expression of very real alarm.

Baron Alain de Treville had been sent by King Stephen expressly to assist the shire reeve of Oakham to keep the peace in this district and Walter of Brinkhurst felt distinctly uneasy at being the man to oppose him on any matter. He fervently wished his daughter had never met and come into open conflict with his most powerful neighbour.

He gave another heavy sigh. 'We may have need of this man in the future, so be circumspect in your dealings with him. Kenrick has come to inform us of another attack on a nearby manor, this time only five miles on the far side of Oakham, more than likely the work of that devil, Mauger of Offen, or the rabble of unruly routiers he keeps to attend him.'

Gisela turned a horrified face to Kenrick. 'Were people killed?'

'Fortunately not. The family was away attending a wedding in Leicester Town. When the place was attacked the household servants fled into the forest land nearby and only returned when it was all over, but the manor house was sacked and its valuables stolen, then the house was fired. It's unlikely it will be habitable this winter.

'Only the sense of preservation of the serfs in the village in running and hiding saved their womenfolk from pillage and rape. As your father says, Gisela, it isn't safe these days for you to ride far from the desmesne without suitable escort. This unrest has been going on far too long. It is time Mauger was brought to justice. Everyone in the shire knows who is responsible for these depredations.'

Sir Walter shook his head regretfully. 'The wily fellow covers his tracks and disowns those fellows who *are* caught. The King is too busied with continued insurrection throughout the realm to be concerning himself with our small pocket of land here.

'In the South, men are suffering far worse. There is talk of merchants being savagely tortured to reveal hidden wealth, nuns ravished and priests murdered while church plate is plundered and no man can trust his neighbours. It is a sorry state of affairs when our King and his cousin, the Empress Matilda, cannot reach an equable solution of their differences.'

Gisela said fiercely, 'Father, you said all men swore allegiance to the Lady Matilda when commanded to by her father, the late King Henry. Why didn't the barons keep faith—simply because she is a woman?'

Her father shrugged. 'There is no binding law which says in England that the eldest son of the monarch must inherit. Even before King William came to our shores from Normandy he believed he had right of inheritance, but the Witan chose Harold Godwinson to be King and William only succeeded in his claim by his victory at Senlac.

'William's oldest son did not succeed him to the English throne. William, called Rufus, became our King and, after him, his brother, King Henry. It is likely that

his son would have inherited but, as you know, he was
lost in the tragedy of the wreck of the *White Ship*, a
terrible blow to his father. Yet life continued to be
unsettled and, on his death, the council almost unani-
mously decided that his sister Adela's son, Stephen,
should be our King.

'I cannot help agreeing that they were right. The
English barons and earls will not readily accept a woman
to rule over them, not even one so strong and formidable
as the Lady Matilda.'

Giscla's mouth set in a hard line. 'Yet many men
do support her. Her half-brother, Robert of Gloucester,
accepts her as sovereign lady.'

Walter nodded, pursing his lips. 'Aye, and so battle
has been waged these many years. I cannot believe now
Matilda will ever ascend the throne. Unfortunately, I
cannot place much hope for peace in the King's eldest
son, Eustace, who has proven himself feckless and
unstable. I wish it were otherwise.

'Stephen is a fine soldier, too chivalrous for his
own good. A King needs to be ruthless to prosper. The
Conqueror proved that. Men are tired of war and the
barons must make soon an acceptable treaty with
Matilda's supporters for the good of the realm. Rumours
abound that the King is ailing. Meanwhile, we continue
to suffer from the unspeakable behaviour of men like
Mauger, who thrive on unrest.'

'And you think this man, de Treville, will be able to
bring order to the shire?' Kenrick asked.

'He is the younger son of a knightly family in
Normandy who came here to make his way in the world.
He has served the King well, they say, and has a repu-
tation as an efficient and ruthless commander.'

'He doesn't appear old enough to have achieved such
a reputation,' Gisela said, 'though I could not see his
features clearly. He was armoured and wore his helmet.'

'He must be in his middle twenties,' Walter mused, 'possibly close to thirty. He's said to be a hard man, but just.'

'Which does not augur well for Sigurd's chances,' Gisela said gloomily.

Kenrick rose, nodding courteously at his host. 'I should be returning to Arcote. My mother worries herself almost into a panic these days if I am even a fraction late returning.'

'Understandable,' Sir Walter grunted.

Gisela scrambled to her feet. 'I will go with you to the stables. My palfrey seemed a trifle lame this morning and I want to make sure the grooms are examining her properly and tending to her if necessary. I was in too much of a hurry to tell Father of Sigurd's plight when I arrived home to give instructions properly.' She slipped her discarded mantle round her shoulders as Kenrick drew on his own which had been draped over a stool.

He watched her as she spoke anxiously with the head groom, who reassured her about her palfrey's condition and promised to keep the animal under surveillance for any signs of further discomfort.

Kenrick's desires were quickened by her nearness as they moved together outside the stable while he waited for his own mount to be brought out. He would have declared himself to her father long ago had it not been for his doubts about his mother's declining health.

She had seemed to ail continually since the death of his father two years ago and, more and more, clung to her sturdy, handsome young son for comfort, so much so that her constant demands for attention were becoming irksome. He looked now at Gisela's radiantly healthy countenance and mentally compared it with that of the sickly, pale creature awaiting him at Arcote.

He longed to wed Gisela and take her to be mistress

there, but knew there would be constant conflicts of wills between the two women and was not sure if he could honourably request Gisela's hand of her father. He was aware also that she was now ripe for marriage and if he did not do so soon, he might well lose her. He must tackle his mother on the delicate subject of his marriage, tonight if possible or tomorrow if she had insisted on retiring early to her chamber.

Gisela watched him as he rode off, a smile lingering round her lips. Kenrick was a kindly man. He would never have uprooted Aldith so ruthlessly and so precipitously brought about this terrible trouble to Sigurd.

She had been considering recently that perhaps Kenrick, who came so often to Brinkhurst on some excuse or other, would ask for her hand in marriage. She had also allowed herself to consider that life at Arcote with so considerate and admiring a young husband could be very pleasant indeed.

She liked the openness of Kenrick's expression, his curling brown hair and wide-spaced grey eyes. At twenty he was not over-tall, but well set up, hard-muscled, an attractive man who could handle himself well with weapons and in the wrestling ring. Despite his prowess he was not boastful and she perceived no hint of cruelty in his make-up.

In fact, secretly, she thought Kenrick too easy on those who served him and much too compliant with Lady Eadgyth, his demanding mother. Were she to become his wife, she would lead him gently in the way he should rule at Arcote.

Alain de Treville strode purposefully into the hall of Allestone Castle and bawled for his squire, Huon. He stopped as he entered through the screen doors to see he had a visitor, who rose from his seat by the fire to meet his host.

'Rainald,' Alain said delightedly, 'how good it is to see you. Do you come on the King's business?'

The two friends clasped arms and Rainald de Tourel stepped back in some alarm when his friendly squeeze of the arms was met with a sharp, hastily suppressed gasp of pain.

'By all the saints, Alain, you are hurt? Have you been ambushed?'

Alain de Treville sank down wearily into the opposite armchair and looked up as Huon came running.

'Not exactly.' He grimaced. 'I was involved in an altercation about the clearance of land in the wood when one of my tenants took strong objection and decided to end me.'

'God in Heaven!' De Tourel snapped at the boy, who was staring in dawning horror at the blood welling up on his master's sleeve through the improvised bandage, 'Get that Jewish physician here at once and bring warmed water and towels. Your master has been wounded.'

The boy scuttled off and de Treville leaned back, grimacing as the pain of the wound was beginning to make itself felt.

'Stand up,' Rainald de Tourel ordered. 'Let me help you off with your hauberk. The boy will be back soon with your physician. How in the name of the Virgin could this happen and you well guarded, I hope?'

De Treville did as his friend commanded and gave only the slightest of grunts as the painful business of divesting him of his mailed hauberk was concluded. He explained briefly what had occurred.

'I cannot, in justice, blame the men for being off guard. My back was turned and I had no expectation of the attack. God be thanked I heard the boy approach over the fallen leaves, though he moved like a cat, and was in time to prevent him stabbing me in the back or, more likely, the neck.' He grinned faintly. 'I have the lad securely locked in the guardhouse.'

'You should have hanged him out of hand,' de Tourel commented tersely, 'and left the body dangling from the keep to show the rest of the villagers you mean business.'

'Yes, I might well do that after he's been brought before me in the manor court, but the lady will not like that. Already she considers me a Norman barbarian and a tyrant to boot.'

'What lady is this?'

'Ah, I forgot to tell you that bit. The two Saxons were defended by a young termagant, the daughter of my nearest neighbour, the Demoiselle Gisela of Brinkhurst. I think she was far more concerned about the boy's fate than my survival, more or less told me the whole business was my own fault for insisting on my right as desmesne lord.'

Rainald made a comical gesture. 'She appears to have made an impression on you, my friend. Ah, here is your physician and the boy with water and towels.'

An elderly Jew, clad in the dark blue gaberdine robe of his calling, came unhurriedly to his master's side and bent to examine the wounded arm. Behind him hovered the alarmed Huon.

'Mmm,' the physician murmured. 'It does not appear too serious, my lord, but we must cut your sleeve and lay it bare, then we shall know more. Our most imperative task is to ensure there is no dirt or fragments of cloth in the wound. It may need to be stitched.'

Alain grimaced again. 'Oh, very well, Joshua, submit me to your torments. I'll not complain.' He set his teeth again as the physician opened his small chest containing instruments and medicaments, extracted a slim, long blade and slit the long woollen sleeve of the tight-fitting tunic de Treville wore beneath his hauberk, then with gentle fingers probed the cut.

The Jewish physician worked quickly and in silence,

gesturing to Huon to come close with the metal dish of warmed water. He declared it unnecessary, after examination, to stitch the wound, but drew the edges together carefully after cleansing it with vinegar and wine, which made de Treville gasp and curse briefly, then he bound up the wound, made obeisances to the two Norman knights and, waving to the boy to withdraw with him, left the hall.

He had advised de Treville to drink watered wine to replace the blood loss, but not to overheat his system with too much wine and to eat sparingly and take himself off to bed as soon as convenient. De Tourel poured for his friend and watched, frowning, as Alain drained the cup.

'That fellow is a treasure. I hear he has saved your life on more than one occasion—but then, you saved *his* hide, I understand. He should be and is grateful.'

'Joshua is a fine physician and, more importantly, knows when to hold his tongue from too much gratuitous advice.' Alain de Treville's long lips curved into a smile. 'As you perhaps do not know, he was taken by routiers, his house burned and his family murdered. It was lucky my company came along in time before they roasted him over a slow fire to make him divulge the whereabouts of treasures he did not possess. We put the fellows to flight and rescued Joshua ben Suleiman. He has been in my service ever since and has saved my hide many times on campaign.' He laughed out loud. 'Faith, I think he was hoping for a quieter life since we settled here at Allestone, but this affair bodes ill for our hopes.'

'Are you having trouble with your villeins?'

'No, just with my neighbours, it seems.'

De Tourel's merry brown eyes met the darker ones of his friend and they both laughed.

'Do you anticipate trouble with her father?'

'I sincerely hope not, since I intend to further my acquaintance with the lady more closely.'

'Ah, then she is pretty?'

De Treville raised one eyebrow as he considered. 'Truth to tell, I am not sure, she was so hooded and muffled in her mantle. I could see by the way she carried herself that her figure is pleasing and she is fair. I saw just a glimpse of tawny hair and—' he laughed joyously '—what counts most with me is that she has spirit enough to match that of two good men. By the saints, Rainald, I was greatly taken with the wench.'

De Tourel looked thoughtfully round the sparsely furnished and appointed hall, noting its lack of tapestries and hangings to keep out the draughts and only the most elementary luxuries.

'You know, Alain, it is more than time you considered taking a wife. This place needs an efficient chatelaine to oversee the work and enhance its comforts. Allestone is a fine castle and you are fortunate to have it within the King's gift, but it could be considerably more comfortable.

'Incidentally, I am on no particular business, as you asked when you first came in. I am on my way to join the royal army. It's likely Stephen will lay siege to Wallingford soon and will need my support. The last time I was at Court he asked after you and, strangely enough, expressed a hope that you would soon marry and get an heir.'

He gave a little regretful sigh. 'He sorely misses the late Queen, you know. That was a love match indeed and he thinks we should all be so blessed. Her death was a terrible blow to him.'

Alain nodded thoughtfully as he sipped his watered wine and experimentally moved his sore arm. 'She was a fine woman and as good a commander as her lord. I do not know what he would have done without her on many occasions. Think what pains she took to have him released when the Empress held him prisoner.'

'So, this little demoiselle is unwed?'

'Yes, so I hear.'

'Not betrothed?'

'I have heard nothing about that.' Alain laughed again. 'Do not take my telling of this encounter too seriously, my friend. I have talked with the demoiselle but once, but I confess my curiosity to see her at close quarters is piqued. She has Saxon blood, as do many of the knights and squires in the shire. If I took one of their women to wife, it might be pleasing to the community and be more likely to achieve their willing co-operation in the defence of the district.

'I think one or two look on me as an interloper, especially since I was born in Normandy. She is young and appeared healthy; she could give me sturdy children, I think. I have no great need for her to possess a large dower, though that, too, would prove beneficial. You might be right. The time has come for me to settle down and marriage could be the first step in establishing myself in the shire.'

'So you will visit her father?'

Again Alain de Treville's eyebrow was raised comically. 'Nothing so definite. She, I am sure, will come to me.'

'How?'

'Well, I hold her young protégé in my dungeon, don't I? His fate is very much in my hands. Unless I am very much mistaken, she will attend my manor court when the boy is arraigned.'

De Tourel's expression became more grave. 'You cannot afford to lose face, my friend, even to please the lady. You must treat this attack upon your person with the gravity it deserves. The boy must be severely punished.'

De Treville's dark brown eyes met his squarely. 'I am

well aware of that, Rainald. My hold on this castle and
the desmesne must be absolute, and my villeins and serfs
made to be aware that I will brook no trace of indisci-
pline. The question is—how do I accomplish this without
further antagonising my neighbour and avoid once more
coming into open conflict with his daughter?'

Chapter Two

Gisela shivered as she, her father and Aldith passed under the grim gatehouse arch of Allestone Castle. Here, somewhere in one of the guardrooms, Sigurd had been confined or, possibly, he had been moved to an even less salubrious dungeon below the castle keep. As they cantered into the inner bailey, grooms hastened forward to take their bridle reins and one helped Aldith down, for she had been riding pillion behind Sir Walter.

Another attentive straw-haired young man, more stylishly dressed, with a round, boyish face hurried to lift up two arms offering to assist Gisela down. She allowed him to help her and waited until her father joined them and their horses were led away to the stables. Aldith stared bleakly at the tall keep before them and then at the ground.

Sir Walter identified himself and his daughter and servant and explained the reason for their arrival.

'I understand, the boy, Sigurd, is to be brought before your lord today and, since Aldith, here, is his mother and naturally very concerned for him, we hope your lord will not be offended by our presence at the manor court. My daughter, the Demoiselle Gisela, was present on the unfortunate occasion of the attack and is anxious to hear his fate.'

The young man bowed. 'I am Huon, Lord Alain's squire. Allow me to escort you into the hall. I know he will wish me to afford you every courtesy. I will see to it that chairs or stools are provided for you.'

Gisela thought he looked very young for a squire; indeed his polished manners and boyish intensity suggested he had only recently completed service at some other household as a page. He led them up the steps to the entrance of the castle keep and stood back politely for them to precede him into the great hall.

Aldith padded silently in the rear, looking neither to right nor to left. Gisela cast her a worried glance. She felt Aldith had little or no hope for her son's survival. After that first day when she had arrived at Brinkhurst and wept hopelessly, they had had hardly one word from her since. She had attended Gisela efficiently as she had formerly when she had been her nurse and, privately, Gisela, who had missed her sorely, was pleased to have her back at Brinkhurst.

As she was escorted to the front of the little knot of villeins and serfs gathered for the manor court to stools brought hastily for their use by servants summoned to attend them, Gisela reached out and placed a comforting arm round Aldith's shoulders as she seated herself. Sir Walter gently but firmly pressed the woman into a stool by Gisela's side while he took another brought for him. Gisela took Aldith's hand and her maid sat listlessly not even gazing round the great hall.

Gisela, for her part, stared round curiously. The hall was circular with a small gallery at one end. There was a central hearth and a lantern trap above it for smoke to escape, but it appeared it was rarely used these days for another, more ornate, hearth had been constructed beneath the gallery near the dais where, presumably, the Baron sat at meat, at the far end.

She gazed up at the huge smoke-blackened roof

timbers and round at the solid stone walls. The place had
certainly been built primarily for defence only, for there
seemed no vestige of comfort to be had here. One arras
near the dais looked dirty and torn and would do nothing
to keep out draughts, nor did it do anything to soften
the uncompromising grimness of the hall's general
appearance.

True, the rushes underfoot had been freshly strewn and
the place was swept scrupulously clean. She tightened her
lips as she thought how this new lord kept discipline
within his desmesne. If his servants feared him, and he
was certainly well and efficiently attended, it did not
augur well for Sigurd's chances of mercy.

There was a little stir behind the dais and the group
of villagers, awkward and undoubtedly worried about
their own summonses to attend this court, stopped whis-
pering together and looked expectantly for their lord to
enter. A door beneath the gallery was opened and two
men stepped through.

Gisela instantly recognised the tall form of Baron
Alain de Treville; behind him came a smaller, grey-haired
man who walked with a stoop and advanced uncertainly
as if he were short-sighted.

'Sir Clement de Burgh,' her father whispered in her
ear. 'The Baron's seneschal. The man served Sir Godfrey
before him for many years.'

Gisela found herself staring intently at Allestone's
lord. For the first time she could see his features clearly,
for today he was devoid of his military garb and wore a
tawny over-tunic over a longer brown one, with a tawny-
lined brown mantle over them for the hall was chilly.
She noted at once that a border of coarse linen bandaging
showed beneath the tight sleeve of one arm and she
swallowed uncertainly.

She had known he was tall and carried himself like a
prince; now she saw he was broad-shouldered and slim-

hipped also, recognising the steel-like strength inherent
in that spare, well-muscled body. His hair was cut short
in the slightly outdated style Norman knights adopted
for convenience beneath the conical helmet. His face was
oval, tanned, smooth complexioned, without the rough-
ness she associated with life out of doors on campaign.

The features were arresting, the nose slightly over-long
and very straight beneath dark level brows, which were
drawn together now as he stood in the doorway and
surveyed the company. His eyes were very dark brown,
almost black, and she felt the chilling quality of their
steady gaze and pitied those poor creatures who were
trembling as they stood before him now, awaiting judgement in the body of the hall.

His mouth was held in a hard line, as if in concentration, but was long-lipped and without the trap-like
rigidity she had noted in men of her father's company
whom she suspected of harshness or even cruelty to their
subordinates.

His eyes, roving the hall, found and recognised his
neighbours. He bowed his head courteously to Sir Walter
and his daughter and smiled approval as he saw they had
been given stools.

'Sir Walter, you are very welcome to Allestone. I confess I rather expected you would take an active interest
in the proceedings this morning.' The mouth relaxed in
a slight smile. 'I bid you good day, Demoiselle Gisela.
As a witness to the attack on my person, I am grateful
that you have placed yourself at the disposal of the court.'

Gisela's lips parted in her shock at the sheer effrontery
of his statement—and in public. Did he expect her to
add more damaging testimony than his own to the evidence which would doom Sigurd?

He was continuing to speak in that low, quiet voice
that she was sure brooked no argument from underlings.

'I hope, Sir Walter, that, at the conclusion of these

proceedings, you and your daughter will stay and take refreshment with me? There are one or two matters, sir, on which I would value your opinion.'

Sir Walter inclined his head. 'I shall be delighted to do so, lord Baron.'

Angered by her father's apparent subservience, Gisela cast him an outraged glance, which he merely met with a smile. Before she could pass comment, there was a noise of rattling chains from the screen doors and all turned to see Sigurd Rolfson hustled between two sturdy guards into the hall.

He was manacled at wrists and ankles and shambled awkwardly forward, his head lowered to the rush-strewn floor so that, for the moment, he did not catch sight of his mother, but at her sharp, heartbroken cry of 'Sigurd', he lifted his head and looked at her dully.

Gisela could discern no signs of mistreatment upon his person and could only put down that uninterested slow gaze to sheer bewilderment at his predicament. She moved to rise and go after Aldith, who had gone to him and sobbed on his shoulder, despite the efforts of one of the grizzled-haired guards, who tried to prevent her, but in an embarrassed fashion as if he misliked the necessity.

'Leave her.' The Baron's voice arrested him in the act of physically pulling her from the prisoner. The Baron said quietly, 'Will you please sit down, mother? You will have a chance to see your son again after this trial. That I promise you.'

Aldith lifted a tortured face to his and then went, unre-sisting, back to her stool. The guards led Sigurd to a place in the centre of the hall near the other villagers, but far enough away from them as to make it impossible for any of his erstwhile companions to talk to him.

He noted Gisela in passing and, for the first time since his entry into the hall, she saw a misting of tears in his blue eyes as he nodded to her in gratitude. Then he resumed his posture of despair, standing docilely between his guards and gazing stolidly down at the floor. Not once did he cast an appealing glance at his lord.

Gisela was too distracted by conflicting thoughts to pay much attention to the minor matters brought before the Baron for judgement. For the most part they concerned quarrels and disagreements between neighbours which were listened to attentively and judgement pronounced unequivocally and swiftly. Two men were accused of failing to do desmesne work which was their duty and each was fined and dismissed.

One youngster stood, like Sigurd, head down, while the desmesne reeve told of his being caught red-handed, poaching in Allestone wood. There was a little hush when the Baron's steel-like tones asked the boy if he had anything to say in his own defence. The youngster shook his head miserably after being nudged by his father, who stood next to him.

All knew this could be a hanging matter; though many guessed the Baron would not go so far, the boy could certainly be condemned to maiming, possibly to the loss of a hand. There was a silence while the Baron conferred with both reeve and seneschal. He looked up and ordered the boy to come forward.

'You have been warned before, I understand,' he said coldly and the boy nodded. 'You realise this is a serious matter for which I could punish you severely, so severely that a maimed son could become totally dependent upon his family. I am informed that your parents have served Sir Godfrey and now me faithfully and for that reason I will show mercy.

'You will be handed over to my marshal for physical punishment. A sore back should teach you to keep to your own preserves in future. A fine could also fall hard upon your parents and so I will not impose one. Be brought before me again and I shall not be so easy on you.'

The youngster looked anxiously towards his father, who was gesturing to him to respond to the sentence. He was not sure what his fate would be, having been too terrified to hear properly. He stammered out some sort of apology and expression of gratitude and was pulled away by one of the attendant guards.

Gisela bit her lip hard now as she saw Sigurd being brought forward to stand before the dais. One of his guards poked him sharply and he looked up at last and faced the Baron. Gisela could not see his expression, but judged from the set of his shoulders that it was still sulky. Aldith gave a little anguished gasp at her side.

'Well—' de Treville's voice was silkily cold now as he eyed the prisoner '—there is little need for me to ask for evidence in this matter since I, myself, was the victim of a deliberate attack. Your guilt cannot be denied as witnesses will attest.' He looked beyond Sigurd's bowed head to where Gisela sat and she started up agitatedly, ignoring her father's urgent pull upon her skirt to try to force her back onto her seat.

'My lord.' Her voice rang out in the raftered hall and she stepped slightly forward, facing the man who sat at the trestle table upon the dais. 'Sigurd cannot deny the charge and, as I was present, I cannot deny the truth of it either, but I came today to plead with you to take into consideration that he was provoked.'

'Provoked?' The dark, level brows swept upwards and Sir Walter gave a little strangled gasp of annoyance behind her.

'My lord, Sigurd loves his mother deeply and she was being evicted from the assart cottage that is very dear to both of them.'

'May I remind you, demoiselle, that the cottage, standing where it did, was unlawfully built.'

'Yes, my lord, I know that too but, nevertheless, it was home to Sigurd and the loss of it and his mother's anguish caused him to lose all control. He is so very young. Had he had time to think coherently I am sure he would not have wounded you. He meant to strike out at one whom he believed had injured his mother and himself and. . .'

'Demoiselle, you were present, you know well enough that had I not been quick off the mark to turn and defend myself, I might not be seated at this trestle now.'

She swallowed, feeling the curious gaze of the guards and the short-sighted one of Sir Clement full upon her. Fortunately for Sir Walter's peace of mind, most of the villagers had now left the hall and the Baron could not consider himself humiliated before his own serfs and villeins.

'That I must acknowledge, but the blow was awkwardly delivered. Sigurd is no trained warrior. He meant to hurt, not kill, I am sure. There was a struggle for possession of the hunting knife. In that you were injured.' He was silent, gazing back at her sardonically and she pressed on desperately. 'You have his life in your hands. Please, I beg of you, be merciful. Forgive his youthful impetuosity.'

Sigurd had lifted his head now and was looking pleadingly at Gisela, for what she did not know. Was he asking her to beg for him even more earnestly, or was he soundlessly pleading with her to keep a dignified silence for his mother's sake?

Aldith said brokenly, 'My lord, I beg you, he is my only son. . .'

Sir Walter stood and cleared his throat. 'While I cannot, nor would I wish to, interfere in your decision, my lord, I would attest to the loyalty of Sigurd's mother, who has served me faithfully since the birth of my daughter as wet nurse. Indeed, without her care, I doubt Gisela would have survived.

'She and Sigurd are foster brother and sister and were brought up together in babyhood. I would add my pleas to hers and those of his mother. The boy deserves to be severely dealt with, but if it is within your sense of pity, I ask you to spare his life.'

Alain de Treville nodded coolly to Sir Walter. 'I have sympathy for this boy's mother, Sir Walter, and acknowledge the debt you owe her. Indeed—' his lips parted in a smile as he gazed at Gisela '—we would all have suffered a great deprivation had your lovely daughter not been present here today.'

Gisela made a little indignant sound deep in her throat. How dare he choose such a moment for meaningless pleasantries!

De Treville continued. 'What has the boy to say for himself? Do you understand you are like to hang for this? Did you intend to kill me?'

There was a shocked silence as all eyes now were focussed on Sigurd. Would the young fool doom himself by some stupidly proud outburst?

Sigurd said roughly, 'I don't know,' then, when prompted to repeat himself as his answer had not reached the Baron's ears, said, more loudly, 'I—I don't know— what I meant to do. No—I thought to stop you from walking away, make you listen—' His voice broke off and he looked down miserably at the floor again. 'I would not have really meant to—hurt you.'

'And do you now regret the attack?' The voice was merciless in its demand.

Sigurd said awkwardly, 'I—I don't truly know. I was angry and—'

'Are still angry?'

'Yes.' This time the voice was more sure, defiant, and Aldith uttered a choking cry of protest at his foolishness.

'I see.'

Gisela was forced down upon her stool by her father and sat utterly still, not taking her eyes from the Baron as he sat tapping his quill lightly against a roll of parchment before him, considering.

At last he looked down at his prisoner. 'Sigurd Rolfson, you are guilty of attacking your liege lord and undoubtedly deserve to die. You tell me that still you deny my right to destroy your cottage for good, military reasons and do not regret your crime. I have little choice but to deal out the sentence required by law.

'However, you are still very young and I must take into consideration that you, at least, believed you were provoked. You are a free man and I could declare you outlaw, but I believe you would not survive long in the coming winter. That might be a more prolonged agony than the one decreed at the rope's end.

'Therefore. . .' he paused and looked straight at Gisela as if she were directly challenging his authority by the very intensity of her fixed gaze '. . .I formally deprive you of your freeman's rights and declare you serf. You will remain within my dungeon at Allestone until I consider you can be trusted to walk the castle precincts without posing a threat to myself and to others. You will continue to serve me and whoever succeeds me to the desmesne of Allestone.'

Aldith gave a great sob and Gisela drew her former nurse hard against her heart, patting her shoulder in a clumsy attempt to comfort. She heard the rattle of chains as Sigurd was led off towards the screen doors, presumably to his prison once more in the gatehouse.

She gave a terrible sigh of relief. The boy's life had been saved and she had not dared hope for that. He would suffer the indignity of serfdom throughout his life and, knowing Sigurd, he would find that hard to bear, but though servitude would be galling, in time, surely, he would recognise the measure of mercy that had been dealt him and be duly grateful for it.

Gisela now saw that the young squire, Huon, had entered the hall and that the Baron had summoned him to the table and was talking to him. The boy turned and looked where they were still sitting and came towards them. He bowed politely.

'My Lord Alain has sent me to request you join him at table, Sir Walter. He has also instructed me to take Dame Aldith to the gatehouse where she will be allowed to speak with her son.'

Aldith rose at once, her face working. 'Thank the Virgin, I thought the Baron would have forgotten. . .'

'My Lord Alain is not in the habit of forgetting— anything,' the boy said with a grin.

Gisela said quickly, 'I will go with you, Aldith, at least as far as the gatehouse,' and the boy nodded again.

Gisela's father was frowning slightly and then, as he realised his daughter would be escorted by the Baron's squire, nodded his agreement. He rose to make his own way to join his host where already servants were laying out jugs of wine, goblets and sweetmeats upon a fine damask cloth which now covered the table.

Huon led the two women out of the main door of the hall and down the steps to the courtyard. Aldith was visibly trembling with excitement and Gisela deliberately slowed their pace. She was afraid that Aldith would collapse in her agitated state. She put an arm around the older woman's waist as they went and could see that tears were glimmering now on Aldith's lids.

At the gatehouse she did not insist on entering with her maid. She was sure Aldith and Sigurd would wish to be alone together at this moment, and she turned back into the courtyard itself to wait for Aldith to return to her. Huon conducted the maid into the guardroom and then returned dutifully to Gisela's side.

The place was a hive of industry. From the stables nearby Gisela could hear the whickering of horses and the cheerful whistling of grooms as at Brinkhurst. The Baron's servants appeared to be happy enough about their labours. A shrill screeching and hectic fluttering of wings from the mews informed her of the Baron's love of hawking. Her own father rode out occasionally; Gisela hardly at all. She had confessed to Kenrick once that, though she admired the deadly skill of her father's hawks, she did not like to see them stoop to their prey and make their kill.

From wooden sheds adjoining the inner bailey wall she heard the sound of hammer on metal as the armourer went about his work and the blacksmith's blowing up of his fires and his hammers, too, beating upon the anvil. Serving men and women scuttled about from keep to bakehouse on various errands and Gisela began to understand just how many people this great fortress kept employed and protected.

A sudden commotion from the stable doorway caused her to turn hurriedly as a small hound puppy skittered across her path with a young stable boy in hot pursuit. Both she and Huon dived for it at the same moment, but it managed to evade them and dashed off towards the entrance to the outer bailey. Just then, a young man-at-arms appeared through the entrance pushing a small handcart containing an assortment of swords, battle axes and arrows.

Huon shouted a warning as the puppy raced across his path almost under the cart wheels. Gisela was before him. She launched herself forward and grabbed the young dog by the scruff of the neck, but she almost overbalanced and fell beneath the heavy iron wheels herself as she stumbled over the skirt of her gown.

Still trying to hold on to the squirming puppy, she was unable to fling out her arms to steady herself and gave

a cry of alarm, but found herself caught and pulled back
as the cart rumbled harmlessly past of its own volition
as the startled soldier let go the handle.

Baron Alain de Treville's voice sounded in her ear as
his arm tightened around her waist.

'What a good thing I came in search of you,
Demoiselle Gisela. I would hardly have dared to return
and inform your father you had suffered injury in my
castle.'

She scrambled frantically to free herself as the horrified man-at-arms stammered out an apology.

'My lord, I am sorry. I did not see the little dog. I'd
my head down and then—then I saw the lady and. . .'

'It was not your fault,' Gisela said breathlessly. 'You
could not be expected to see the pup. It is so small.'

The Baron nodded to his man to proceed and as the
cart trundled by them, he looked down, eyebrows raised,
at the squirming hound pup in Gisela's arms.

'One of Freya's litter. I hear there is one constantly
escaping. It's probably this one. I see you are fond
of dogs.'

Gisela dropped a kiss on the smooth fawn-coloured
head as the puppy was struggling to reach up and cover
her face with kisses.

'He's quite beautiful.'

De Treville was thinking the same about the pup's
rescuer as she stood, trembling slightly from her recent
fright, her hood fallen back, revealing her smooth fair
braids beneath her fluttering head veil. Her mantle was
slipping back from her shoulders and he had a tantalising
glimpse of her tight, hip-hugging woollen gown beneath
as the wind swirled its folds against her legs.

Her bosom was heaving from her recent exertion and
her cheeks were tinged with pink, her eyes sparkling. He
thought he would have given much to bring that tender

glow to her face as she gazed down, smiling, at her still-wriggling burden.

'He will dirty your gown,' he said quietly and gently took the hound from her, handing it to Huon. 'Return him to his mother, she'll be fretting.'

Gisela stood watching as the boy ducked his head beneath the stable door and went inside with the still-agitated stable boy.

'I came to escort you back to the hall. You must be getting very chilled out here.'

'No, no,' she said hastily. 'I was waiting for Aldith. She's—she's with Sigurd.'

'Yes.'

'It was good of you to allow her to see him.'

'I promised I would.'

'Not all men keep their promises,' she responded.

He smiled. 'Forgive me, demoiselle, but I would have thought your extreme youth would have prevented you from finding out that sad truth so soon.'

'I am almost seventeen.'

She bridled as she saw his long lips curve into a smile again and added hurriedly, 'It is just that I have heard Aldith and the serving wenches say that. . .'

She broke off in confusion, then her eyes caught sight of the bandaging on his left arm and widened. 'Oh, my lord, I hope you did not hurt your arm again in helping me.'

'No, but had I done so it would have been damaged in a worthy cause.'

'You are making fun of me,' she said reproachfully. 'I regret that I have not yet asked you how serious it was. I would not have believed that the knife could have pierced through the rings of your mail.'

He grimaced. 'A sharp blade can pierce through anything if wielded with sufficient force, as can the iron tip of a good arrow. No, it is but a long scratch. The blade grated on the bone of the forearm and was deflected. It is sore and needs to be kept covered to keep clean, but it pains me little now.'

Her expression had become sweetly grave. 'I must thank you, my lord, for listening to our pleas and granting Sigurd his life. I know he was in grave peril. Many lords would not have shown such mercy.'

He shrugged in that Gallic way she had noticed before.

'Do not trouble yourself unduly about the boy. He will do well enough. He will resent the loss of his status. Freemen guard their rights with pride, but a hard winter can cause many of them to starve, while serfs fill their bellies at their lords' expense.'

'Not always. Compassionate lords will deal with their serfs responsibly but some are neglectful and some are worse—they treat them less kindly than they would their horses.'

'Demoiselle Gisela, if you know how costly a good courser is to buy and maintain, you would understand the possible reason for that,' he said, smiling again.

She turned away, her cheeks burning, as she resented his teasing once more.

'Sigurd can be—difficult,' she said stiffly. 'As you have said, he will resent his loss of freedom.'

He shrugged again. 'We shall manage him, never fear. He lacks a father, I understand, and has needed a firm hand for some time. Your former nurse must have worried about him constantly.'

'Will he be beaten?'

'If he proves—difficult, as you put it. A sore back will teach him obedience and will do him no permanent harm, as it has done no harm to Huon, nor did to me when I was undergoing my training as page and squire.'

She looked at him thoughtfully, trying to imagine this tall, authoritative man as recalcitrant page and squire and finding it hard.

'Shall we go back into the hall? Your father will be concerned about you. Huon will wait for your nurse and escort her back to you.'

He held out a lean brown hand and she reluctantly placed her fingers within his grasp and allowed him to lead her back towards the keep steps.

Sir Walter was palpably relieved to have his daughter return to the hall and smiled his pleasure. A panting Aldith, breathing hard as if she had been running, hurried through the screen doors and made for her mistress. There were visible marks of tear stains on her roughened cheeks and she curtsied dutifully to the Baron to show her gratitude.

Gisela seized her by the hand and dragged her to the far end of the table to question her about her interview with Sigurd. De Treville followed her progress regretfully and signalled to Huon, who had entered with Aldith, to carry the wine jug, sweetmeats and goblets to the two women.

He took a long pull at his own wine cup and then looked steadily at his guest.

'You have a very beautiful and spirited daughter, Sir Walter.'

'Aye.' Sir Walter followed his gaze fondly. 'Too spirited for her own good sometimes. She can be headstrong. I put that down to a lack of a mother. My beloved Hildegarde died soon after her birth and Gisela is as lovely as she was.' He sighed a trifle lugubriously. 'I fear I spoil her outrageously.'

'I imagine you will be looking soon for a suitable husband and protector for her. In these difficult times that can be a worrying business.'

Sir Walter shook his head. 'The truth is, my lord, I cannot face the prospect of life at Brinkhurst without her.'

'I can understand that.' De Treville sat thoughtfully silent for a moment, then he leaned forward in his seat slightly towards his guest. 'Demoiselle Gisela has Saxon blood, I understand.'

'Her great-grandmother was Saxon. Her husband was killed at Senlac and she married a Norman knight. My wife, Hildegarde, also had Saxon blood.' His lips twitched. 'Many men in the shire are proud of their Saxon inheritance, my lord.'

'Of course. I am equally proud to know my Norman ancestors came from Viking stock.' De Treville twirled the wine round in his goblet, watching the firelight behind them glimmer in its red depths.

'You will see, Sir Walter—' he looked up and gestured towards the stark bare stone walls of the hall '—that my castle lacks a chatelaine.' He gave a short laugh. 'My friend Rainald de Tourel, who visited some days ago and has now left to return to the King's court, took me to task over this matter and brought a message from the King himself that I should be thinking soon of taking a wife.

'I am twenty-six years old and my hectic life on campaign at the King's side left me little time to consider that possibility, nor had I sufficient means to do so. Now that I have obtained the castle and desmesne of Allestone, my bachelor state begins to gall me.'

He saw his guest's body become rigid in his chair and his eyes wary. De Treville looked pointedly at Gisela, who was talking excitedly to Aldith. Her lovely eyes were flashing and she moved her hands expressively as she was obviously engaged in attempting to comfort her maid for the loss of Sigurd's company.

'Your daughter tells me she is nearly seventeen, Sir Walter, an age when she is ripe for the marriage bed. In our short acquaintance, I have come to have a healthy regard for her unequivocal honesty. She is not only beautiful but brave, and kind to both people and animals. I find both qualities admirable. I take it there is no prior arrangement for her betrothal or you would have mentioned it. I could keep her safe at Allestone. I ask you now, formally, for the honour of her hand in marriage.'

Sir Walter blinked rapidly and, in order to give himself time to think, he helped himself to more wine and drained his cup.

He said deliberately, 'I have said Gisela can be headstrong, my lord. Naturally I believe she has every quality finest in womanhood—she is my beloved daughter—but I have to face the fact that she could prove—difficult.'

De Treville laughed. 'That is the way she described Sigurd to me, just now. I assured her I would manage the lad.'

Sir Walter's eyebrows flew upwards and de Treville shook his head very gently.

'Have no fears, Sir Walter, it is not my way to be cruel to women nor unduly so with my servants. I would deal well with the Demoiselle Gisela and I believe she would make me an excellent wife. Her Saxon blood and standing in the shire makes her eminently suitable. With her at my side, I am confident I could achieve the ready co-operation of my neighbours that, perhaps, my Norman heritage may render open to reserve.

'I am the third son of Sir Gilles de Treville. Our manor is close to Caen. I came to serve in the Earl of Leicester's household as squire when I was but fourteen and have lived in England serving the King since then.'

His dark eyes brightened somewhat. 'I have no mistress established here at Allestone and, since my mother is some distance away, there would be no other woman here to challenge the Demoiselle's rule. My seneschal's wife, the Lady Rohese, is a very gentle lady and would prove helpful and friendly. She would be delighted to have the company of another female within the bower.

'Gisela would have a totally free hand, which I believe would be important to her. I recognise in her a nature as formidable as that of the Empress Matilda, and I have, on occasion, met that lady.' His dark eyes twinkled and Sir Walter could not hold back an answering smile.

'On the matter of dower. . .'

'I am sure we could come to some sensible arrangement, Sir Walter. My needs are not great on that score.'

Walter of Brinkhurst gave a little sigh. 'My lord, will you allow me time to consider?'

'Of course. Naturally you will wish to speak with the Demoiselle Gisela.' He put one hand gently upon the older man's arm. 'I know you are reluctant to give her in marriage, but Allestone is very close. You will see her often and—in these hard times, you will need a man who can hold her safe. Think well on what I have said and send me word soon.'

Sir Walter said doubtfully, 'Though Gisela lacks a mother, Aldith taught her well all the housewifely skills but,' he hesitated, 'she is so very young. . .'

'Not so young that she will not learn quickly.'

'No.'

He turned in his chair as Gisela also turned and caught his eye. Both she and Aldith were looking happier but, as if she read in his expression the gravity of the matter in discussion, her vivid blue eyes clouded over somewhat and one fair brow arched upwards as if in interrogation.

He said heavily, 'If you will excuse us, my lord, we should be riding back to Brinkhurst. I promise I will think very hard on what you have said.'

'I know you will.' De Treville rose and held out his hand to the other, who grasped it.

'Thank you again for your forbearance in the matter of the boy.'

De Treville bowed his head.

Gisela came hesitantly to her father's side and curtsied as he took his leave of his host.

As they rode home together she was aware of his

absorption in his own thoughts. She ceased her chatter about Allestone and rode silently beside him.

Over supper he seemed just as quiet and, at last, she ventured to challenge him.

'Father, what is it? I saw you were talking intently to the Baron. Had he some information about the course of the war which has troubled you or are you still worried about Sigurd?'

'No, Sigurd will be safe enough at Allestone. Sooner or later the lad would have come to grief without discipline and I had no real authority over him.' Sir Walter tackled a chicken leg bone with unusual ferocity and Gisela watched him doubtfully.

'Then did he take you to task over my behaviour? I know you think I was unwise to challenge him there in open court.'

He put down the leg and looked at her deliberately. 'On the contrary. He appears to have admired your spirit in outfacing him. He asked for your hand in marriage.'

Colour drained from her face and she sat unmoving, her eyes growing larger and larger before his gaze. He waited for her to speak but she continued to sit rigidly still. Then, at last, she said very quietly, 'And what did you say to him?'

'I told him I needed time to consider.'

She drew in her breath in a little hiss.

'But you cannot be thinking of saying yes!'

Again he regarded her directly. 'Why not? It is a fair match. You would be mistress of Allestone. Many maidens in the shire would give their eyeteeth for such a future.'

'I am not one of them,' she said, again speaking so calmly and softly that he leaned towards her to both hear and catch her expression. Still she appeared deadly pale.

He said almost jovially, but in a tone patently false,

'You have never considered such an honour I know, but...'

'Honour?' The single word was suddenly shrill with outrage. 'You cannot believe I would welcome such a match?'

He turned from her, embarrassed, and once more gave his attention to his food.

'Child, I cannot afford to simply dismiss this offer. All fathers have a duty to provide for their daughters fittingly and I cannot deny that your welfare and protection would be assured at Allestone.'

She shivered as she had done when they had ridden below the gatehouse arch this morning. 'The place is a prison. I cannot face the prospect of being immured behind those defensive walls.'

'That is just it, Gisela. They *are* defensive. I have to consider, first and foremost, your safety. You heard Kenrick talk the other day of the attack on that manor near Oakham. It seems the shire reeve is powerless to curb that man's excesses. Baron Alain de Treville has both the ability to do so and the King's warrant.'

'Father, are you afraid of the Baron de Treville?'

He met her unflinching gaze steadily. 'I would not wish to offend him.'

'So I am to be sacrificed so that you can keep the favour of this King's man?'

'That could be the size of it, daughter,' Sir Walter admitted. 'What have you against him? He is young and personable. He did not appear to me to be excessively harsh. You could do worse.'

'I could do better. What of Kenrick, whom I have known and loved since childhood?'

He was visibly flustered. 'Kenrick of Arcote has spoken to you of love?'

'No, he has not,' she replied quietly. 'That would have been dishonourable without asking your permission to court me first and Kenrick would not behave so.'

'Kenrick is a fine, upstanding young man, Gisela, but he is not for you.' The statement was made bluntly and she winced at the finality of his tone.

'What if I were to say I loved Kenrick?'

'Frankly I would not believe you. You know nothing as yet of love. Your mother did not love me when we met, nor I her, but we grew to love one another. My father chose her for me and I obeyed him as was right and proper. I have spoiled you, Gisela, for you to so defy my wishes in this.'

'Why do you object to Kenrick?'

He turned to bluster, not finding it easy to put into words his doubts about such a mating.

'He is simply not the man for you. He is kind and honourable, I am the first to admit that, but he is weak-willed, easily swayed, too much under the influence of that mother of his. I do not believe you would be happy or fulfilled in such a marriage.'

'But you think I would be, wed to this man you hardly know.'

'I believe I have the measure of Alain de Treville.'

'And,' she said bitterly, 'the fact that he is a powerful baron and in the King's favour does not weigh with you in the slightest. Will you not have to beggar yourself to provide a suitable dower for me? That is usual in such alliances, isn't it?'

'We did not discuss a possible marriage contract.'

'I will not do it,' she protested stubbornly.

'Gisela, do not be foolish. I have seldom opposed your wishes. In that I was, perhaps, unwise, but this is a serious business. I will not be defied. I have not yet made up my mind but I tell you plainly, every instinct impels me to accept this proposal. I shall inform you of my final decision tomorrow. You can retire to your chamber if you have finished your meal.'

He was dismissing her as if she were an unruly page or servant. She was trembling with distress and fury. Never had he showed his anger so plainly. She could find no words to answer him so she stood and curtsied formally, an action rare with her to this man she knew only as a loving and generous father, then she walked in dignified fashion from the hall.

She felt her limbs still trembling as she climbed the stair to her chamber where she found Aldith sorting gowns in her clothing chest. Aldith had fallen easily into work as her personal attendant from the moment she had come to Brinkhurst on the afternoon of Sigurd's arrest. Now she slept on a truckle bed within her mistress's chamber and to Gisela, it seemed her beloved nurse had returned to her as if she had never left to live with Rolf and Sigurd in the little cottage in the assart.

Aldith saw at once that something was terribly wrong. She did not make the mistake of enquiring, knowing that if the matter concerned Sigurd she would have been informed at once and sensing Gisela was not yet ready to tell her what was distressing her so badly.

Gisela walked to the little casement, its shutters not yet drawn to, despite the cold outside, for Aldith knew that her mistress liked the still-scented air from the herb garden to freshen the little room behind her mother's bower, which was warmed from below by the hearth fire and could become stuffy.

Gisela stared bleakly over the darkened garden. She said without turning, 'Aldith, I want you to find a reliable servant to take a message for me to Sir Kenrick of Arcote at first light tomorrow.' Her voice shook slightly. 'Kenrick does not read well so it must be verbal. I want him to meet me at noon tomorrow in the clearing in the wood near the stream. He knows the place. We have ridden there often together.'

Aldith frowned. She was aware, without being told,

that this message must not be repeated to others, or reach the master's ears.

'Mistress, you do not intend to ride out tomorrow without escort? That would be very dangerous.'

'I must, Aldith.' The words were whispered.

She turned from the window and Aldith hastened across to draw to and fasten the shutters. The room was illuminated now only by a single candle on a chest by the bed but, by its light, she saw how white her young mistress was, especially round the mouth.

Gisela had sunk down upon the wolf-pelt coverlet of the bed and was stroking its fur absently.

'What is it, child?' Aldith questioned gently, reverting to her former familiar attitude when Gisela had been her loved charge. 'You would not disobey your father without cause. It is not your way.'

'He intends to wed me to Baron Alain de Treville.'

Aldith's lips rounded in an 'o' of astonishment but she uttered no sound.

Gisela said woodenly, 'I love Kenrick of Arcote. I—I somehow never questioned the fact that, in time, we should wed.'

Aldith chose her words with care. 'It is within the right of your father to choose for you.'

'I know that, but it never occurred to me that he would gainsay me in this, my deepest desire.'

Aldith hesitated, then pressed on, 'Few girls expect to marry the man of their own choosing. The Baron is the wealthiest man in the shire. It is natural your father should consider this the finest match for you.'

'I do not wish to be mistress of Allestone.' The words were ground out through gritted teeth. 'This man is an arrogant stranger. Look how he treated Sigurd.'

'He granted him his life when it was in his power to hang him,' Aldith reminded her softly. 'I shall pray for him to the end of my days for that mercy.'

'But if he had not thrown you both from your cottage, the attack would never have happened.'

Aldith sighed. It was not for her to challenge the decisions of the great ones.

'What do you think Kenrick can do about this?' she said at last diffidently.

'I don't know,' Gisela said desperately. 'Surely he can plead with Father. . .'

'Suppose it is not in his mind to—offer marriage,' Aldith ventured, 'since he has not declared himself? It is my opinion that Sir Kenrick will be guided by his mother in this.'

Gisela stared at her dully. 'I am sure he loves me,' she said desperately. 'I could be happy at Arcote.' She seized her maid's hand. 'You will do this for me, find me a messenger and help me to get out of the house?'

Aldith nodded slowly. She was kneeling close by her mistress's side. She rose heavily. Everything appeared to be happening suddenly to disrupt the even tenor of their lives. She felt cold to her bones. Surely this was a natural sense of foreboding for the problems facing them and not the acute approach of old age!

Chapter Three

Gisela rode fast for the little clearing in the wood once she had managed to get free from the village. She had not found it as difficult as she had feared; her father had risen early and ridden out on the desmesne, obviating the need to lie to him about her destination and purpose for the ride. Since the latest attack on the manor near Oakham, he had been more and more adamant that she be escorted and it was essential that she should ride alone this morning.

In the end, it had been the head groom she had had to convince that she needed no one to accompany her, giving as her excuse that she was going no further than the church in the village. Aldith had stood by the manor gate, clearly alarmed. Had Sigurd been available, he could have run by his mistress's saddle bow and afforded her some protection.

Aldith's heart misgave her as Gisela put spurs to her palfrey and rode out of sight. Not only was her mistress at risk, but the necessity to urge Kenrick to declare himself also worried Aldith. Suppose her mistress was to be disappointed in the man and humiliated by a refusal to help her? Gisela was so sure that Kenrick was a suitor. If she were wrong, she would be brokenhearted.

Aldith had sent off Gisela's message as promised.

Since there was no time for a reply she could only hope
Kenrick would be at the trysting place as Gisela had
requested. She sighed and went wearily back into the
manor house. She had slept badly, still worried about
Sigurd and concerned for her mistress.

Gisela knew she was early when she reached the clearing.
She had been too impatient to wait before leaving
Brinkhurst. She walked her palfrey to a large flat stone
she had previously used as a mounting block and managed to dismount unaided, then secured her palfrey's
reins on a low branch of overhanging alder and moved
unhurriedly to the stream.

She had encountered no one in the wood. The villagers
had been working at the final autumn tasks within their
own cottages. There were still rushes to be dipped, apples
stored and inspected and the final sealing done on salted
pig-meat barrels.

She frowned as she tapped her riding whip against her
booted foot. If Kenrick had been from home when her
message arrived, this last desperate measure to avoid
what she considered an enforced marriage could well be
doomed for, somehow, she knew her father would give
his decision later today. He would not keep Baron Alain
de Treville waiting and last night he had been so defi-
nitely in favour of the match. Only Kenrick could give
her hope of rescue from this sorry fate by declaring
himself today, as she prayed he would consent to do.

She heard sounds of movement on the track and turned
instantly to find Kenrick's sorrel hack entering the clearing. She waited by the stream, her heartbeat quickening,
as he sprang down and almost ran towards her. He took
both her hands in his and squeezed them tightly.

'Gisela, oh, my dear, I came the moment I received
your message. I was out when the man came but he
waited, praise God, and found me as I rode through the

gate. There is no trouble at Brinkhurst? But, surely not, your father would have sent word.'

His greeting was so ardent. She scanned his face anxiously; she could not have been mistaken about his feelings for her.

She went straight to the point. 'I thought you should know at once. My father proposes to wed me to Alain de Treville.'

Shock registered instantly on Kenrick's good-humoured countenance. For a moment he looked almost haggard. His gloved fingers tightened upon hers and he pulled her a little closer to him.

'He has given his word?'

'Not yet. I think it will be soon. De Treville asked for me yesterday, at the manor court. Did you hear about Sigurd?'

Kenrick nodded. 'Yes. I am sorry for the boy, but I suppose it was the best we could hope for him, under the circumstances.' He drew her away from the clearing some way so that they would not be seen so easily by any passer-by on the track. 'Tell me, Gisela, you are not in favour of this match? He would make you my lady. . .'

'Of course I am not. Father was angered with me last night more than he has been for years now. I was vehemently against it. I told him I would not be coerced. I cannot imagine why the Baron should want such a marriage. We have been at odds from the first time we met and he does not strike me as a man who would accept a rebellious wife lightly. Surely he could make a more advantageous marriage at the King's court?

'I am at a loss to understand it. The proposal has come out of the blue.' Her eyes appealed to him and she hesitated, then plunged on. 'I—I had hoped that—' she swallowed hard '—Kenrick, I must humiliate myself by asking if you have any feelings for me. . .'

'Of course I have,' he said forcibly. 'I would have

declared myself months ago had not my mother been so
against it.'

'You have spoken with her about it?'

'Aye.' He looked away momentarily. 'We have quarrelled. I rode out early this morning to clear my head of
wine fumes. We had a fierce engagement only last night
when I informed her of my intentions regarding you and
I drank more than I should.'

'She does not approve of me,' Gisela sighed. 'I feared
as much.'

'She would not approve of anyone I wished to marry,
if the truth were known,' he said angrily. 'She is unwilling to allow any other woman's rule at Arcote, but I
informed her last night that I would brook no more tearful
scenes, that I would go to your father soon and request
your hand in marriage'

Gisela expelled a tiny sigh and he bent and kissed her
gloved palm. 'Do not be afraid, my love. I will ride back
with you today and ask for your hand. When he is made
aware that we both want this match, I do not think he
will force you into a marriage that would be odious
to you.'

Gisela was doubtful. Her father had been determined
last night that Kenrick was not the man for her but surely,
as Kenrick said, he would listen to reason? She had
to try. She looked into Kenrick's young frowning face
intently.

'You are sure? I would not press you. It is just that—
we have always dealt well together and—and this has
come so suddenly. . .'

'Aye,' he said bitterly, 'and this man de Treville is far
more noble than I. Your father will take some per-
suading.'

'Oh, Kenrick, what shall we do if he will not listen to
reason? He has never been so adamant before, about
anything.'

Kenrick's brows drew together. 'Let us meet this squarely first, Gisela. If your father refuses me outright, we must think again.' He paused and looked down at her steadily. 'Would you—would you be prepared to defy him and—and run from Brinkhurst?'

She caught her breath in a great gasp, her gaze directed from him now, looking wildly about the little clearing, at the trees almost denuded of leaves now and the short grass where the pigs had grazed. 'I don't know, I—' Then she turned fully back to him. 'Yes, if it is necessary. I will escape this forced marriage by any means but, Kenrick, where could we go, what could we do if my father refuses his consent to our betrothal?'

His mouth set in a stubborn line. 'Why, then we must wed without his consent. I will take you before a priest in Leicester Town. There we are not known and any priest will wed us, given the right inducements. Afterwards—' he gave a click of the tongue indicating distaste for his next words '—afterwards your father will not wish to have the marriage annulled, not if—if you are truly mine. Do you understand, Gisela?'

She nodded, but her eyes were misting with tears. 'Yes, but I pray the Virgin that it will not be necessary. I love him so, Kenrick. I would not wish to live in enmity with my own father, nor will you wish to be at odds with a neighbour.'

Alain de Treville rode at ease through Allestone wood. He was accompanied only by his squire, Huon. Today he expected no displays of hostility from his own people. He had proved to them who was master and he hoped they would recognise the degree of mercy he had shown. True, he was leaving the desmesne of Allestone but only for a short time; he intended calling on his neighbour, Walter of Brinkhurst, so he rode without mail.

The reason, or was it excuse, for his visit was curled

up in a rush basket within a pannier secured to one side of his saddle. He smiled down at the hound pup fondly. He had been assured that it was correctly weaned and would make a suitable gift for Gisela of Brinkhurst. Had she not said he was beautiful? He was humming an old Norman folksong sung to him in childhood by his own wet nurse, which he had not remembered in years. The air was cold but the day was bright and his hopes were high.

Huon, keeping a respectful distance behind him, watched the jaunty set of his master's shoulders and wondered. Alain de Treville had proved himself a good and fair master but, so far, Huon had seen little sign of jollity in his character. Throughout these past months the Baron's one abiding desire had been to ensure the defences of Allestone Castle. He had not ventured into Oakham or Leicester Town to seek feminine company and since he kept no leman at Allestone, he had apparently lived like a monk throughout the time Huon had been assigned to him as squire.

Now, without warning, his master's mood had lightened and he had gone about the castle joyfully. Huon gave a little secretive smile. He had glimpsed the light in his master's eye when he had spied the Demoiselle Gisela within the manor court assembly and knew their destination now was Brinkhurst. If Lord Alain was not yet in love, Huon believed he could soon arrive at that delectable state. Huon was in favour of whatever it took to keep Lord Alain permanently in this pleasant mood which eased the lives of all in service at Allestone.

As they entered the clearing that led to the track to Brinkhurst Lord Alain checked, drew rein and Huon drew up close. Two horses were tethered in the clearing, one a sorrel hack, the other a lady's palfrey. Huon believed he had seen that dapple mare once before. He made a little sound deep in his throat that was checked by his master's upraised hand.

De Treville's eyes gazed warily round the clearing. The two horses paid him little attention and seemed intent on grazing quietly. Neither appeared to be soldiers' mounts and would pose no threat. He made to move on again, then stared hard once more at the palfrey. His throat tightened as he realised he had seen it before in the assart by Aldith's cottage. It was Gisela's palfrey.

Some movement to his right alerted him and he put one hand to his sword hilt, swinging round in the saddle and motioning silently for Huon to move back and keep quiet. His watchful eyes swept the clearing until he saw the two people half hidden by coppiced beeches. The man, young by his stance, unknown to de Treville, was bending low to kiss the girl held close in his arms.

De Treville drew a harsh breath as he knew, without even glimpsing her features properly, for she was half-hidden from him by the man who held her, that Gisela of Brinkhurst was in the arms of a lover. How could he be mistaken in the poise of that head, the slim perfection of the youthful form?

He kept his mount perfectly still, one hand gentling the animal, so it made no sound, not even a whickered greeting to the other horses in the clearing. Skilfully he turned the horse and motioned for Huon, who was waiting warily by an oak nearby, to do the same.

Keeping his courser to the softer ground where its passing would not be heard by the two lovers, de Treville headed back to Allestone, Huon falling in behind. He looked down at the puppy who woke suddenly and began to wriggle, wag its tail and make little squeaks demanding attention. His lips curved into a rueful smile.

'Not the right moment, my boy,' he said regretfully. 'Perhaps one day soon you can meet your new mistress again.'

Huon noted with some concern that the humming had stopped. He had not emerged into the clearing to see what de Treville had seen, but he was convinced that, whatever it was, it had disturbed his master's peace. He gave a heavy sigh of disappointment.

Gisela rode in silence by Kenrick's side as they made for Brinkhurst, watching him covertly. His brows were drawn together and his lips compressed. She knew he did not relish the coming interview with her father, neither did she. She was not sure why she did not feel as comforted by Kenrick's nearness as she had expected to be.

He had greeted her as warmly as she had hoped, had promised immediately to do what she asked, indeed, had drawn her into a tender embrace. Everything had gone as she had planned it in her dreams, yet she was neither as sanguine nor as happy as she had thought she would be.

Kenrick's kiss had been warm, tender, caring, but had not drawn forth in her the passionate response she had dreamed of and heard about in the troubadours' tales. She castigated herself for her own doubts. Those tales were foolish, for entertainment only, not intended to be taken seriously by any sensible maid. Aldith would have said as much. Kenrick was like a brother to her; she held him in high esteem, trusted him utterly.

It was unlikely that at their first proper kiss—for on other occasions he had kissed her lightly in her father's presence on cheek and forehead many times, in greeting and in taking farewell—her heart would pound madly or her bones melt or strange tingles run through her body as the troubadors declared. It would take time for such love to come to fruition, when they were wed and he held her close on their marriage night.

She had not managed to convince herself either that her father would so readily consent to their betrothal as Kenrick predicted. And what if he did not? Although she had promised Kenrick she would, Gisela was not sure

she wished to steal from Brinkhurst secretly and shame-
fully wed in direct disobedience to her father's wishes.
She stirred uneasily in the saddle and, catching Kenrick's
eye, managed a weak smile in response to his own
assured one.

It was in the action of turning and, once more, giving
his attention to the track that Kenrick suddenly froze in
the saddle, pulled up his hack sharply and seized Gisela's
bridle rein. She stared at him in astonishment as she saw
that his usually ruddy features drained of all colour and
his lips tightened in alarm.

'Kenrick, what is it?'

His eyes were focussed dead ahead in the direction
of Brinkhurst manor and she followed his gaze in utter
bewilderment. Then she saw it, black smoke curling up
above the trees, oily, thick smoke that could not be mistaken for the normal emissions from hearth fires and
cookhouse and bakehouse. She gave one frightened cry.

'Kenrick, it cannot be Brinkhurst!'

'I'm afraid it is.' His tone was grim. 'You must wait
here, Gisela, while I ride forward to reconnoitre.'

She dragged his hand free of her bridle rein and, putting spurs to her mount, flew on ahead of him. She heard
his quick curse of surprise and anger faintly on the wind.
Her mount was docile but powerful and she was soon
well ahead of Kenrick on the track. If something had
happened at Brinkhurst nothing and no one was going
to prevent her reaching her father.

As she pounded along, Kenrick riding hard in pursuit,
she tried to tell herself that whatever had occurred, her
father could not be involved. He had been away from
home when she left and that had not been so long ago,
yet—she knew in her innermost heart that her father
must have seen the smoke just as she and Kenrick had
and must, even now, either be on route for the manor or
had already arrived.

The gate was unguarded as she thundered through and the courtyard deserted, though horses were milling about, confused, bridles trailing. She was breathing in the smoke now, coughing and retching as she rode. There was no mistaking the sounds of conflict assailing her ears from the hall as she kicked her feet free of the stirrups and sprang down.

She neither knew nor cared now if Kenrick were following. Her one desperate need was to get to her father. Her riding gown was hindering her headlong dash and, impatiently, she bent and tore her feet free of it as she ran on. A serving lad, coughing as she was, and crying at the same time, blundered past her near the screen door and she shouldered him aside and rushed on.

The noise of men shouting and women screaming was almost deafening now as she burst into the hall then stopped dead, stricken to stone momentarily by the sights that met her eyes.

Trestles had been overturned, bodies lay still or twitched in pain where they had fallen. Men clad in mail whooped their triumph as they rushed about the hall seizing anything of value they could find. She stared round blindly for sight of her father, but the brief fight appeared to be over. The manor had been taken completely by surprise by this band of marauding routiers and now all that was left was for them to loot the place, see to it that no man could pursue them and get away from the scene of destruction without being captured.

A girl's sharp scream of utter terror froze Gisela once more to the spot. Try as she might she could not turn and run. It seemed that her feet would not carry her away, for she realised instantly that there was nothing to gain by remaining. Her only chance was to follow that boy who had fled from the chaos. In their wild lust for destruction, the attackers had thrown torches up to the roof timbers, which were already engulfed in flames and giving out the thick, lung-wrenching smoke that had alerted her and Kenrick to the scene.

Her eyes roved the hall while, for a blessed moment, no man appeared to notice her entrance for the intruders were too intent on enriching themselves, taking in the smaller signs which she found so touchingly horrifying: the spilt wine, the wooden mazers and platters that had been hacked about in the acts of senseless destruction, all marks of the dread scene, and her father's favourite elderly hound lay slain, horribly blood-smirched.

Gisela found her voice to let out one long howl of anguish. Instantly she alerted one of the routiers, who was in the act of wrenching a wall hanging from behind her father's chair. She registered the fact, dully, that she had been told that it was especially prized as her mother's work when Lady Hildegarde had first come as a bride to Brinkhurst.

The man turned and let fall the hanging. He let out an animal yell and leaped for Gisela and bore her to the ground. She fought him desperately with teeth and claws, crying out curses to the god who had let this disaster overtake them and pleas to the mother of all to protect a virgin, as she was herself.

She was suddenly wrenched free and rolled clear, sobbing, clumsily attempting to hold together the torn parts of her gown, to see Kenrick in mortal combat with her attacker. The two men were rolling over and over, panting hard, scrambling for mastery and thrusting with their daggers in frantic attempts to find vulnerable spots to aim for and finish this fight.

Gisela crouched some feet away, too winded and frightened to even try to rise and run. She was too shocked even to be fearful for Kenrick's safety. She watched each move with horrified fascination, not even aware that there were other men in the room, men flushed with victory, their hauberks smeared with ominous bloodstains, their faces soot blackened.

They were all laden with pillaged goods, linens, fur pelts, metal drinking cups, weapons. They stood and cheered on the combatants as if this was one special entertainment put on for their amusement, for the moment too engrossed in the fight to take note of the girl crouched some feet from them.

Gisela gave a terrible sob of desperation as she saw Kenrick's opponent strike down ruthlessly, giving a panting gasp of triumph that was echoed by his fellow routiers.

Alain de Treville saw the betraying plumes of smoke almost at the same moment as Kenrick of Arcote had done so. He reined in his horse abruptly and stared back towards the clearing he had just left. Huon rode up to his side and peered in the same direction.

'A cottage fire, got out of hand, my lord?'

'I doubt it. There's too much smoke for that. It could be the manor house.'

'My lord?'

'There have been several attacks on property near here, recently. Huon, take the pup. I'm going back. Ride straight for the castle and tell Sir Clement I want a company of men to mount up instantly and follow me to Brinkhurst. Impress on him the urgency of my need.'

He scooped up the wriggling, protesting puppy from the pannier basket and thrust it into the boy's arms. He could see he needed to say no more to have Huon realising his need and obeying his orders instantly. The boy's young face was set. He made no attempt to protest that he should accompany Lord Alain. Obviously his lord's prime need now was to have reinforcements at his back. He nodded and spurred his horse in the direction of Allestone, firmly holding in his squirming burden with one arm.

De Treville cursed inwardly at low-lying branches that impeded his headlong ride down the track. His one thought was for Gisela. As he thundered through the clearing he saw at once that the two horses were gone. Gisela and her youthful swain had left and were, doubtless, heading back to Brinkhurst and certain danger.

He rode on, straight into the smoke blown his way by the wind, gritted his teeth and soothed his courser, which was rearing and squealing in dismay at the obvious signs of fire his master was deliberately aiming him into, through the gate arch into Brinkhurst's courtyard, where he saw now only three riderless horses. His expression hardened as he jumped down and gave a curt command to his mount. Well-trained, despite his natural fear of fire, the destrier would wait docilely for his master's return.

De Treville made for the hall steps at a run, his hand on his sword hilt. It would seem that what opposition to this attack there had been, had been easily subdued and most of the marauders had already left. His body went cold as he thought Gisela might have been carried off by one of them. Her one champion would have had little chance to foil any attempt to abduct her. He burst through the screen doors to the scene of destruction.

He'd been right. Most of the looters had departed. One man only, laughing and whooping with delight, was engaged in pulling along a scratching, biting girl, whose gown and head veil were torn, a girl whose wrists had been bound with some cloth, possibly torn from a damaged wall hanging.

At the sudden entrance of a newcomer, her abductor raised a hand in guffawing greeting, as if to a companion, then his eyes narrowed as he recognised a stranger. He let go of the girl, who fell back against an overturned trestle, and, drawing his sword, got ready to defend his prize.

De Treville leaped into the attack, his soldier's eye

taking in the fact that the man appeared to have recently been engaged in conflict. He would be tired. There was no need for haste now. He could be defeated simply enough by being worn down.

De Treville called a curt command to Gisela. 'Stand clear. Leave the man to me.'

She was distraught and totally exhausted and was only too glad to obey. She scrambled up from her tumble and moved warily to the side of the hall, her eyes never leaving the combatants. She looked across once at the sprawled form of Kenrick and hastily averted her eyes.

This contest at arms lasted very little time at all. She watched, dry-eyed, as de Treville skilfully fought the man back and back until he was tight against a trestle. One well-aimed move and her erstwhile captor had been thrust headfirst over the fallen trestle and de Treville leaned easily down and dispatched him with one thrust. The fellow gave only one strangled grunt as if utterly surprised.

Alain de Treville rose and moved towards the distraught girl. He sheathed his blood-smeared blade and, after freeing her hands and took one shaking hand within his, his head jerking upwards as two men came thundering down the stair behind the dais. They took in the sight of their fallen comrade and, laden down with valuables, thought it best to take to their heels and flee.

One made it, scrambling through the screen doors, dropping most of his trophies, but de Treville sprang over another fallen trestle and engaged the other swiftly. Taken as much by surprise as Gisela's former captor, the man took a thrust beneath the arm where his mailed hauberk was weakest and dropped with scarce a murmur and the clatter of metal cups as they fell from his hands.

Gisela had run towards Kenrick's body. He was lying face down and, frantically, she tried to turn him, the tears she had held back till now streaming down her face.

De Treville reached her and bent down to draw her aside gently. 'Let me.'

She sat back on her heels, mutely entreating him to inform her that Kenrick still lived. He turned the young man, noting grimly the gaping chest wound and blood soaking the rushes beneath him. His questing fingers sought the side of the neck for sign of a pulse and he looked up quickly to meet Gisela's agonised gaze and gently shook his head.

'I am sorry.'

She let out a terrible sob and put one shaking hand to her lips.

'He died protecting you?'

She nodded mutely.

'Then you must be glad for him that he died a true man's death, fighting for one he cared about.'

'I—I have known him all my life. He. . .he is Kenrick of Arcote. . .'

He nodded, rose to his feet and, slipping off his mantle, he covered Kenrick's form after gently closing the staring eyes.

Gisela gave another great gulp of terror. She looked round wildly at the sprawled bodies. So far she had not been able to recognise individual servants, womenfolk and—and still—still—she had not identified her father.

De Treville put his hands to her shaking shoulders and drew her to her feet, then he led her to a bench, which he righted, and pushed her gently but firmly down upon it.

'Was your father at home?'

'I—I don't know. He was out when—when I left about an hour ago. He could have returned.' Her eyes were searching those bodies near her.

Suddenly the shrill sound of a trumpet broke the deadly quiet that had struck the hall and she clutched at his sleeve desperately.

He reassured her. 'My men. I sent for reinforcements

the moment I saw the smoke. I was riding in
Allestone wood.'

She shuddered as she thought that less than an hour
ago Kenrick had been kissing her in Allestone wood and
now she would never see him bend towards her, laughing
again, hear his merry voice tell some joke about one of
their neighbours. She thrust aside the thought and, with
it, the gnawing pain of loss, and rose agitatedly.

'I must try and find my father and—and Aldith. Oh,
sweet Virgin, for a while I forgot Aldith had been here
at the manor. She may have perished with all the rest.'

The hall was beginning to fill with men who wore the
blue chevron device of Allestone. The sergeant whom
she remembered as the man she had challenged outside
Aldith's cottage came to salute his lord and, behind him,
Gisela saw the young squire who had greeted her at
Allestone castle, Huon.

Lord Alain directed his men about the grim business
of assembling the corpses decently and arranging for
prayers and, finally, burials.

'One of you ride to the village and find the priest. Tell
him he is needed urgently. I want a search made for any
wounded. We must take them for tending to Allestone
and Sir Walter must be found.' He acknowledged Huon
with a drawing together of his dark brows.

The youth said hastily, 'I thought you might need me,
my lord.'

'Well, since you are here, go with the other men and
see what can be done for any survivors, then I shall want
a complete report of all damage.' He nodded approvingly
as the sergeant was already ordering a posse of men to
deal with the still-smoking rafters. The fire could be
checked but the damage was considerable.

Huon called to him as he made his way towards the
hearth and the door near it that led up to the ladies'
bower. Here was the high trestle where Sir Walter and

Gisela sat at meat. The trestle, like all the others, had been overturned and there were stains of blood upon the white linen cloth that had been laid upon it, as if a hand had grasped at it in an attempt to pull a body upwards after having fallen.

'My lord, I think I have found Sir Walter. He still lives, but is sorely wounded. He had fallen behind the table.'

Gisela gave a choking cry and made for the spot. Lord Alain followed her.

Her father was deathly pale; his eyes were closed and there was evidence of a great deal of blood loss. He had not been wearing mail and would have had little chance against his attackers.

Lord Alain stooped and discovered a seeping wound soaking the thigh and right leg. He gently cupped Sir Walter's face between his two hands and then very lightly cuffed him upon the cheek in an attempt to rouse him to consciousness. The eyes flickered open, the injured man made an abortive effort to sit and was gently but firmly pushed back.

'Lie still, Sir Walter. We will check the bleeding and get you to a physician. Don't try to move or speak for a moment. I think you may have suffered a blow to the head. Your daughter is here, safe. Do you know me, Alain de Treville? The attack is over and my men in control.'

Sir Walter gave a little bubbling sigh, clutched at Gisela's hand as she knelt beside him and he could vaguely make out the shape of her beloved form, then he lapsed off into unconsciousness again.

Gisela sobbed but Lord Alain said quietly, 'Do not concern yourself. He is better so. The leg may be broken and the setting can give agonising pain. He has lost a lot of blood but he should do well enough when we get him to Allestone. I have an excellent physician there who is used to dealing with battle injuries.'

'Oh, no,' she said brokenly, 'surely to move him will make him worse? Can he not be put to bed here?'

He gestured up to the still-smoking and dripping rafters after the firefighters had done their work. 'You cannot stay here, demoiselle, either of you. Those timbers may not be safe. You could have the roof down later and, in all events, that roof will not keep out bad weather. Your father needs shelter and careful tending. I will see to it that a stretcher is procured and he is taken very carefully to Allestone.'

She opened her mouth to protest but thought better of it. He was ripping up linen cloth from the table with hands and teeth and winding an improvised bandage tightly around her father's leg, frowning in concentration. 'This must not be too tight or stay on too long or it could cause trouble later. We must move him as quickly as we can now.' He stood up and called to two of his men, who hastened out to fashion a litter.

Gisela watched numbly as the Allestone men went about their work efficiently. As yet she could not tell how many of her own people had survived. She tried to pull her straying, grieving thoughts into some sort of order. She should be making arrangements for the care of the injured. If the house was not safe, where could they be accommodated?

Lord Alain returned to her and reached down a helping hand as she attempted to stand. Her legs were still shaking. She allowed him to take her by the shoulders and turn her and hold her close to his body.

She experienced a surge of utter thankfulness that he was here. She had never felt so comforted since she had been a child and Aldith had lifted her on to her knee and kissed away her tears after some minor accident. She felt an idiotic desire to just rest against him, close her eyes and allow him to take her to some place away from all this pain and ugliness where she could feel warm and safe.

Abruptly she pulled away. This would not do. She was no longer a child and Aldith—Aldith might even now lie stiffening somewhere. . .

As if in answer to her thoughts, a voice called to her from the direction of the screen doors, which had banged open suddenly.

'Demoiselle Gisela. Oh, dear God, no. Demoiselle Gisela. . .'

Relief flooded through Gisela. 'Here, Aldith, I'm here,' she cried and the older woman dashed across and enfolded her mistress in her arms and rocked her to and fro in an anguished mixture of joy and distress at what she had discovered here.

'I was in the village,' she cried. 'I saw the smoke and started to run and then when I saw some of those men coming out of the gate laden down with goods and I thought—I thought. . .I ran and hid, Demoiselle Gisela. I'm sorry, but I was so frightened I couldn't do anything—I know I should have come and. . .'

'You did quite the most sensible thing, Dame Aldith,' Lord Alain said firmly. 'Had you not done so you would have been murdered as some of the other women have been and proved no use at all to your lady. Now she will be very glad of your tending.'

Aldith was patting Gisela's bent head as they clung together.

'My master, Sir Walter?'

'Is injured, but I pray he will recover,' Lord Alain informed her. 'But—' he glanced significantly at the figure shrouded in his mantle. '—I'm afraid Sir Kenrick of Arcote was killed bravely trying to defend your mistress. Someone must be sent to inform his people and allow them to make arrangements for masses to be said for him and for his burial. I will see to it that his body is guarded until he can be carried home.'

Gisela gave a great sob again and Aldith, whose face had expressed yet more shock and horror at the news, bent to whisper soft words of comfort.

Aldith then hastened off to pack necessities for her mistress once she had assured herself that Gisela could be left alone for some moments with the company of strange men from Allestone. She glanced briefly at Lord Alain as if assessing his character, then with a little nod she left the hall.

Lord Alain returned to Gisela's side. 'There are six fatalities, four men and two women. Several more of your women are in a distressed state and I have ascertained that they have kin in the village who could come and fetch them and accommodate them until it is fit and safe for them to return here. Two more of your men are quite seriously injured and should be conveyed to Allestone with your father. The rest can manage here, I think.

'Many have fled into the woods and will return later. As yet there is no word of your reeve, which is a pity. I had hoped he would take charge of the household, but I will leave one of my more reliable men to see to things here. Now we should leave. The litter is prepared and the sooner your father is being tended properly, the better.'

Aldith had returned with a bundle and he nodded approvingly. 'I'll see to it that one of my men takes you up pillion, Dame Aldith.'

'I can ride,' Gisela faltered.

'No,' he said decisively. 'You are in no fit state to do so. You will ride with me.'

She was about to protest when the men appeared in the hall with the litter and she was more anxious about her father, as she moved to see that he was lifted carefully and placed comfortably amongst the skins and cushions the men had found, than wanting to argue with her imperious rescuer.

As they were about to leave, men arrived from Arcote. Obviously they had ridden hard and Gisela crossed to Kenrick's reeve, who was looking hastily about the disordered hall for the whereabouts of his master's body.

'I am so very sorry,' Gisela said chokingly. 'Please convey my deepest condolences to Lady Eadgyth. How—how did she take—this terrible news?'

The man shook his head, his eyes misting with tears. 'Demoiselle Gisela, I do not think she has realised it yet. I don't think any of us have. He was—' he gulped '—a fine gentle master. We shall not see his like again. I've—ordered a bier prepared and all is at hand at Arcote to receive his body and—and the priest has arrived and will begin to say prayers—' He broke off and blinked rapidly as Lord Alain approached before adding, 'I hear your father is hurt, not too seriously, I hope. . .'

'Seriously enough,' Lord Alain said grimly. 'I warn you to keep a careful watch at Arcote. We have six dead here and several more injured and women ravished. If you've cause to fear attack, send to Allestone at once. There will be more of these raids, I'm afraid.'

'Aye, my lord.' The man looked to the wrapped form of his young master and took a step closer. 'You can leave all to me, my lord, to see that all is arranged reverently. Thank you for all you did here.'

Gisela touched the older man's hand just once in sympathy. She knew Kenrick was popular with all his household and this would be a terrible blow to them and was likely to kill Lady Eadgyth. Once she had composed herself somewhat after this shock and seen to her father's care, she must go and speak with Kenrick's mother, though how she would find the right words to express herself adequately, she did not know.

In the courtyard the Allestone men who were escorting the party home were seeing to their mounts. The litter carrying Sir Walter, who had stirred briefly, opened his eyes and then relapsed into unconsciousness again as Gisela bent over him and kissed his forehead, had already begun to make slow progress on its way back to the castle. A groom waited with Lord Alain's destrier and another man was pulling Aldith up behind him. Her bundle had been taken by another.

Lord Alain mounted and reached down a hand to Gisela. 'Do you need one of my men to lift you up?'

'No, no.' She put one foot up on to his stirrup and he easily lifted her and settled her before him in the saddle. She turned and gave a last look at her ravished home and he drew her close to his body with a supporting arm, drawing his fur-lined mantle around her.

'It is cold. You are shivering. We shall have you warm soon.'

She was still too upset to resist. It seemed that all effort to think for herself had deserted her. Again she felt comforted by the nearness of his strong body. The shock of Kenrick's death was now beginning to make itself felt and her teeth chattered. She must not give way to tears again.

Was she responsible? Had she not met with Kenrick illicitly in Allestone wood, he would not have ridden with her to Brinkhurst—to his death. Lady Eadgyth, she was sure, would see it that way and yet—had not these two men come to her rescue. . . She was trembling so violently now as she began to comprehend the sheer horror of what would have been her fate had she been present at the beginning of the raid.

The man who held her close had saved her. Kenrick had died in the attempt. She felt sick and forced back the bile rising in her throat. She owed Lord Alain her life—and probably her father's for, if he had lain untended in the hall, he would surely have died. Yet she was aware that his presence here and the debt she owed him placed her at a disadvantage in her dealings with him.

She was deeply grateful for his intervention, and for his responsible control of the situation, but she had an innate dislike of the man. He was like no other man she had met. Their first clash had stirred her to an awareness of his essential masculinity.

Other men had deferred to her, even her beloved father, and she knew Kenrick had worshipped her, yet from the first, Baron Alain de Treville had treated her with respect, but never once had he given in to her wishes—except in his judgement of Sigurd, and that mercy might well have been due to his own reasons for showing clemency rather than a desire to please her.

In their conversation within the castle courtyard after the incident with the puppy she had felt at a total loss. He had received her gratitude for his leniency towards Sigurd with quiet gravity but there were times when she could not understand his attitude towards her, his teasing which made her resistance to his wishes appear childish and worse—churlish.

She was too weary now to pull away from him, though his physical nearness disturbed her. His arm compelled her closeness; she was glad of the warmth of his body and the mantle, which shielded her from the damp chill of the approaching evening, enfolded her like protecting wings.

On their arrival at the castle Huon hastened to help her down and she was instantly conducted to the hall and a chair near the blazing hearth. Lord Alain swept off his mantle and placed it round her shaking shoulders, for her own garments were dirtied and torn during the struggle with her intended captor.

Wine and food were brought to her and Lord Alain moved off, murmuring that he intended to check on her father's condition and he would return with news quickly. He also assured her that a chamber within the tower was being made ready for her and Aldith.

Servants scuttled about, attending to the needs of the new arrivals, but they kept a respectful distance between themselves and Gisela as if ordered to afford her the dignity and privacy she required.

Gisela felt too sick to eat but Aldith insisted.

'You must, dear heart. You will need your strength. Your father will need to rely on you for a while.'

Listlessly Gisela obeyed her and, meeting her former nurse's enquiring look, hesitantly and very quietly told of her meeting with Kenrick and how he had ridden back to Brinkhurst with her and come by his death.

Aldith sighed heavily and glanced warily round the hall at the servants who were casting them curious looks.

'Mistress, I think you should not tell anyone else of this meeting. It would certainly do no good for Lady Eadgyth to discover the truth of it and I doubt if your father will wish the world at large to be informed of the circumstances. All it needs to be believed is that Sir Kenrick had come on a visit to the manor and naturally went to your defence as any man of honour would do.'

Gisela swallowed hard. 'You think it should be kept from the Baron?'

Aldith avoided her gaze. 'If your father is still of the intention of wedding you to him, yes.'

'Oh, no, Aldith, do not even think of it,' Gisela whispered agitatedly.

'Well,' Aldith said firmly, 'he has proved himself a man of fine-tempered steel.'

She broke off as the Baron returned and came to Gisela's side. 'If you would like to come with me and see your father, you can question my physician yourself and be assured of his good judgement. Your attendant can be taken to prepare your chamber. I have arranged for a truckle to be taken in there for her use.'

*　　*　　*

Sir Walter had been installed in a small chamber within the thickness of the tower wall on the second landing. As they approached, the leathern curtain that served as a door was thrust aside and a tall, elderly man stepped outside to greet them. Gisela was instantly relieved at sight of him. She liked his grave, dignified bearing and air of quiet confidence. She saw that he was a Jew by his dark gaberdine robe.

He bowed in Eastern fashion, his fingers brushing his heart and forehead.

'The wound is deep, demoiselle, and has cut into thigh muscle. I can detect no broken bone. The blood loss has been considerable but is now checked. I am most concerned about the head wound, which might have come about as he fell or was administered in the struggle with his antagonist, possibly by a sword hilt. He comes in and out of consciousness so I do not fear too much for his eventual recovery, but he must be kept very quiet.

'I have administered a mild dose of poppy juice so he will not continue to be restless in the night and I will watch by him later when I have tended the rest of your wounded.'

'I would like to stay with him. . .'

'I do not think that sensible, demoiselle. You are very shocked, naturally, by the events of the day and have taken some slight injuries yourself. You need your rest and I venture to say I can gauge your father's condition more efficiently. I have experience of this type of injury.'

'Thank you,' she said softly. 'May I see him, master physician?'

'Of course, demoiselle, but I beg you not to wake him.'

Her father appeared somewhat diminished in the small cot thrust close to the wall. His face seemed drained of all colour, but the steady rising and falling of his chest told her he was resting comfortably. She bent and kissed him very carefully upon the forehead, then did as the physician had asked and left him to the care of one who was more knowledgeable about such battle injuries than she was.

As they mounted the spiral chair to her chamber on the third landing, Lord Alain informed her of the man's credentials.

'Joshua ben Suleiman trained at Salerno and is capable and totally dedicated to his art. He has been with me some years and has treated me on several occasions after battle. You can leave your father to his care in total confidence.'

She nodded tremulously.

'I—I have to thank you once again, Lord Alain, for your immediate response to our need—and—and for your rescue of me. I—I haven't even asked if you were hurt further in that encounter. . .'

'Just a few scratches,' he said smiling. 'I see you have some marks of battle upon you. Joshua has sent up a pot of salve for your attendant to deal with your minor wounds. Should she feel that you need his care, she should send down at once and summon him. He has also provided you with a mild poppy drink for I think you will find it hard to rest tonight although I am sure you are exhausted.'

At the entrance to her chamber he bent and, turning her palms upwards, kissed them gently in farewell, then turned and ran lightly down the stair towards the hall.

Inside the small chamber, constructed as her father's had been within the defensive thickness of the tower wall, Aldith had already turned down the fur pelt that served as a coverlet. A warmed brick had been brought up for Gisela's added comfort.

Gisela sank thankfully down on the bed.

'My father is in good hands,' she said tiredly as she reached up to remove her ruined head veil and fillet.

'The physician seems confident that he will recover and I trust in the man's abilities.'

Aldith's truckle had been pushed close to her own and Gisela noted it thankfully, for she could not have borne to be alone tonight. Indeed, she wondered if she would ever feel entirely safe again.

She started as there came a male voice from outside the enclosing leather curtain.

'It is I, Huon, Demoiselle Gisela. The Baron sent me to assure himself of your complete satisfaction with your chamber and that everything had been done for your comfort.'

'Thank you,' Gisela said. 'Tell him all is well.'

Aldith thrust aside the curtain and the boy was revealed clutching tightly to a small, round rush basket from which came the sound of frantic scratching and whimpering. He looked down at it defensively.

'Lord Alain saw how you admired him and thought this gift might comfort you, demoiselle, but if he is troublesome or you too weary to cope with him I will take him away again.'

Gisela reached mutely for the basket, her lips parting, in spite of herself, in a little delighted smile. Within sat the hound puppy she had tried to rescue in the castle courtyard. Great round eyes regarded her solemnly and a small pink tongue lolled happily at sight of her. She took the basket from Huon and, placing it down on the bed, lifted him out and nuzzled her nose against his velvety brown head.

'Tell your master I am very touched by his gift,' she said brokenly, 'and I will certainly keep him with me tonight.'

The boy sighed his relief and moved to the doorway again.

'Thinking that you might be glad of someone you

know well to guard your chamber tonight, Lord Alain has made provision for that, too.'

He made her a courteous bow and withdrew.

Gisela stepped out of her chamber, still clutching the squirming pup as a shambling figure rose from a crouched position on the landing and gave her a respectful salute. She gave the second glad cry of that terrible day.

'Aldith, come and look. It is Sigurd, released from his prison,' she said.

Chapter Four

Pale light was streaming into the chamber when Gisela woke. For the moment she lay bemused, unable to recall why she was not in her own chamber at Brinkhurst. Then realisation came and she sat up with a little sob and gazed wildly round for Aldith. She was alone, so obviously her maid had gone down to the hall to ask for warm water to be brought.

As she pushed back the coverlet to stand up, Gisela heard a sharp yelp from somewhere near the window and turned to see her newest acquisition, the hound pup, straining to reach her from his tether, a long piece of rope Aldith had secured to the soft leather collar he wore and had tied to the strong iron hasp on a chest beneath the unshuttered lancet window. Obviously this had been to prevent him from dashing after her down the stair.

Gisela untied him and returned with him to the bed where she sat nursing and kissing him. He returned her show of affection with wags of his tail and continued efforts to lick her face.

The terrible grief that had assailed her when realisation had struck was somewhat relieved by the love she was able to lavish upon this small creature. She wept and kissed him and was still doing both when Aldith pushed aside the leather curtain in the doorway and entered with a ewer of hot water and towels.

She said, frowning in mock annoyance, 'You will spoil that dog outrageously if you go on like that.'

Gisela pushed back the heavy waves of her hair and blinked back tears.

'Aldith, I'm sorry, crying doesn't help. It all came upon me suddenly when I saw I wasn't at Brinkhurst. As for this little chap, don't be hard on him. He's still just a baby and probably missing his mother. Have you heard any news of Father?'

'Not yet. The seneschal tells me the Jewish physician is in attendance and you can see him later.'

'You don't know then if he has regained consciousness?'

Aldith shook her head. 'Try not to worry. He will sleep late after the drug they gave him, doubtless.'

As Gisela made to stand up again, the puppy renewed his attentions and Aldith quelled him with a little slap and fastened him again to the chest hasp.

'You little devil dog, stay there. I woke up to find him chewing one of your shoes. I will find some milk for you soon and later, Sigurd will go in search of some meat for you and, perhaps, take you for a walk in the bailey.'

Gisela washed and dressed hurriedly. She was impatient now to go to her father. 'Have you seen Lord Alain this morning?'

Again Aldith shook her head. 'I'm told he has gone over to Brinkhurst to look over the damage and to order craftsmen to come over from Oakham.'

Gisela frowned. '*I* need to do that. He takes too much on himself.'

Aldith looked at her sharply. 'There's gratitude. The man takes upon himself your problems when, I imagine, he has plenty of his own and you find fault with him.'

'Don't speak to me as if I were still a child,' Gisela snapped, then regretted her burst of temper immediately and reached out for Aldith's work-worn hand. 'I'm sorry. That was unforgivable. I know you have only my welfare at heart, Aldith, but. . .'

'But you still resent the attentions of your suitor,' Aldith said pointedly. 'What would have happened had he *not* come to your rescue, I dread to think.'

'I know that,' Gisela said defensively, 'and I am very grateful to him for that and for the care of my father but—he is too arrogant. He assumes we shall instantly follow his advice and all this without consulting us.'

'Your father is in no state yet to be consulted upon anything,' Aldith said, 'and I do not think you are either—yet.'

Gisela fastened her girdle. She was thankful that Aldith had brought changes of clothes from Brinkhurst, for the gown she had worn last night was beyond repair. Just to look at it made her shudder at the remembrance of how close she had been to ravishment and death. And she had Alain de Treville to thank for her salvation!

She was ashamed of her previous pettish outburst. She avoided Aldith's eye. She knew her resentment was due, not to the Baron's officiousness, but to the fear that was haunting her mind. Her one hope of escape from a forced marriage with this man had lain in Kenrick—and Kenrick was lying cold and stark upon a bier in the hall at Arcote.

She descended the spiral stair with Aldith and went to break her fast in the hall, where a trestle had been laid for her near the hearth despite the late hour of the morning. Sigurd stood waiting to serve them and Gisela managed to give him a wan smile.

'You have not been harmed in your prison, Sigurd?'

He shook his head. 'No, mistress. They kept me shut up but they fed me. The Baron sent word last night I could be released to tend you and my mother so long as

I gave my sworn word I would not try to escape.'

'And you gave it?'

His young mouth turned down at the corners. 'He is my liege lord. I had no choice and—and I wanted to come to your help, mistress.'

'Then see that you keep your word, for I shall feel responsible should you break it.'

He poured ale for her and she began to toy with a piece of fine white manchet bread as Aldith pushed the honey pot to her.

'Sigurd, you must accept your new status with as much good grace as possible. You know you have been treated leniently.'

'He's been told that,' Aldith snapped. 'I want to hear no more of his complaining. We all have to make the best of our lives that we can. How would he have fared if I had given up after Rolf died?'

Gisela lowered her head. She felt that Aldith was censoring her too in this dour statement. Aldith believed that Gisela should accept her fate with good grace, obey her father and marry Baron Alain de Treville. No one, she thought furiously, will understand just how I am grieving for Kenrick, not only because he is lost to me but because I know I brought about his death.

I must go and pay my respects to Kenrick's mother, she decided, just as soon as I have seen my own father and assured myself that he is no worse and receiving every care.

Walter of Brinkhurst was awake and, to her relief, fully cognisant of all that had happened, when she was allowed to see him about an hour later. He still looked bloodless and was obviously exhausted, propped up on pillows, when she sank to her knees by the bedside to kiss his hand.

He bent to stroke her veiled head. 'You were not harmed, my child?' His question was sharp, his meaning only too clear. 'I hear you arrived in the middle of all that destruction.'

'No, Father. Baron Alain de Treville arrived by good fortune and rescued me from one of the routiers who— who—' She averted her head. 'He killed the man after— after the man had killed Kenrick.'

'Aye, I have been told that.' Sir Walter compressed his lips. 'He was a fine, honourable young man—we shall all miss him about the shire. I understand his reeve arrived to convey his body to Arcote.'

'Yes, Lord Alain took charge of all that and has arranged for the burial of our people.'

Sir Walter nodded. 'De Treville is a capable man. We are fortunate to count him as a friend.' He glanced down deliberately at Gisela and she bit her lip. He meant more than a friend and his expression had told her that. She was determined that he should not press the matter of a betrothal further. She had no wish to distress him in his weakened state.

She rose to her feet. 'The doctor tells me you are doing well, Father, but should rest a great deal over the next few days. I shall come and see you again soon. In the meantime, I shall see to it that all that is necessary is done at Brinkhurst so we might return there as soon as possible.'

Her father grunted. 'I understand there is no sign of Oswin. He was not numbered amongst the dead so must have run off to safety—not that I blame him. De Treville informs me that the roof at Brinkhurst is so badly damaged that it will be weeks before we can go back, especially as the weather worsens. He offers us his hospitality here at Allestone for as long as is needful.'

Which situation will suit him very well, Gisela fumed inwardly, but dared not express her irritation to her father. She kissed him hastily and withdrew.

*   *   *

Gisela found Sigurd in the hall and asked him to take her to the stables. She wished to know if her palfrey had been brought from Brinkhurst since she had every intention of riding over to Arcote to see Lady Eadgyth.

As they were about to cross the bailey, their progress was checked by a company of Allestone men-at-arms coming through the gatehouse arch. Gisela saw Baron Alain de Treville was at their head.

Sigurd slunk back behind her and she waited a little nervously as Lord Alain dismounted and began to come towards her. To her horror, she saw that the last man to ride in was tugging a prisoner who, like Sigurd had been on that dreadful day of the attack on his lord, was secured by a rope to his captor's saddle.

Lord Alain reached Gisela's side and bowed.

'I trust you slept adequately and were comfortable. I could not hope that you slept soundly after all that happened, but I hope to make your stay here as pleasant as possible.'

'Thank you, everything has been done for my own and my father's pleasure.'

She shielded her eyes against the low wintry sun to peer at the prisoner who was being taken in charge by the sergeant, struggling and making hoarse, pleading cries. The Baron followed her gaze and shrugged somewhat regretfully.

'I am sorry you should have seen that.'

'I'm sure you are,' she retorted hotly. 'You appear to make a habit of brutality towards your people, my lord. What has the man done that he should be treated so?'

Again Lord Alain followed her gaze, his own expression unmoved by her protest.

'He has committed the unforgivable sin, demoiselle. He has disobeyed my direct orders, issued to all my men this very morning.'

'I see.' Her own expression revealed her distaste for his severity.

He smiled grimly. 'To be explicit, he was caught in the act of looting property at Brinkhurst. I will not have my men behaving like the routiers who caused the damage in the first place.'

She made a little sound of distress and he nodded, then, pushing his hand into the embroidered opening of his tunic, he withdrew a small reliquary hanging from a heavy gold chain. 'I think this may be yours.'

She took it from him, touching it reverently, her eyes blurring with sudden tears.

'Yes, it was my mother's. I was wearing it when—when I was attacked. It must have come loose in the struggle.' She swallowed hard. She still could not think of that dreadful fight without breaking into a cold sweat of terror.

'Just so.'

She turned again to watch as the struggling prisoner was led away.

'What do you intend to do with him?'

'Why, hang him, of course.'

'Oh, no, you cannot.'

His eyebrows rose eloquently. 'Demoiselle Gisela, I cannot for ever be giving way to your misguided pleas for those who offend against my laws. This must serve as an example to my men.' He did not add that it was by no means an easy task to hold in check a company of armed men whose general taste ran to acquiring the spoils of war whenever possible.

She said huskily, 'I understand, my lord, but—but since this was my property and—and no one was hurt. . .'

'Do you think these men of mine possess any more principles than those who attacked your manor yesterday? They are bred to fight, live hard lives and expect to profit from victories. They are disciplined only by the strength of will and power of the man who leads them. Believe me, I know. I have experienced more aftermaths of battle than you can imagine.

'My men will expect me to punish the man. If I show weakness, they will not respect my orders in the future— and you will be no more safe with them than with any other masterless men.'

She swallowed and turned from him, fighting for control. She knew in her heart that he was speaking plain common sense and that her father would have agreed with him, yet she could not resist one final plea.

'This is not war, my lord. . .'

'It is worse than war, it is pillage,' he interrupted coldly. 'This giving way to unbridled greed leads on to more serious crimes—like rape.'

Colour flooded her cheeks and her lips parted slightly in remembered distress.

'However—' he shrugged again in that Gallic fashion she was beginning to know '—since it is *your* trinket and you plead for him so eloquently, I will forgo hanging him.'

'Then what will you do with him?' she enquired diffidently. She knew she was unwise to press him further and yet needed to know for her own peace of mind. If the man were to be maimed, he could die a more lingering death and that would be her fault.

His opaque dark eyes regarded her steadily. 'You are determined to know what other maidens would prefer to ignore.'

'Yes.' It was a faint whisper and he gave a short barked laugh.

'Why, then, know you must. I suppose my best plan would be to have the fellow soundly flogged and dismiss him from my company. I'll not have one I cannot trust in the service of Allestone.'

She nodded with a little sigh. She knew, well enough,

that the punishment was severe. In this coming winter, masterless men could starve, but the fellow would have a chance. She thrust back the thought that he might well join the very company of mercenaries who had attacked Brinkhurst.

'I have to thank you again, my lord,' she said.

'Then let us turn to more pleasant matters. I hear your father is improving.'

'Oh, yes, he has regained consciousness and knows everything about the attack. Master ben Suleiman is pleased with his progress.'

'Excellent.'

She was aware of Sigurd stirring awkwardly behind her. 'I have to thank you for allowing Sigurd to attend me,' she said, her voice, for the first time, expressing real warmth, 'and for my little puppy, of course. How kind of you not only to make me a present of one but to remember just which one it was I took such a fancy to.'

His dark eyes lit up with sudden fire as his brooding gaze dwelt on her proudly held young form. 'I could never have forgotten the sight of you with the puppy in your arms, demoiselle. Every detail was engraved on my memory.'

Dark colour suffused her cheeks again. She was never sure just how to take such remarks. She would not have taken him for a gallant, though he had served at the King's court. Was he making fun of her?

He said abruptly, 'May I ask just where you are bound?'

'To the stables. I wished to know if my palfrey is there.'

'Certainly she is. I gave orders that she was to be brought here. I felt sure you would want to ensure that she was being well cared for. You were not intending to ride out?' His gaze took in her mantle and hood.

'Yes,' she replied evenly. 'I wish to ride to Arcote and pay my condolences in person to Sir Kenrick's mother, Lady Eadgyth.'

'Do you think that is wise?'

She was startled by the sharpness of the question and turned wide blue eyes upon him.

'Of course. Sir Kenrick was our nearest neighbour and friend. It is only right that I should do so.'

'Would it not be better for you to leave this for some days?'

'No, I want to go at once. Sir Kenrick died defending me and. . .'

'Then I will ride with you. You cannot go alone.'

She was instantly alarmed. The very last thing she wanted was for this man to accompany her on what she knew would prove a very delicate mission. Her true relationship with Kenrick was as yet unknown to all but herself and the dead man, but Lord Alain must not be allowed to guess at the nature of it.

'No, no,' she protested. 'You rose early on my business. I cannot put more upon you. It is but a short ride and Sigurd can run at my saddle bow. He has done so before, often.'

'Sigurd has given his word not to leave the castle,' the Baron replied smoothly, his dark eyes set on the boy who was regarding him doubtfully. 'Come, Demoiselle Gisela, if you are determined to go to Arcote, you must accept my escort.'

She was forced to give way with good grace and waited docilely while her palfrey was led out, then submitted to being lifted into the saddle by Lord Alain. He commanded four of his men to accompany them.

They were both silent throughout the short ride. Apparently Lord Alain had no more to say to her and Gisela was too wrapped in her own gloomy thoughts as they approached Arcote to try and distract him by light conversation.

On their arrival at the door of Arcote Manor, Lord Alain dismounted and hastened to assist her down.

'I am not known to the Lady Eadgyth so it would not be seemly for me to intrude upon her grief at this time. I will wait for you here in the bailey.'

She nodded thankfully and hastened up the steps and passed into the hall itself. Instantly she halted as she saw that the bier holding Kenrick's body held pride of place in the centre. Four candlesticks stood, one at each corner, and an elderly priest knelt in prayer beside the shrouded form of Arcote's lord. Kenrick's reeve came soft-footed to Gisela's side and bowed low.

'Greetings, Demoiselle Gisela. I trust your father is improved.'

She glanced nervously from the body of the man who should have been her betrothed back to the elderly man at her side.

'He is, thank you, Osric. How is Lady Eadgyth? This must have been a terrible blow to her. Will you tell her I am here?'

'She has been distraught, demoiselle, naturally. She had no intimation that Sir Kenrick had been near Brinkhurst at the time of the attack. She has kept strictly to her chamber. An apothecary from Oakham was summoned and he prescribed poppy juice, which has quietened her first hysteria.'

Gisela's lips trembled. 'I am so deeply sorry that he should have come to this attempting to help us.'

Osric bowed again and withdrew to the ladies' bower to acquaint his mistress with the news of Gisela's arrival.

Gisela hesitantly approached the bier and knelt by the priest's side. Kenrick's face was uncovered and appeared serene. Indeed, one would have thought he was sleeping, she thought, as a lump rose in her throat and threatened to choke her. She managed to recite the prayers for the dead with the priest and rose finally as Osric re-entered the hall.

He crossed to her side; as he lifted his head to face her, she saw his expression was grave and embarrassed.

'Demoiselle, my mistress thanks you for your presence and your condolences and bids me inform you she is much too ill and grief-stricken to receive visitors. She knows you will understand.' He hesitated. 'She also requires me to tell you that—that Sir Kenrick's burial will take place tomorrow within the village church and—in the presence of his family and members of his household—only.'

It was clear he found his message distasteful as Gisela gave a little hurt gasp. She lifted her chin slightly.

'I see. I understand, Osric. How terribly Lady Eadgyth must be suffering. My father and I wish her to be aware of the high regard we had for Sir Kenrick. We shall hold our own prayers for him. Will you convey to her that—that I will respect her wishes.'

She turned hastily before he could be aware of the depths of her distress and sense of outrage. Kenrick had been their dearest friend at Brinkhurst. Since her father could not be present at his obsequies, it was only right and proper that Gisela should attend. Lady Eadgyth was showing her displeasure for the past attentions her son had shown Gisela.

Now, more than ever, the secret of their planned marriage, even their plans for elopement should all else have failed, must be kept by her alone. She turned once more to the bier with its softly murmuring attendant, then quietly left the hall.

Outside she was close to tears when Lord Alain came to her.

'She—blames me for his death,' she said shakily. 'She

will not receive me and—and she has more or less forbidden me to attend his funeral.'

He nodded gravely. 'I thought that might be the case. I have heard much about the temperament of the Lady Eadgyth and feared she would treat you harshly. Though it is no fault of yours that Sir Kenrick was killed, undoubtedly she believes that had he not been attempting to save you he would still be alive and with her now. She is obviously beside herself. You must forgive her.'

'Yes. Yes, I know.'

She turned towards her palfrey and was about to be assisted into the saddle when another visitor rode into the courtyard, attended by two men-at-arms.

He dismounted quickly and came towards the two, bowing almost obsequiously to acknowledge Lord Alain's rank.

'My lord de Treville. I presume you, too, have come on the same melancholy mission as I have done. I heard at Offen how Sir Kenrick had died and decided to offer my condolences to his grieving mother.'

His bold eyes raked over Gisela's slim form as she turned hastily to face him.

He was a big man, heavily muscled, who would run to fat in the future probably, but at present his height and arrogant bearing and striking good looks would prove attractive to many women, Gisela thought. He pushed back his mailed coif to reveal a mop of dark curly hair and his bearded lips parted in a broad smile as he gazed insolently at her.

'I do not think I am acquainted with your companion, my lord.'

Lord Alain's greeting was as curt as the other's had been effusive.

'This is the Demoiselle Gisela of Brinkhurst. She and her father are my guests following the unfortunate attack on her manor, in which business Sir Kenrick met his death, Sir Mauger. It seems the news reached you quickly at Offen.'

Gisela recoiled almost visibly as if the man had struck her a blow and only Lord Alain's gentle, restraining hand upon her wrist prevented her from making some angry response. This, then, this flamboyantly swaggering man was Mauger de Cotaine of Offen whom all in the shire credited with the sheltering of the men who constantly raided their property. How dared he call so impudently to condole with Lady Eadgyth!

She looked from him to Lord Alain as if she expected her escort to make some accusation. He did not do so, though his manner to the other was decidedly cool.

Sir Mauger appeared to take no offence. He continued to smile and bowed exaggeratedly low to Gisela.

'I am sorry to hear of your misfortune, demoiselle. I suppose you, too, have been to see Lady Eadgyth, an unfortunate business. I take it your father is indisposed following the incident or he would be with you now.'

Gisela felt the bile rising in her throat and could not answer him but Lord Alain did so for her.

'Yes, Sir Walter was injured. However, he is progressing well and will be soon seeking some reprisal for this unprecedented attack from the shire reeve at Oakham.'

'Ah, then he knows who was responsible?'

Gisela drew a hard breath but again the grip on her wrist counselled her to silence.

'Unfortunately, no. I, myself, was present shortly after the attack and saw some of the looters. They wore no distinguishing device, but one would not expect them to do so. Those who fell in the attack died and so were unable to give us information about their protector. The men are being harboured somewhere in the vicinity and it should not be too difficult to apprehend them soon.'

The other man continued to smile broadly, slapping

one mailed glove he had removed on his other hand. 'One would believe so, my lord, but since these raids continue to go on unchecked, it will not prove an easy task.'

'No,' Lord Alain replied evenly. 'There is talk, of course, suspicions, but unfortunately no proof against anyone—as yet. Lady Eadgyth is distraught, I understand, and you may find she is unable to receive you. Excuse us. We must return to Allestone. You will understand, with many of the household of Brinkhurst quartered at my castle, I have much to do.'

Sir Mauger nodded and bowed again to Giscla. She was deeply afraid he would offer to touch her hand and she thrust her free hand behind her hastily. She could hardly bring herself to look at the man. His bold dark eyes passed over her almost as if she were unclothed and she was not so naïve as not to realise that his first thought upon seeing her with Lord Alain had been that she was his mistress. Her flesh crawled and she was grateful for Lord Alain's presence and his skilled handling of the situation.

As the man bowed again and moved off, followed by his men, she allowed Lord Alain to lift her into the saddle and found she was trembling violently. He stood back a little and regarded her intently. She swallowed and tilted her chin deliberately. He nodded in acknowledgement of her rigid control over her own violent revulsion against this encounter, then he mounted and signalled to his own escort to mount up and they rode out.

She was still shaking when he lifted her down in the bailey at Allestone. As he moved to lead her into the keep she burst out angrily, 'Why did you not accuse him?'

'Mauger of Offen?'

'Yes, of course, Mauger of Offen.'

'Of the attack on your manor?'

'You must know he is sheltering those men who did it.'

He shook his head. 'Unfortunately, I do not know that. There is no proof. I had hoped to find one prisoner alive. Had that been the case we could have questioned him, put on some pressure, but that was not to be.'

'Everyone believes that. . .'

'What most people in the shire believe is not evidence. Had the shire reeve been sure of his ground he would have summoned Mauger to face charges long ago.'

'They are all afraid of him,' she burst out.

He turned her to face him, looking intently into her eyes.

'That may be the truth but, nevertheless, until Mauger of Offen is found to either be in possession of looted property or have routiers living under his protection, it is difficult to see what can be done. The King himself could not act without direct proof.'

She thrust off his grasp on her arm and marched defiantly up the keep steps.

He stood for a moment watching her, his eyes troubled, then he turned towards the stables, deciding it best not to follow her in her present mood.

Later he went to see his guest and was relieved to see Sir Walter much better. The Jewish physician confirmed his belief that all seemed to be well, then gathered up his chest of medicaments and left host and guest together, having indicated outside the small chamber that Sir Walter had wished to speak with Lord Alain the moment he returned to the castle.

'The head wound is not as serious as I first feared,' he explained, 'but he does seem restless and it is imperative he speak with you now as he has requested.'

Lord Alain had thanked ben Suleiman and now came to stand beside Sir Walter's bed.

'How can I serve you, Sir Walter?'

'I hear you escorted my daughter to Arcote.'

'Yes.' Lord Alain hesitated and then quickly told Sir Walter what had occurred at the manor house and of the later encounter with Mauger of Offen.

The older man frowned and sat staring into space for a while.

'I thought at one time Kenrick of Arcote would ask for Gisela's hand,' he said at last. 'Such an alliance would not have been suitable. That harridan of a mother would never have accepted Gisela with good grace and—' he smiled bleakly '—as I have said before, Gisela is not one to accept the rule of another, especially that of another woman, however senior in age.'

Lord Alain gave an answering smile.

'I do not think, either, that Gisela would ever have been contented with young Kenrick. He had an easy, pleasant manner and I'm sure he would have striven to please her, though he would not have wished to quarrel with his mother either. That was ever young Kenrick's problem. He was too ready to please everyone and anxious to avoid giving offence to others. In time, that attitude would have irritated Gisela. She would have come to despise him, finally.' He moved restlessly. 'I fear you are thinking me too ready to speak less than admirably of the dead.'

'No,' Lord Alain conceded. 'You knew Kenrick of Arcote far better than I.'

Sir Walter turned abruptly to stare into those dark, opaque eyes. 'I'll come straight to the point. Are you still willing to wed my daughter, my lord?'

There was no fraction of hesitation before the answer came. 'Certainly, Sir Walter, I wish to wed the Demoiselle Gisela—as soon as possible.'

'Aye, the way things are, I would have her under your protection.' His lips parted in a little regretful sigh. 'I warn you, my lord, Gisela will not accept my decision easily and I hesitate to press her while she is distressed by recent events and yet—' he pressed irritatedly at the fur coverlet '—I must. Will you have a clerk come so we might discuss the marriage contract immediately?'

Lord Alain nodded. 'I will send for Father John in the village. He is learned in such matters.'

'Aye, I have always found him honest and sensible.'

Lord Alain paused in the doorway. 'Do not fret yourself, Sir Walter. Whatever you consider fair I will accept and—do not be anxious about the Demoiselle Gisela. While I intend to see that she is kept safe here at Allestone, and rule her with a firm hand despite her desire to go her own way, I shall not expect too much of her—at first.'

Sir Walter gave that same bleak smile again and waved his acceptance as Lord Alain withdrew from the chamber.

In the afternoon Gisela's father sent for her. She hastened after Huon who had come with the message, fearing his condition had worsened, but she found Sir Walter sitting well up on his pillows, drinking some of Lord Alain's finest burgundy, and apparently much improved.

She sat down upon a stool placed near the bed. 'You look better. Does your wound pain you?'

'Aye, a little, when I move. The sawbones tells me that is to be expected, but let that be, child. Lord Alain tells me you were refused entry to Lady Eadgyth's bower.'

She bowed her head, avoiding his gaze. 'I'm afraid—she thinks I am responsible for Kenrick's death. She made it plain she did not wish me to attend the funeral tomorrow, but I intend to disobey her and go.'

'You will not.'

Her lips parted at the angry note in his voice and she looked up at him, startled.

'But, Father. . .'

'You will stay right away from Arcote.'

'But he was our dearest friend. . .'

'We are not kin. If Lady Eadgyth does not wish it, for you to attend in direct contradiction to such an avowed wish would cause grave offence. I know you were fond of Kenrick, but unpalatable as the truth is, Gisela, he is dead to you. You must grieve in silence. You cannot add to Lady Eadgyth's distress by causing gossip in the shire and that is what you would do if you flagrantly attend in contravention of a request to refrain from doing so.'

Tears blurred her eyes and she looked away from him. Did he guess at that last meeting she had had with Kenrick in Allestone wood? Did Lady Eadgyth? No, surely Kenrick could not have informed his mother of his intention to meet with her when she had enjoined on him the need for secrecy!

Sir Walter waited until she had gained control, then he said quietly, 'We have already discussed Lord Alain's request for your hand in marriage and I made it plain to you at the time what my wishes were. Now more than ever, Gisela, I must insist that you obey me and accept him.'

She gave a furious gasp and sprang to her feet.

'Father, you cannot ask this of me now. . .'

'Now, more than ever. Child, I have been lying here wondering what would have happened to you had I been killed.'

Her hand sprang to her mouth. 'Father, you have no intimation of. . .?'

'No, no,' he said testily. 'I have told you I am much improved, but the fact remains that I am in no condition to protect you adequately if such an occurrence happened again. It has made me think very hard, Gisela, that your one assurance of safety lies in becoming the Baron's bride.

'I have spoken with him again this morning and he

has expressed a wish for the marriage to be solemnised very soon. He also told me of your meeting with Mauger of Offen. Child, do you realise you could very easily become that man's prey?'

A terrible shudder passed through her body and Sir Walter did not miss her reaction.

'Yes,' he said grimly, 'I see you *do* know, only too well, what might befall you should you fall into his hands. Do you tell me that marriage with Lord Alain de Treville is equally abhorrent to you?'

'No,' she said hastily, 'but—I cannot express it properly—I cannot like the man. He seems too stern, too restrained—too cold. . .'

'You are afraid of him?'

Her blue eyes met his grey ones squarely and he could see she was struggling to come to terms with her own feelings of revulsion for the match.

'No,' she said at last quietly, 'I do not think I am afraid of him, yet. . .' She broke off, biting her nether lip. 'I cannot see us living in amity together—as—as I had hoped to do with—Kenrick.'

'Ah,' he said gently. 'You were easy in Kenrick's company. He made no effort to thwart your wishes. You were children together, but life with a husband is very different, Gisela, and I think, in time, you might have discovered that Kenrick had faults, too—weaknesses would perhaps be a better word—and life would not have been so fanciful as the troubadours tell.'

She blushed as she understood that he had divined her most secret longings.

'There will be much to be done here at Allestone. Life could be a challenge for you and I think, in time, you will enjoy that. Alain de Treville will prove no compliant husband, but I believe he will not prove too hard a master either.'

'You think I am afraid that he will beat me?' she asked shakily.

'That is possible,' he said laconically, 'knowing you as I do. You might well deserve it—on occasions.'

'He will not break my spirit,' she retorted, her chin lifting defiantly.

'Nor do I believe he would wish to do so. You can deal well together, Gisela, provided you are willing to make the best of the marriage.'

She was silent and he could see by her heightened colour and the suspicion of tears upon her lashes that she was very close to breaking down.

He sighed inwardly. He loved this beautiful, wilful child so dearly that it almost broke his heart to force her into this match she so vigorously opposed, yet he was sure it was the best arrangement he could make for her and he resisted the temptation to weaken now.

'You will obey me?'

Her lips trembled as she turned to face him again. She could not continue to oppose him. As he had said, the continued protection of Baron Alain de Treville could assure the safety of all at Brinkhurst. She nodded and, bending, kissed his hand, which was gripping the coverlet with unaccustomed tenseness.

'It is for me to obey. I *must* obey.'

He reached out and ruffled the smooth band of fair hair showing beneath the veil's edge at her forehead.

'Your mother would have been proud of your resolve. Go and talk to Aldith about finery for the ceremony.' He pushed her gently towards the doorway as she stooped to kiss him.

She went reluctantly to seek Aldith and found her within their small chamber, attempting to find some suitable hanging space for the gowns she had managed to bring from Brinkhurst.

'We shall have to send for more from Brinkhurst,' Gisela said baldly as she sank down dispiritedly upon the bed. The puppy jumped on her lap and she kissed his ears, finding comfort in his demonstrative loving.

'Then the marriage contract is to be signed?'

'Yes, my father insists. I have no choice, Aldith.'

'It'll be no bad thing,' Aldith said cheerfully. 'I've said as much before. You'll be my lady and a fine chatelaine you'll make. I know.'

'You are very confident.'

'He's a handsome bridegroom and most likely a skilled lover.'

'How would you know such a thing?' Gisela demanded indignantly.

'A woman of my experience can make a fair guess at such matters,' Aldith replied, smiling.

'So you think he is handsome?'

'Don't you?'

Gisela considered. 'I don't think I have considered that. He is well built and his features are not unpleasing, but he is too dark for my liking and his expression too stern and unrelenting, almost arrogant,' she conceded, 'but,' she added with a little cynical smile, 'he is not too old.'

'There you are, you are making the best of it already.'

'Perhaps, but there will be many a tussle for dominance between us, I'm thinking.'

She was ruffling the puppy's fur when she laughed and said, 'I will call you Hereward, after the Wake. He spent his life opposing the Normans.'

'And lost,' Aldith replied succinctly.

Chapter Five

To her surprise, Gisela was invited to take supper in the hall that evening. Huon came to her chamber and made the request from his master. So far, arrangements had been made for her to eat in her own chamber, except for breakfast, which she had taken alone after the Baron had already left the castle.

She accepted the invitation issued so courteously by Huon in a voice which suggested he was afraid she might refuse and so anger his master. Gisela saw by his expression that he was greatly relieved.

She dressed with care but soberly, mindful of the fact that she would really have wished to don mourning garb for Kenrick, but that was patently impossible.

She descended the tower stair with Aldith in attendance. Sigurd had taken charge of Hereward, who resented being deserted by his adoring mistress.

Lord Alain rose at once to greet her and led her to the dais where a chair had been placed for her next to his own. She felt tongue-tied in his presence. She had given way to pressure. She would be this man's bride, but she could not be easy in his company. Now she felt his eyes upon her, appraising her, and she glanced briefly at him, acknowledging the fact that he, too, had dressed with some care in a fine scarlet over-tunic, which enhanced his dark good looks.

She seated herself, knowing that her legs felt weak, and waited while Huon approached with a ewer and bowl of rose water for her to rinse her hands before beginning the meal which he proffered on bended knee. Unused to such ceremony, she felt even more ill at ease.

Lord Alain was speaking and she turned politely to face him.

'I hear the hound pup has become extremely devoted. I hope he will not be too much trouble for you.'

'No, no,' she disclaimed hastily. 'He is very gentle natured. I treasure him already.'

'Good.' His lips twitched slightly. 'I understand you have named him Hereward. I hope that is no incentive to him to hold my Norman blood in despite.'

Her own lips curved into a smile in answer and she said a little defensively, 'I have always admired the exploits of the Wake as I think most of us of Saxon blood continue to do.'

'He was a fine soldier. How could any of us deny that?'

He served her delicacies as they shared cup and trencher and she was gratified to note that though he ate heartily, his manners were good and he did not drink too frequently from his wine goblet. She could not have borne to be wed to a drunken sot.

He said without ceremony, 'Your father informs me that you have consented to become my bride. You honour me greatly, Demoiselle Gisela. I shall make every effort to assure your comfort and happiness here at Allestone.'

Her own fingers trembled on the wine cup as he offered it to her and their hands touched.

'My father wishes the match, sir. It is not for me to gainsay him.'

He regarded her gravely. 'I know it is usual for maids

to be reluctant at first, especially as you know so little about me.'

'You know even less about me, my lord,' she countered. 'I cannot but wonder at your choice. Surely there are more noble ladies at court who would make more suitable chatelaines for Allestone?'

'I think not. I know all I wish to know about you. You are beautiful, and—' his lips parted in a broad smile '—strong willed enough to make an efficient and capable mistress of my household and a fit mate for me.'

She said dutifully, almost mechanically, 'I shall strive to please you, my lord.'

He laughed out loud. 'If you constantly do that, I shall be both surprised and somewhat disappointed.' Meeting her puzzled gaze, he explained, 'I have always enjoyed our verbal engagements, Demoiselle Gisela. It was this quality that first drew me to you.' He lifted their wine cup in a smiling toast and was amused to see her blue eyes blaze back at him.

She looked down at the body of the hall, meeting boldly the avidly curious glances of Lord Alain's retainers who had this opportunity to view Lord Alain's betrothed for the first time. She noted that Sir Clement, his seneschal, and his lady, Rohese, were absent, apparently taking their meal in their own apartment.

'I hope, in time, to take you to Normandy, to present you to my lady mother and the rest of my family. I have just sent off a message to her, informing her of my good fortune in acquiring so lovely a bride.'

She turned back instantly. Strange, she had not thought of Lord Alain as having a family. It was ridiculous, of course, and she listened with interest while he talked enthusiastically of his boyhood home and how he had come into service in England and, eventually, to fight beside the King's side.

She realised how hard it had been for him, a younger

son, to make his way in the world and could only admire him for that for, it seemed, he had done so by sheer grit, hard work and loyalty.

A man-at-arms entered the hall and approached the dais, deferentially saluting his lord. 'We discovered a man entering Brinkhurst soon after noon, my lord, and mindful of your strictures against looting, we arrested him and brought him to Allestone. He begs to speak with either Sir Walter or the Demoiselle Gisela. Since Sir Walter is indisposed and now settled for the night, I wondered if. . .' He blinked in Gisela's direction apologetically.

'Keep him within the guardroom tonight.'

Gisela said quickly, 'He may have news of another survivor. There are still men missing from the household, I hear, or—or he may have information about the mercenaries. I would like to see him at once, with your permission, my lord.'

'Very well. Bring him here, but see he is well guarded.'

A man was hustled into the hall and pushed unceremoniously towards the dais. The prisoner kept his head bent, as if ashamed, but there was no mistaking that rotund figure and Gisela gave a little relieved cry.

'This is Oswin, my father's reeve. Where have you been all this time, Oswin? We feared you were dead.'

Oswin's clothes were torn and dirty and, as he lifted his head, she saw his round cheeks were besmirched by tears.

'Mistress,' he cried brokenly, 'tell them I would never steal from Sir Walter. Forgive me, Demoiselle Gisela, I was so afraid when the attack began and when I saw what those men intended—I—fled. When I saw the manor was in flames I hid in the forest and—afterwards—afterwards—I was too ashamed of my own cowardice to come back. Then—then, today, I. . .'

'There is nothing to be ashamed of, Oswin. You were

wise to run. Of course I understand. I am sure my father. . .'

She was interrupted by the Baron's voice speaking authoritatively. 'Well, now we know who this fellow is. Keep him locked in the guardroom. I shall wish to question him further.'

'No.' Gisela rose angrily. 'Oswin must not be treated like a criminal. . .'

'Do as I say,' the Baron commanded. He turned a set, stern face towards Gisela.

'Demoiselle, please accompany me to my desmesne office.' He held her wrist in a light but tight hold and she was half-pulled from her place. She turned to protest but caught sight of the angry jut of his jaw and understood that this time she had really infuriated him. She watched helplessly as Oswin was hustled out through the screen doors again, still volubly protesting his identity and his reasons for entering Brinkhurst manor.

Only then did she allow herself to be drawn towards the door behind the dais, registering the fact that Lord Alain had signalled for Aldith to follow them.

He led her into a small chamber within the thickness of the tower wall. It contained a table, a fald chair and stool. Two rolls of parchment and an unrolled one, beside inkwell and quills, showed this was the Baron's place of business where he discussed with his reeve and seneschal, as well as his sergeant-at-arms, the household accounts and gave out his instructions for the running of the household and defence of the fortress in time of need. He pushed her down upon the stool and went to stand behind the table, arms folded, his dark eyes smouldering.

'You need not fear. Dame Aldith is just outside the door and will come if called.' He leaned forward until his face was very close to her own. 'Demoiselle, do you enjoy deliberately contradicting me before my men?'

She drew back, for the first time confused and really afraid of his anger.

'Please—please, I do not understand.'

'You understand very well. I need to question that man. He may be a trusted servant of yours but he made himself scarce at a very convenient moment. At the very least he should be charged with dereliction of duty. Now he comes snivelling back to you and you want me to treat him as if he were a child in arms. I want to know where he has been skulking all this time, what his real excuse is for absenting himself. He could have been back hours ago.'

She was shocked to the marrow. 'You cannot mean that you suspect. . .?'

'These mercenaries make their attacks after being given good information. Your father was conveniently away from the manor and only returned later to become embroiled in the fighting. Someone in your household was responsible for giving a signal inviting those brutes to attack. I have been questioning all your men, aye, and your women, too. It may be that this fellow wished you well and arranged the attack after he knew you had ridden out. At all events, I intend to get to the bottom of it and a spell in my guardroom will make him hesitate before lying to me.'

She gave a great gasp of horror.

'I cannot believe that. . .'

'Obviously not. You are too trusting, demoiselle.' He was glaring at her across the table. 'We shall deal better together as husband and wife if you do not openly continue to oppose my decisions. I said I admired your spirit and I will, on occasions, listen to and defer to your judgement, but not before my retainers. Do you hear me?'

'Yes,' she stammered, too shocked by his outburst to argue. 'Yes, my lord, I—I understand that I put you in an unfortunate position and. . .'

'Go on thinking about that.'

He stood upright abruptly and eventually sat down at the table, fingering the unrolled parchment moodily, as if he was striving to regain his temper.

She was not sure if he had finished with her and sat on for moments, watching him uncertainly, her eyes huge in her pale face, then, as she made to half-rise, he pushed the parchment towards her.

'Do you read? This is the marriage contract Father John drew up in the presence of your father and me earlier today. I wished to inform you of the conditions.'

She nodded. 'I do, a little, but I am sure it is satisfactory if my father has agreed to it.'

'The provisions are simple. Your father has promised a dower, subject to his means. I shall not insist on any hurry about that since the damage to Brinkhurst is considerable and, of course, he must have lost an amount of coin in the raid. The Michaelmas rents had only just been collected.'

She had not thought of that. In the event, the Baron might well have changed his mind about his offer of marriage, since her father's possessions had been greatly lessened by this attack.

He continued. 'I have made over to you land that is mine to give freely should I die without heir and the King, as is his right, could repossess this castle. You will be adequately provided for and, since you are your father's sole heiress, Brinkhurst will eventually become yours unless he marries again.

'That seems unlikely since your mother died so long ago but—' he shrugged lightly '—who knows what will happen these days? Your father is still relatively young and entitled to some future happiness, I'm sure you will agree.'

Her tongue seemed frozen and she could not reply to him, though she was puzzled by her own reaction. All

these arrangements were to be expected and he was showing unwonted civility in making her aware of them.

He said abruptly, 'I also wished to discuss with you
arrangements for the ceremony.'

Her head jerked in spite of her resolution to make no
objections or even to appear opposed to the match.

'I think the ceremony should be soon, before the holy
season of Christmas, if possible. After that, the bad
weather may well be upon us and the knights and your
friends in the shire might not be able to attend and bear
witness.'

As soon as that? Her heart began to thump uncomfortably and he could not avoid noting the dawning alarm
mirrored in her eyes.

'If your father should die,' he said deliberately and
put up a hand to prevent her from crying out in horror
and interrupting him. 'I did not imply there was any
likelihood of that. He is making good progress, Joshua
informs me, but he has been over-hot today and unduly
restless. He himself is not unaware of the dangers of
infection from his wound and is anxious to make absolutely sure of your safety. If anything were to happen
before we are formally betrothed or bedded, you would
become a ward of court and matters would be delayed.
I am sure the King would give his consent to our
marriage, but for a time you could be at risk, an heiress
ripe for the plucking. Your father knows that, and has
agreed to our hasty marriage because of it.'

Bleakly she reviewed the situation. Yes, she had
realised only too well that she could become prey to
some creature such as Mauger of Offen. It had happened
to many maids and widows during these uncertain days
of the war. She looked back at Baron Alain de Treville
directly. She had doubts concerning this marriage, but
not the terrible fear that would assail her if faced by a
forced alliance with some ruthless mercenary.

She bowed her head in mute acceptance of the common sense of his words. 'As you wish, my lord.'

She rose and made for the curtained doorway, thinking, now, that they had finished with this distasteful business, but he had come very close to her and, with a hand upon her shoulder, turned her gently but firmly to face him.

'Am I not entitled to the customary kiss to seal our betrothal?'

He was so very close and she could smell the maleness of him, the clean tang of soap and the hint of leather and the oil he used for cleaning armour. She knew, instinctively, that he had bathed just before descending to the hall. Even his dark hair was damp from bathing. His breath was faintly wine-scented but not overpoweringly so.

She felt trapped and longed to protest, turn and run, but knew that would be both foolish and useless. She was to become his bride—and soon. It was pointless to refuse him the promise of greater rights soon to come.

He drew her close, his arms reaching up behind her waist, pressing her to him. She had expected him to kiss her brow or cheek formally, but his lips suddenly closed upon hers, gently at first, then demandingly, so that she was forced to open her own and respond. Her head swam as she felt his hard-muscled body, so hard against hers, and she could both feel and hear the steady beat of his heart, which quickened even as her lips received his.

She had been kissed only once before this by any man other than her father. Kenrick had kissed her in the wood and she remembered, guiltily, that she had been vaguely disappointed. Now she was not sure how she felt about this. Certainly she was not disappointed, was disturbed by her own response, even alarmed. She sought to pull away and after a moment he released her gently and stood regarding her, his head slightly on one side.

'You must not be afraid of me.'

'I am not,' she said huskily. 'I—'

'Good. I shall not expect too much of you—at first.'

Hot colour was flooding her cheeks and throat. She tried to move back from him and he reached out and caught her wrist again.

'I shall ask Father John to hear our betrothal vows tomorrow.'

'Yes,' she said hurriedly, 'if my father agrees.'

She managed to make her escape then and found Aldith's frankly curious eyes upon her as she made her way quickly up the spiral stair to her own chamber. Aldith made no attempt to question her and as she lay sleepless, her mind went over and over the events of the day.

Her rejection by Lady Eadgyth had been devastating and then the meeting with that creature, Mauger—she shuddered at the recollection. Then her final surrender to her father's will, and finally there had been her objection to the Baron's summary treatment of Oswin and his unexpectedly furious response to her behaviour.

She had had a distinct reminder there, in the office, of what life would be like for her—she would be mistress of Allestone, but still Alain de Treville's chattel, and fury rose in her throat like bile. Then he had kissed her and her response to that kiss had been overwhelmingly sudden and frightening. Though she had immediately sought to withdraw from close contact with him, her traitorous body had wanted to remain in his arms.

She remembered the moment when he had held her after his rescue of her at Brinkhurst. She had felt so safe and secure then, so assured of his complete protection. She was confused. One moment she was castigating him as a tyrant in his own household and afraid of his threatened domination over her, the next she was grateful for his nearness, as she had been when Mauger of Offen's eyes had dwelt upon her so insultingly.

Not for one moment had she been afraid then, since Alain de Treville had been with her. She had hated and despised the flamboyant knight and recognised instantly the naked desire that had flamed in his eyes. She knew that the kiss had awakened Alain de Treville's desire but he had put her from him, had not continued to press unwelcome attention upon her.

The difference between the two men, she was sure, was not the depth of passion but the amount of control that each exerted upon his own desires. Mauger of Offen would make no fight against his carnal needs; Alain de Treville would hold himself under restraint until he felt the time was ripe to possess what was his. She sighed as she sank back against the pillows. That time was very close now.

Her father appeared less restless next day and the Jewish physician assured her that he was now less concerned about his patient's condition. Sir Walter was relieved when Gisela expressed herself satisfied with both the marriage contract and the arrangements for the ceremony, set for two days before Christmas.

When Father John arrived from the village, Gisela had stood docilely in her father's chamber beside Alain de Treville and they exchanged their betrothal vows. She felt a tremor pass through her as the Baron placed his heavy signet ring upon her finger, the outward symbol of his possession of her.

Over the days that followed she tried not to think of her looming marriage day—or what would follow. When Aldith had sought to prepare her, she had hastily cut off the approach and Aldith had been silenced.

She set herself to take stock of the interior of the castle as its future chatelaine. The autumn slaughter had been completed and the meat salted down and stored in barrels within the commodious cellars beneath the keep, apples and pears gathered in, sorted and stored carefully, soft fruit preserved in honey in jars sealed with hogs' fat. Rushlights and candles were being prepared for the dark days of winter ahead.

She had inspected the well in the bailey and saw with relief that water was drawn daily and stored in barrels within the keep in case of siege. Lord Alain informed her that one of his projected tasks was to have a well dug beneath the keep itself and she understood his concern. A month ago she would have derided such panicky plans, as she had his clearance of the land around the castle. Now, dry-mouthed, she was only too aware of the urgency.

Once or twice she rode over to Brinkhurst with Lord Alain to see that repairs were in progress and was finally relieved to see Oswin once more back at his work in the manor house.

Lord Alain said coolly, 'It appears he took shelter with his friend, one of the woodsmen. I can find no evidence to suggest complicity with the attackers, but I have pointed out to him the necessity of total dedication to the needs of your father. I do not think he will prove negligent again.'

She had watched her betrothed closely over this short time of freedom left to her and tried to make a fair assessment of his character. She had considered him stern and austere, but found this was not entirely correct.

True, he was hard on his men, insisting on excellent discipline within the ranks. The men were forbidden to molest the women within the villages nearby, or to swagger and annoy through overindulgence in drink, but she saw that these hard-bitten men held Lord Alain in grudging respect. Even Sigurd succumbed to a sulky acceptance of his control, though Gisela understood he was still yearning for the old freedom of movement he had formerly had.

One evening she sat in the hall with Aldith and Lady Rohese, the buxom, pretty, brown-haired wife of Sir Clement, the castle seneschal. Gisela had been afraid that this lady would resent her as the new chatelaine-to-be but found Rohese to be good-natured and easygoing, perhaps far too much so with the household servants, who were inclined to be slack unless they came under the frowning countenance of their lord.

Lady Rohese smilingly requested that Huon, who was sitting near, should play the lute to entertain them as they sat stitching at a new wallhanging for the hall.

Huon instantly complied, lifted his instrument from a nail on the wall near the hearth and began to strum and sing in a pleasing tenor voice. He sang one of the troubadour songs Gisela loved and she paused in her work, listening to him.

Lord Alain strode into the hall. He had obviously been riding on demesne business for he still wore his mail hauberk and coif and had missed supper in hall. He stood listening to his squire; Gisela noted that, after a while, the stern expression faded from his face and he drew up a stool and sat with them.

At the close of the song Huon looked up at him questioningly and Lord Alain reached out and took the beribboned instrument from the boy's hand. He strummed experimentally for a moment or two, then struck up a merry tune he had obviously heard in one of the English villages on campaign. His voice was a rich baritone and his playing accomplished. He finished with a swirl of fingers across the strings and grinned at his rapt feminine audience.

'Please sing us one of your Norman songs, my lord,' Rohese begged.

Lord Alain looked towards Gisela as if asking for her encouragement and she nodded her head, blushing rosily.

He sang, as Huon had, one of the ballads of heroic deeds then, suddenly, with a jangling chord, changed rhythms and began to sing a hauntingly romantic song of Provence, of a handsome young knight betrayed by his lady, of his desperate love for her and his death in battle in deep despair when she married another. Gisela was transfixed.

She had never known her betrothed in this mood and could not take her eyes from his blunt, skilful fingers on the strings. She knew his powerful, melodious voice would live in her memory—she had not heard a professional jongleur who had pleased her more. Her own fingers lay idle on her work and her mouth parted a little as she listened. Hereward stirred at her feet and she hushed him hastily with a gentling hand on his collar.

Lord Alain finished and rose, handing back the lute to Huon.

'You must excuse me, mesdames, I have not yet eaten and must retire to my chamber.' He bowed and left them.

Gisela sat on, thoughtful, and Lady Rohese glanced at her curiously. 'He is accomplished, is he not? I suppose he learned those skills as a page in France.'

Gisela nodded, swallowing the lump that had risen in her throat at the beauty of the music.

Huon said, laughing, 'All pages learn to entertain, but few are as accomplished as my lord, and, of course, he is passionately fond of music. He likes to read the troubadour tales too.'

The boy hurried up to his lord's chamber and Gisela was left to wonder. It seemed that Lord Alain had another side to his nature she had not guessed at.

*   *   *

The next day Aldith broached the matter of Gisela's bridal gown.

Gisela dismissed it. 'Oh, any of my gowns will do, Aldith. I have several I have worn only once or twice, quite fine enough.'

Aldith put her hands on her hips. 'Mistress, you must not disgrace Lord Alain. He is a baron, an important man in the shire and there will be many curious eyes on both of you at this wedding.'

Gisela pursed her lips then sighed. 'I suppose you are right,' she said grudgingly. 'I must seem to go willingly to this sacrificial altar.'

Aldith snorted and Gisela could not help giving a little embarrassed laugh.

In Gisela's clothing chest they discovered a length of white samite, which, worn with a warm undertunic, for the chill in the village church was likely to permeate the cloth, would prove fine enough. Aldith cut and sewed and produced a gown to be proud of, close fitting in bodice and to the hips, its hem and long, flowing sleeves bordered with marten fur.

Gisela was to wear with it a long double girdle of white and gold ribbons, plaited together and tasselled at the ends, which were long enough to reach to the hem. Aldith fashioned for her a simple fillet of gold and white silk, also plaited, which she would place over her loosened hair and she would wear the reliquary Lord Alain had rescued for her from the looter.

When attired in her bridal finery for the first time, Gisela twirled for Aldith's approval and her attendant nodded, satisfied. 'We must look out your warm fur-lined tawny-velvet mantle for it's bound to be cold in the church and possibly in the hall afterwards, despite the fire in the hearth.'

Gisela agreed. She had no intention of shivering with cold at this wedding and the feast to follow, which could

be interpreted by onlookers as fear of her wedding-
night duties.

Alain de Treville stood before the crude little altar in
Allestone church, awaiting his bride on his wedding day.
He, too, had been persuaded to dress with some attention
to current fashion, for such frivolity had always been
seen by him as unnecessary. Despite the new style
Normans now affected in wearing their hair longer, he
continued to wear his close clipped and on most
occasions wore his serviceable tunics or mail.

Today he wore a long tunic of blue damask cloth from
the East, shot with silver thread, over a longer undertunic
of unbleached fine wool. The neck and sleeves of his
overtunic were bordered with strips of cloth of silver and
the neckties were of silver cord ending in tassels. Over
this he wore a fine wool mantle in blue, lined with cloth
of silver, caught at the shoulder with an ornamental silver
brooch, which bore in its centre a polished round of
bright blue opaque stone his brother had informed him
was lapis lazuli.

Odo had been on Crusade and had purchased several
trinkets in Jaffa as gifts for the family. He had surprised
Alain by sending this brooch and the damask and cloth
of silver with his congratulations, following the receipt
of the news that Alain had been granted the lordship of
Allestone.

His older brother had jocularly remarked in the letter
that had accompanied the gifts—penned by a clerk, for
unlike Alain Odo had never bothered himself to acquire
the writing skill—that he hoped both cloth and pin would
prove useful when Alain found himself a bride, which
he prayed would be soon.

The gifts had been consigned to a chest within Alain's
chamber, but a week ago Alain had found a tailor in
Oakham willing to make up both tunic and mantle for

him in haste. This morning he had gazed at his hazy
reflection in his scratched iron shaving-mirror and wondered if he were making a fool of himself, parading like
a peacock before an unwilling bride.

A movement behind him informed him that his bride
had entered the church and he turned hastily to watch
her approach the altar. Sir Walter had made the journey
from Allestone in a covered carriage and had been carried
to a chair placed near the altar.

Alain's heart gave a sudden jolt of combined joy and
desire as he gazed at Gisela. Never had she appeared
more beautiful and it appeared she had gone to some
trouble to honour him in her becoming apparel.

Her tawny mantle had been flung back over one shoulder so Alain could see how the silky cloth, cinched in
tightly by the girdle, clung to her high, firm breasts and
the altar candles glimmered on the gold of her heavy
masses of hair that fell loose below her waist, putting to
shame the gold braid of her fillet.

She walked superbly and there was no trace of either
nervousness or artificial modesty that some women used
as an aid to coquetry. Her blue eyes met his directly and
her lips parted in a half-smile as she slipped her hand
within her father's on reaching his side.

She made her vows clearly and distinctly as he had
expected. Her small hand trembled a little as he placed
his marriage ring in place and Father John bound their
wrists together with the folds of his silken stole and
pronounced them one flesh. Her lips were cool under his
as he sealed their union with the customary kiss, then
her hand was in his and he led her out of the church to the
porch to be greeted by rousing cheers from the assembled
villagers.

He sat beside her proudly at the high table above the
salt and looked down with pleasure at the revellers below,
the assembled knights and squires of the shire who had

come to wish him good fortune. Sir Walter looked a trifle flushed, but happy now that this was finally concluded and Gisela was truly the baron's bride. He received congratulations from all around him—his daughter had won the hand of the most influential lord in the shire, an intimate of the King himself.

As he looked across at her, seated at Lord Alain's side, he experienced mingled emotions of satisfaction and concern. She looked calm enough but pale and abstracted. His heart misgave him and he gave a little inward prayer that he had made the right decision in her best interest.

Lord Alain leaned towards his wife. 'You are eating little and drinking less. Our cook has done us proud.' He glanced, gratified, at the groaning board set before them upon pristine white drapery. 'You are not unwell?'

'No, I am just—' she gave a little rueful moue '—excited by all this.'

'I cannot find words to tell you how much I appreciate your choice of wedding garments. You have never looked lovelier.'

'You must thank Aldith for her skill,' she said. 'She insisted I must do you great honour before all your guests. This is a joyous occasion.'

'And you cannot find it so?' he murmured.

She flushed and her lips trembled. 'It is difficult for me, strange, as it must be for all new brides.' But she was soon smiling at the antics of an acrobat, from some troupe that had arrived in Oakham for the festive season, who had been persuaded into service at the castle feast with the promise of a very generous reward.

It was when she was alone with Aldith in Baron Alain's private chamber at the rear of the hall, now to be their conjugal chamber for the long years that stretched ahead, that Gisela thought achingly of her dead mother. Would

she have held her close, comforted her fears? As she
undid the tasselled ties of her undertunic, Gisela looked
anxiously towards Aldith who had fulfilled that function
for her over the years and who came now to her, smiling,
offering a final cup of wine.

'This will warm you.'

Gisela drained it obediently and climbed into the
marriage bed made fragrant with clean linen and the scent
of herbs to guarantee fertility. The fire in the hearth
blazed up brightly but Gisela shivered, though she knew
she was not really physically cold. Aldith bent to pull
up the furred coverlet tightly round her.

'Be blessed in this marriage bed, with happiness and
fine, strong children,' she murmured formally.

As she made to withdraw, Gisela reached out and drew
her close.

'You have been as a mother to me now I am a woman,
even more than you were as my wet nurse. I love you,
Aldith, and I am glad you are with me now. . .'

Aldith's grey eyes glimmered with tears as she hugged
her former charge. 'Your mother would have been very
proud of you this day,' she said hoarsely. 'Remember
tonight can make or mar this marriage, but you know
that, I'm sure.' She kissed her tenderly upon the forehead
in blessing and stole from the chamber.

Alain de Treville came in soon after Aldith left her
and Gisela was glad that he had not left her time to dread
the coming intimacies of the night. His step was firm
and determined and he came to the bed and stood looking
down at her.

'You are warm enough?'

She had pulled up the coverlet defensively and now
felt somewhat foolish and cowardly.

'Yes,' she murmured, glancing away from his
searching gaze.

'Your father has been carried to his chamber. I

think he has taken just a little too much wine.'

'He is consoling himself for the loss of his daughter. He is no habitual drunkard.'

'I know that well enough.'

She had watched her husband throughout the feast and noticed he had drunk sparingly. She wondered if he had drunk more immoderately after she had withdrawn, but she doubted it. There were no signs that he had over-indulged and she doubted that he ever needed wine to bolster up his courage. He was too composed, as ever, too sure of himself; in her eyes a little more than human and, so, intimidating.

Kenrick, she thought, with a sudden pang, would have come to her tonight excited, a little awkward and more than a trifle drunk on the mead he had so loved.

Her husband had now turned from her and was beginning to undress. She heard the betraying chink as his sword belt was unbuckled and placed upon a stool near the bed. She did not look at him. She could hear the rustle of cloth and the susurration of fine damask as he drew his elegant overtunic over his head, then, determinedly, she opened her eyes and watched as he stood in fine linen drawers and short undertunic, still turned away from her.

The muscles of his back rippled beneath the cloth, then he had divested himself of everything and stood in the power of his manhood, fully revealed to her. The firelight flickered over taut ribs, the spare, perfectly proportioned body, the broad shoulders and slim hips.

He came towards the bed and she could not avert her eyes from his manhood, but neither could she draw back the coverlet in simple welcome as she had promised herself she would do.

He bent and pulled back the coverlet, revealing her nakedness, and she drew back with a barely restrained cry.

He frowned and, as she sought desperately to cover herself, deliberately restrained her. She gave a faint sob.

He said harshly, 'I suppose you are wishing it was Kenrick of Arcote who comes to your bed tonight.'

His words affected her like a douche of cold water. She sat up straight and glared back at him.

'Kenrick of Arcote was a friend of—my father. You dare to imply. . .'

'I saw you—in the wood together.' His dark eyes never left hers and they widened in part shock, part terror.

'I—I do not understand. There was nothing between us of which I would be ashamed. . .'

'You were in his arms.' He gave a little cynical smile. 'I was on my way to make you a gift of Hereward. I rode into the clearing—and there you were, totally absorbed in each other, unaware of any passerby, I imagine.' His lip curled. 'I suppose it was fortunate I was so near. I saw the smoke very quickly, you see, and was able to come to your rescue immediately.'

Her brain was racing, her eyes darkened and huge in her pale face.

'Knowing that—that he was very dear to me—you continued to press for this marriage?'

'I wanted you.'

Her breath was coming uncommonly fast. 'You believed that—that—there in the wood. . .'

He shrugged. 'I don't know what to believe except that—I do not think your father was made aware of the situation.'

'You have not—told him?'

'No, why should I? Kenrick of Arcote is dead.'

It was a brutal statement and she covered her face with her hands.

He stood looking down at her and, at last, he climbed into bed beside her. She retreated from him as far as she could and he reached out and took her by the shoulder.

'I should not have spoken to you like that, tonight of all nights, but your instinctive rejection of me made me aware of. . .'

She tried to push against him but he took possession of her two hands and held her hard to his body.

'Whatever you might think, whatever you and he did together, I still want you and today in the church—you became mine.'

'We did nothing together but kiss,' she said wildly. 'I met him there alone and secretly for the first time because. . .'

'Because?'

Her tongue froze to the roof of her mouth. How could she explain that her meeting with Kenrick was a desperate attempt to escape this marriage, this very moment—?

He said mockingly, 'You met him in secret to discuss my offer of marriage. Was that it?'

'Yes,' she said defiantly. 'Kenrick loved me and. . .'

'Then why had he not declared himself before that?'

'He—he—was waiting for the right moment. He. . .' She broke off on another faint sob. Why, oh, why had Kenrick waited? Because he had been afraid to face the wrath of his mother? Had he been so weak? She was so very close to the man who held her now. He would not have been deterred by any opposition, not even by the will of the King himself. He would have taken what he wanted and risked losing everything.

His hold was painful yet she no longer sought to struggle. He would make her his, and there was nothing she could do to prevent it—yet she would hold back from him her true self.

He had been granted rights over her body by Holy Mother Church and she could not deny him, but he could never make her love him. She would be his dutiful wife, control his household efficiently, submit to him in bed, bear his children, but she would never be really his. Her

small teeth gritted together as if in painful determination
to resist his possession of her.

He was furious with himself that he had antagonised
her at this vital moment. She had angered him by her
instinctive withdrawal. He had never had need to force
a woman. Proud dames at the King's court and whores
in the army baggage train he had taken for his pleasure,
though without declaration of love. He had never
deceived a woman or taken any unwillingly.

Now he cursed his own stupidity that he had frightened
her, yet his control over his rising passion was fast
deserting him. He released his hold on her and she fell
back against the pillows. The firelight glimmered on her
lovely ivory form and desire clawed at his vitals. God,
how he wanted her!

At first, when the determination to make her his wife
had been mooted in his talk with Rainald de Tourel, he
had thought his need for a suitable bride to enhance his
role in the shire had been the motivating factor. Now he
knew that the sight of her in another's arms had inflamed
him beyond reason. She was his, and, by God and the
Holy Saints, he would take her tonight and force her to
dismiss any other man from her thoughts.

He put out a hand and twisted a long tress of her
curling hair. It was silky and scented with rosemary and
lavender, as her pale smooth flesh.

'Come now, *chérie*,' he murmured throatily. 'I will
make you forget. . .' He pressed his lips to the beating
pulse in her throat.

She could not fight him and win, she knew that. She
had to submit. She steeled herself and, this time, did not
withdraw from his lean body as he drew her close again,
though she became so breathless with apprehension and
untamed excitement that she feared she would die. Would
he punish her for what he considered her deception? Yet
she had never allowed him to think that she loved him,

even liked him. He could not blame her for having wished
to escape from a marriage she had thought abhorrent.

She knew that losing her maidenhood would be painful. Now she feared he could be exceptionally harsh with
her in his present mood or even think she was no longer
a virgin and treat her with scant consideration. She determined to make no outcry or protest whatever he did.

In actual fact, he exerted supreme control over his own
desire and forced himself to treat her gently. He could
feel her violent trembling as he lowered himself upon
her supine form and bent to gently kiss her forehead.

'*Doucement, doucement,*' he murmured softly. 'There
is no need to fear. I have sworn to make you love me.
Allow me to teach you the delights of love. There is no
need for haste.'

She felt his lips lightly touch the more sensitive parts
of her body; first her throat, the nape of her neck, her
breasts, then ventured lower to her taut belly and groin.
She was very close to tears yet the sensations were first
delicately gentle, then tantalising until, despite herself,
her body arched against his and she gave a little moan
of half-pleasure, half-fear.

His lips closed on hers as they had done in the office,
this time scorchingly demanding, and her own opened
to receive the kiss she had dreamed of since her woman's
body had begun to waken from childhood.

When he entered her at last it was painful, certainly,
but he had waited until she was ready and the pain was
swept away on the overwhelming tide of her response.
She had never conceived of such ecstasy and, afterwards,
she lay shuddering with pleasure within his arms.

He gave the lightest chuckle of triumph and she sought
to turn her face from him, but he bent and, taking her
chin in his strong, lean fingers, he whispered, '*Chérie*,
how right I was to believe that you could respond with
such ardour, though I feared it might take longer for you

to learn so thoroughly the delights of love.'

She wanted him to take her again and burned with
shame at the thought. He had been a gentle, considerate
lover and she had found that, despite her resolve to with-
hold her responsive emotions, this man could take her
to the heights of passion. She had been so totally
unprepared.

She had known what must be endured, dreaded the
embrace of this man who had entered her life an arrogant,
antagonistic stranger and, in so short a time, had come
to dominate her existence, yet she realised, as heat suffused her body, that she would now ache for his caresses.
She had thought him to be cold, restrained, a demanding
master who would take his own pleasure without considering her needs, but now knew herself mistaken.

Alain de Treville was possessive, dominant, even
tyrannical, but his blood was as hot as the knights she
had dreamed of, that he himself had sung of only days
ago. He lay at her side now, spent, his arm tightening
round her, signifying his possession even as he slept. She
leaned over slightly and looked at him as his chest rose
and fell rhythmically in contented sleep.

Her own lips curved in a sudden rush of tenderness.
Perhaps, after all, her life here at Allestone would not
be totally bereft of the pleasures she had dreamed of.
Aldith had spoken truth. This night could well have
marred her whole life, if her remembrance of it had been
as horrifying as she had feared.

Whatever occurred between them now, she would
always give thanks that he had spared her humiliation
and pain—and despite the knowledge of her feelings for
Kenrick of Arcote that she had tried, so desperately, to
keep hidden from him.

Chapter Six

Gisela knelt by Kenrick's tomb, her tears spilling onto
the slab of marble which had been hastily set over it.
Soon an image maker would be summoned from the
West country, where such skills were prized, to fashion a
statue of the young lord brought so untimely to his grave.

Gisela had not found the courage to visit the tomb
until today. She had not attended the funeral, as Lady
Eadgyth had requested; and since Alain de Treville's
blunt statement that he had seen Kenrick and herself
together in the wood, she had baulked at angering her
husband by coming near the church. Today she had been
assured that Lord Alain was well away from the village,
and with Aldith she had managed to venture out without
disclosing her destination.

'Kenrick,' she whispered, brokenly. 'Oh, my dear, do
not think I will ever forget you. I loved you well and
our happy days together will always live in my heart,
but now I am wed and my duty is to my husband and—
I think—I believe—that, given time, I can come to love
this man.'

She broke off in confusion. It seemed so strange and
wrong that she should be confiding her innermost
thoughts and fears to the shade of the man who had been
her constant companion. Was this a betrayal of her former

love? She prayed that Kenrick would understand her desperate need and not condemn her.

The days following her marriage had been hectic since the Christmas feasting had been on them almost immediately. In her bewildered state of mind Gisela had found that comforting, for she had had little time to consider her chaotic feelings about her husband.

The day after her marriage she had expected that Alain de Treville would perhaps rise early and be off riding, leaving her to come to terms with her new state of wifehood. When she had woken, he had indeed left her. As the wintry sun forced its way between the cracks in the still-closed shutters, she had risen up on one elbow to stare blearily at the place where he had lain beside her. She had missed the warmth of his body instantly and yet was relieved that, for the moment, she would not have to meet his eyes.

Aldith had come later and been completely satisfied by the marks on the soiled sheets that informed her that her mistress was now true wife indeed and lady of Allestone. She had questioned Gisela with one simple look and smiled happily when Gisela flushed darkly and hid her head, then raised her eyes to her former nurse.

'It was—very good for me,' she confessed huskily. 'Has my husband left the castle so early?'

'No, no, mistress.' Aldith laughed back at her. 'Leave his new-made wife so soon on the first day of their married life together? No, he is even now chivvying the servants to prepare breakfast and to harry the remainder of the men out of the hall so you might eat together in peace.'

'Oh!' Gisela was somewhat disconcerted. She had hoped for some little time alone to reorganise her thoughts. 'He is expecting me down in the hall soon now?'

Aldith nodded and hastened to provide warm water for Gisela's toilet and to lay out her morning clothes upon the bed.

'Where is Hereward?' Gisela said as she struggled into her gown.

'Sigurd took care of him last night since Huon was in attendance upon Lord Alain. He has taken him out into the bailey.'

Gisela's conscience had smitten her somewhat when she had suddenly remembered her pet, who had been used to sleeping upon her bed with her and Aldith. In her anxious concern, when she had first left the marriage feast, she had given no thought to the puppy. Now she was relieved to hear he had been well cared for.

She hastened to descend to the hall, determined not to keep her lord waiting.

He, too, was dressed plainly this morning in a tunic of dark brown wool over grey chausses, cross-gartered. As yet he had not donned mail so he seemed in no hurry to be off out on manor business and to take his leave of her. His dark hair was damp and swept well back from his freshly shaven face and she saw that already he had bathed.

He stood up to greet her. 'Come to the fire. The morning is very cold.'

She joined him near the hearth fire where one of the smaller trestles had been set for them.

'I left you to sleep on. I had one or two matters of business to discuss with my seneschal.'

She nodded, glancing at him shyly then down at the table, which appeared to be groaning under the weight of food. There was fine white manchet bread, cold meats and cheese, buttermilk and ale, even some of the last of the autumn apples. She drew a swift breath even as a serving wench came hastening in through the screen doors with a tray on which smoked basins of oaten porridge.

'I can never eat even a fraction of this,' she protested, but he laughed.

'I think you will find you are more hungry than you think,' he said. Already he was tucking into his own bowl of porridge, after first sprinkling it with salt from the ornate salt cellar that had graced the table in pride of place at their marriage feast.

He pointed to it, with a faint grimace. 'A marriage gift from the shire reeve.'

'Oh,' she said, 'it is very fine.'

He shrugged. 'I might have been better pleased with a box of good grey goose-feathered arrows.'

There was no answer to that and she helped herself to honey and began to eat her own porridge. He was right. She was, indeed, hungry, and recollected, with a flush which she felt mounting from her throat to her cheeks, that she had once overheard one of their grooms remarking that he always felt exceptionally hungry after indulging in bed sport.

She ate her way appreciatively through porridge, bread and meat and even a rather wizened apple. He watched her over the rim of his ale cup, then, as she wiped her fingers upon a napkin one of the servants had placed ready and sat back a trifle guiltily, his lips curled into a grin of approval.

'What did I tell you?'

'Yes,' she said, then a little defensively, 'I did not eat very much at the feast. I was—'

'More than a trifle apprehensive,' he finished.

He leaned back and surveyed her, his smile broadening. 'You have nothing to fear from me ever, unless—'

'I disobey you?' Her blue eyes opened wide as she looked back at him directly.

He shook his head. 'Oh, knowing your mettle I am

sure there will be times when you disobey me. No, that was not what I meant.'

'You think I might—betray you?' Her eyes were sparking indignant blue fire at him now.

'I know, Gisela, that you do not love me.'

'I shall make every effort to make you a good wife.'

He inclined his head. 'I know, but that is not the same thing. However. . .' He paused, then rose and walked to a wall niche where wine cups and jugs were often set so that guests might help themselves when pages were not present. He withdrew a canvas-wrapped parcel from the stone shelf and returned to her.

'To show my appreciation—for last night.'

She coloured hotly. He was offering her the traditional morning gift, given by a husband whose wife had pleasured him well on their marriage night. With unsteady fingers she undid the ribbon that tied the parcel.

Upon a folded length of fine tawny velvet lay a gleaming torque, such as those ornaments formerly worn by Saxon men and ladies, thick and shining and inscribed with an antique linear curving design that she had heard described by her mother, but had never seen before. She touched the circlet wonderingly. 'It is beautiful and so very old.'

'I set the goldsmith in Oakham to find me one. I remembered your pride in your Saxon blood and hoped it would please you.'

She glanced up at him quickly. Had he been so sure of his own sexual prowess, believing that he would arouse her to such transports of delight that she would be ready to please him in all things? Possibly not. He might well have kept this gift for another important occasion, such as the birth of their first child. No, his whole manner suggested that he was indeed pleased with her.

'Thank you, my lord,' she said with quiet dignity. 'I shall treasure it for ever.'

He stood for a moment longer, looking keenly down at her, then he stood upright and gave her his familiar little half-bow.

'And now, Gisela, you must excuse me. There is much about the castle still to be done and I am sure your father will be anxious to receive a visit from you.'

At the screen door he paused and turned back to her. 'Can you find it in your heart to call me by my given name, at least when we are alone together?'

She lifted her chin slightly and looked steadily across to him. 'Yes, Alain,' she said softly and he bowed again, his long lips parting in a smile of real pleasure, then he was gone from her.

During the days that followed Gisela was hectically engaged in overseeing final preparations for the Christmas feasting itself. She found herself bustling about from kitchens to buttery and cellar throughout the hours of daylight, a panting Aldith in attendance, and spent her nights cradled within her husband's arms. He was considerate and gentle with her and she was grateful for the comfort of his warm muscular body pressed so tightly and protectively to her own. Yes, she told herself, before she slipped off into slumber, she was truly fortunate in her husband. She saw evidence that he could be a stern master with his own men and hard, though just, with all wrongdoers, but, it seemed, he had pledged himself to be patient with her.

He had expressed his regard for her expert handling of the Christmas arrangements. She had made a dignified hostess at the high table and she knew her father was as proud of her as her husband was.

*   *   *

Now she knelt in the gloomy, silent little church trying to come to terms with her own mixed feelings. There would be a great deal to do at Allestone over the coming winter months, plenty to occupy her mind. Surprisingly, she no longer found the castle so gloomy or oppressive as she had feared.

She worked with Aldith whenever she had a free moment on a large arras for the hall to cut out the worst of the draught from the screen opening. The bright wools were a delight to her eye as they spilled out across the sober hue of her gown. She could find contentment at Allestone if only she could come to terms with her own confused feelings for her husband.

She was about to rise from her place near Kenrick's tomb when she was startled by the sound of mail-shod feet approaching her down the nave and turned to find her husband coming determinedly towards the altar. He halted suddenly at the sight of her and she scrambled a little uncertainly to her feet to face him. His eyes went deliberately to the tomb of his erstwhile rival.

'I am sorry to disturb you.' His voice was cold. 'I had not known you were here. I came in search of Father John.'

Gisela wished he had not found her engaged in praying so intimately near Kenrick's tomb. For the moment she could find no words to explain herself.

'I see you need to be private with your dead. I shall see Father John gets my message some other time.' He turned from her and was about to retrace his steps up the nave when she pattered hastily after him.

'I—I had finished my prayers,' she said a little hoarsely. 'I came because—at this joyful time of Christmas it seemed so dreadful that—that he could not be with us and. . .'

'Christmas is so much a family occasion that the loss of those we held dear is always more poignant,' he said mechanically. 'You must come here whenever you feel the need, only. . .' he hesitated for a fraction of a second '. . .you must inform me or Sir Clement, my seneschal, and he or I will arrange an escort for you. You must realise by now that it is simply not safe for you to go any distance from the castle unprotected.

'You must not fear the men will intrude upon your need for privacy. I will see to it that they are given strict instructions to remain well back from you while keeping you in safe sight.'

His tone was more than a trifle bitter and she recognised that he believed her need to weep for her dead lover was her paramount reason for coming alone to the church. Aldith had actually accompanied her but had remained outside in the churchyard.

As if to press home his point, he added, 'Your father will back me up in this, I am sure.'

'Of course,' she said. 'I do understand your care for my well-being, my lord—Alain,' she added a trifle belatedly. 'Aldith is nearby looking for winter herbs, I believe.'

'Good,' he said curtly, 'but Aldith is no adequate protectress in these uncertain days.'

'I will do as you ask,' Gisela responded tonelessly. She gave a sigh. It was pointless now to wish he had not found her here.

She was to discover over the next two days that her surmise was correct. Though he did not reproach her either in words or by indirect action, she realised that her visit to Kenrick's tomb had cast a real shadow over their relationship for, though she still mourned for the old days with Kenrick, she was beginning to accept a deeper understanding both of her husband's character and her own growing fondness for him.

She had believed him to be an austere man, yet found he could be both witty on occasions and could appreciate the humour of a situation even when he was mildly annoyed by it. She recalled his amusement when Hereward had dropped heavily upon her legs as she climbed into bed on the second night of their marriage.

The puppy had been merely asserting his right to his proper place with his mistress but Alain, with a grin, had simply seized him by the scruff of the neck and had dumped him unceremoniously on to the floor. 'Oh, no, my lad,' he had said firmly. 'I have no intention of sharing my marital bed with you. Go and find comfortable quarters for yourself elsewhere.'

Hereward had scrambled up against the bed, his forepaws pressed against Gisela's side, his liquid eyes appealing, but, laughing, she had been forced to harden her heart to him. After jumping up for the third time, Alain de Treville had shouted for Huon to come and take possession of the dog.

'See him tethered somewhere in the hall, Huon,' he had ordered. 'Really, he should be housed in the kennels, but since he has already made himself into a lapdog we must not cruelly part him from his mistress. However, he's not to come into our bedchamber even if he has been used to sleeping here in the past. He has a master now who will see to it that he obeys.'

Huon had gone off smiling. Gisela knew she could rely on the young man to guard her pet well.

She had found herself laughing with her husband on several occasions over the Christmas feasting when they had entertained many of the knights of the shire with their ladies, and had also been gratified to note that he was in no way cruel by word or deed to the entertainers, amongst whom was a young hunchbacked dwarf.

On her return to the castle after their meeting in the church she sensed at once the barrier between them. He greeted her courteously and, at supper, plied her as usual with the delicacies set for them upon the table, but that night he did not join her in the marriage bed.

The following morning, he excused himself, saying he had been kept up late with Sir Clement, discussing some important matter concerning the castle defences, and had not wished to disturb her since the hour was so late. Gisela was by no means convinced by such a tale. The period of the Christmas feasting was no time to consider such matters and she doubted that Sir Clement would leave the side of his buxom wife at bedtime unless the situation facing Allestone was very grave indeed.

Some of their guests had already left Allestone though the feast of Twelfth Night had not yet come, but the atmosphere within the castle was not nearly so welcoming and the household seemed aware of it, though no one dared to gossip about what might be the cause of friction between the bridal pair.

On the third day following the incident, Gisela came unexpectedly into the hall to find Sigurd standing defensively before his lord, who was seated at the high table in the attitude of judge.

The Baron's voice came to her clear and curt, though not raised. He was not in the habit of shouting. He did not have to—his hold over his men was decisive. 'I have told you, boy, I will not tolerate any breaking of forest law upon my land. It has come to my notice that you were, in the past, guilty of doing so on more than one occasion. If I allow you occasionally to leave the castle, that will cease immediately.

'I hold your mother in high esteem, as does my lady, but that will not exonerate you if caught in a misdemeanour. Since I do not wish your mother to suffer, and she will, if I am forced to punish you severely, you will heed my words and obey them.'

Though Sigurd's back was to her, Gisela could tell

by his dejected attitude that he was shamefaced. She could hardly catch his whisper of, 'Yes, my lord.'

'Then take yourself off and find yourself something useful to do.'

The boy bowed low and turned to face Gisela. He made a second hasty obeisance but, as he passed her on his way to the screen doors, she saw there was a sullen cast to his mouth and a determined gleam in his eyes.

Gisela bit her lip and hoped there would not be further trouble with this lad whose life had always been a free one, risking detection from foresters and warreners in his poaching activities while he and his mother had lived happily and without restraints in their assart cottage.

That same afternoon Aldith sought her mistress out in the small tower chamber near the cellar that Gisela had commandeered as a still room. Gisela saw at once that her attendant was very worried.

'It's Sigurd,' she blurted out. 'I can't find him anywhere. He's wanted in the stables but no one seems to know where he is.'

Gisela had been pounding powdered tansy into lard to make a healing ointment. She rubbed her hands on a towel and sank down on a stool.

'Has he been ordered to work in the stables?'

'Not permanently, but Huon says Baron Alain sent for him this morning and told him to make himself useful. Apparently the head groom was told to find Sigurd work to do.'

'Yes,' Gisela said thoughtfully, 'I happened to hear some of what the Baron said to Sigurd. Has he been managing to get out and do some poaching, Aldith?'

Aldith shook her head. 'He tells me very little but he resents——' She broke off, her eyes clouding. 'He misses his freedom and lately. . .'

'Lately?'

'There is a girl—in the village—the daughter of one of Sir Alain's villeins. I haven't seen her but one of the serving wenches told me of her. She is very pretty and the young lads in the village have all been vying for her attention. I suspect Sigurd has been taking her tokens of his prowess. . .'

'He is a skilled archer, I know.'

'Aye, his father taught him well.' Aldith sighed, remembering. 'My Rolf was a champion at the butts.'

'So you think he has gone after small game to give to this girl?'

'Aye, the young fool. And if he has—' Aldith's anger showed in her fierceness of tone '—and if he's caught, it'll be serious punishment for him.' Her face went white. 'My lady, he could lose his right hand.'

Gisela made no attempt to console Aldith with the notion that that would be most unlikely. Only this very morning she had heard her husband warn Sigurd and she had also seen with her own eyes the smouldering resentment in the boy's expression as he had left the hall.

'Have you any idea which part of Allestone wood he frequents?'

'Aye, I think so.'

'Is there any one of Sir Alain's men who could be trusted to keep close-mouthed about Sigurd's activities?'

'He has made two young friends who allow him to practise with them at the butts in the bailey, Edwin and Algar. They are about his age.' Aldith thought again. 'If he isn't to be found where I said, he might be at the rabbit warren. He knows that Winfrith likes tender meat.'

Gisela rose. 'I will go to Sir Clement and ask if Edwin and Algar can accompany me for a ride outside the castle. You can ride pillion with one of them. I happen to know Sir Alain is in Oakham at the castle this afternoon and unlikely to be back here before dusk. We must try to find Sigurd before men are sent out to search for him, for I'm pretty convinced that suspicions are already roused and that is why the head groom has sent for him.'

She shook her head, frowning. 'How could Sigurd be so foolish as to deliberately flout Sir Alain's orders on the very day he has been specifically warned?'

'The boy is mad for the girl,' Aldith declared bitterly, 'and he fears his rivals will score over him, being freer to see her more often, living as they do outside the castle.'

'Aldith, go and see if you can find those two archers and ask one to bring out my palfrey while I inform Sir Clement of my intentions, so the Baron will not be concerned when he returns and finds me gone from Allestone. We should manage all before dark if we move quickly.'

Gisela found Sir Clement in the tower basement, checking over spear heads and arrows in the room designated as the armoury. He looked up a little shortsightedly as she approached.

'My lady, you did not need to come here and soil your gown with dust. I would have come to your chamber or to the hall had you sent for me. What can I do for you?'

Gisela gave the man her brightest smile. Sir Clement de Burgh was approaching forty, a thin stick of a man with a slight permanent stoop. His thin face constantly bore a vaguely harassed look and Gisela thought that might well be due to his increasing shortness of sight, for Sir Clement was an efficient seneschal of whose work Baron Alain de Treville rarely had cause to complain.

'I would not put you to so much trouble, Sir Clement,' she said. 'I was told you were here. I have a fancy to visit the church. Edwin and Algar have agreed to escort me so I should be safe enough.'

'Well, well—' Sir Clement was genially agreeable and anxious not to interrupt his work in the armoury to come up to the hall and find other men to escort his lord's lady '—that should do very well. Edwin, in particular, is a sensible young fellow, but you will not ride too far from the castle, my lady, will you? Darkness comes very quickly at this time of the year, and it has been a particularly cloudy and dismal day today.'

Gisela beamed at him. 'I promise.'

She hastened to her chamber to find a warm lined hooded cloak and hurried to the bailey to find the two young men-at-arms waiting with Aldith just outside the stable. Already her palfrey had been saddled and Edwin held the bridle and drew the horse close to the mounting block, then assisted Gisela into the saddle. She padded the voluminous skirt of her gown comfortably beneath her and took the reins from him.

'Good, then we should go,' she said crisply. The young Algar had mounted and pulled Aldith up behind him and, once Edwin had mounted likewise, the little group rode out of the bailey through the gatehouse and clattered over the drawbridge, then turned in the direction of the church and Allestone wood.

They rode through the village and Aldith pointed out one small cottage as the place where Winfrith lived, then they were bypassing the three big fields, still brown and barren. The winter ploughing would soon be done and afterwards the green shoots of wheat and barley would show themselves while the fallow field—the north field this year—could be used later for grazing.

Soon they had reached the outskirts of the wood and since Gisela was uncertain of her way, approaching the clearing Aldith had mentioned from the Allestone side of the greensward, not from Brinkhurst, she allowed Algar to lead the party with Aldith to point the way. Soon they had left the main ride and were picking their way with some difficulty on a lesser track.

Aldith gave a little click of her tongue in annoyance as there was no sign of Sigurd. 'There's a charcoal burner's hut over there.' She pointed to where a tall oak guarded the northern end of the clearing. 'When it is wet or very cold I've known him to shelter there. We are about half a mile from the Baron's main rabbit warren so it's very likely he would head in that direction. He mustn't be caught with the carcases.'

Algar grunted agreement and turned in the saddle to seek his lady's approval to ride in the direction Aldith was indicating.

'Yes,' Gisela said, 'let us try that way. If we have no luck there, we must return to the village; I must call on Father John before dusk as I promised Sir Clement I would do.'

Edwin fell in behind Gisela's palfrey. 'Young fool,' he commented. 'Baron Alain is fair but severe. If he gets caught after this morning's warning, the Virgin aid him, I say. It'll be a thrashing—or worse.'

The autumn leaves of the past months had carpeted the track and their horses made little sound as they moved carefully after Algar, the two men peering from side to side for any mark of their friend's passing.

Occasionally, one or the other made some slight, quaint sound like a bird call, unfamiliar to Gisela, which was obviously used as a signal between them. Apart from that no one spoke, as if each thought there might be others in the woods, searchers or one of the Baron's warreners about his work.

Gisela's palfrey gave a shrill whinny suddenly; she pulled her up sharply. Algar was some yards ahead, Edwin quite close in behind her. A slightly built figure stepped from the undergrowth and Gisela saw two dead rabbits dangling from one hand.

Aldith snapped, 'Sigurd,' and made to struggle down from behind Algar.

The boy stepped closer and placed a warning finger on his lip. His eyes went from Gisela to his two companions and his mother and he moved cautiously towards

MILLS & BOON®

AN IMPORTANT MESSAGE
FROM
THE EDITORS OF MILLS & BOON®

Dear Reader,

Because you've chosen to read one of our romance novels, we'd like to say "thank you"! And, as a **special** way to thank you, we've selected <u>four more</u> of the <u>books</u> you love so much **and** a mystery gift to send you absolutely **FREE**!

Please enjoy them with our compliments...

Tessa Shapcott   Editor,
Mills & Boon

P.S. And because we value our customers we've attached something extra inside...

EDITOR'S
FREE GIFT SEAL
THANK YOU

PEEL OFF SEAL AND PLACE INSIDE

EDITOR'S FREE GIFT
"THANK YOU"

1. Peel off the gift seal from the front cover. Place it in the space provided to the right. This automatically entitles you to receive four free books and a mystery gift.

2. Send back this card and you'll receive four specially selected Mills & Boon® Historical Romances™. These books are yours to keep absolutely FREE.

3. There's no catch. You're under no obligation to buy anything. We charge you nothing for your first shipment. And you don't have to make any minimum number of purchases - not even one!

4. The fact is, thousands of readers enjoy receiving their books by mail from the Reader Service™. They like the convenience of home delivery and they like getting the best new romance novels at least a month before they are available in the shops. And of course postage and packing is completely FREE!

5. We hope that after receiving your free books you'll want to remain a subscriber. But the choice is yours - to continue or cancel, anytime at all! So why not accept our no risk invitation. You'll be glad you did!

6. Don't forget to detach your FREE BOOKMARK. And remember... just for validating your Editor's Free Gift Offer, we'll send you FIVE gifts, ABSOLUTELY FREE!

We all love mysteries... so as well as your free books, there's an intriguing gift waiting for you! Simply return this card and when we send you your free books, there'll also be a gift enclosed specially for you!

THE EDITOR'S "
FREE GIFTS
► Four Mills & Boon
► An exciting Myste

P
FRE
S
H

YES! I have place

the space provided above. Ple
mystery gift. I understand th
purchase any books, as expla
opposite page. I am over 18 ye

MS/MRS/MISS/MR   IN

SURNAME

ADDRESS

POS

Tha

▼ DETACH AND POST CARD TODAY! ▼

MILLS & BOON®

WITH OUR
COMPLIMENTS

THE EDITORS

THE READER SERVICE™
FREEPOST SEA3794
CROYDON,
Surrey
CR9 3AQ

If offer card is missing write to: The Reader Service, P.O. Box 236, Croydon, Surrey CR9 3RU

Gisela's mount, which was now standing quietly enough after she had soothed it by gently stroking the glossy neck.

'My lady,' Sigurd whispered hoarsely, 'you must all be very quiet and begin to move back towards the clearing. There are men in the charcoal burner's hut, dangerous men. We must not be caught here.'

Edwin's eyes narrowed. 'Fighting men? Here, in Allestone woods?'

'Aye, routiers, I'm sure. They are settled in up there for an hour or two, I'd think. They have butchered a fallow deer and are roasting the meat.'

Algar gave an infuriated intake of breath and reached behind to settle Aldith again more safely. Edwin placed a warning hand on Gisela's bridle and whispered, bending close to her ear, 'Best we do as Sigurd advises, my lady. We must get clear of this place. We are too few to guard you adequately.'

As Gisela turned her mount carefully on the narrow track she thought she caught a sound of raucous laughter ahead of her. Her first instinct was to forge on in spite of advice to the contrary and see these men for herself, possibly force a confrontation, but better sense prevailed. As Edwin had said, there were too few of them to subdue a company of experienced and well-blooded mercenaries. At least when they were out of earshot she could find out more from Sigurd.

Once they were back in the clearing she leaned down to the boy, her expression stern.

'How many are there? What do you think they are doing there and so close to the Baron de Treville's stronghold?'

Sigurd had clearly been alarmed by the sight of these men settled in his own bolthole and had been frightened enough to make himself scarce at once. His breath was coming raggedly. Probably when he'd heard horsemen approaching he had taken cover, fearing to encounter more of the mercenaries. He sank down on the ground, clutching his prizes and trying to avoid the accusatory glances his mother was casting him.

He found his voice at last. His two friends were waiting impatiently and he strung out, between gasps, most of what he'd seen.

'I was making for the hut.' He looked shamefacedly at Gisela. 'I use it sometimes. It's been abandoned for some two years or more. I wanted to—skin the rabbits for—'

'Winfrith,' his mother put in grimly.

His look slid away from hers guiltily. 'Aye, for Winfrith. When I was in sight of the hut I saw this fellow come out, then another from behind him. They'd made a fire and were roasting meat, venison, I'm sure. I could smell it. They don't concern themselves about forest law.'

'I know one or two others who don't either,' his mother said tartly.

Sigurd winced at her sharpness. 'One of them is a big hulking brute with flaming red hair and a beard.' Gisela gave a desperate little cry, hastily suppressed.

Aldith looked at her quickly.

'You know something of such a man?'

Gisela shook her head doubtfully. 'I saw a man like that at Brinkhurst, but I cannot be sure it is the man Sigurd has seen here. He had red hair, certainly, and was ordering the others—' She broke off, biting her lip.

Catching Edwin's eye, Sigurd went on with his tale.

'Aye, well, then I took cover and watched the hut for a little while. One after another came out with chunks and gobbets of meat to roast over a sort of tripod made of branches they'd torn down. I can't say how many there are, at least six, possibly more. They were talking of loot, as far as I could gather, they were laden down with it, taken from some manor near Oakham and laughing about—' he gulped in an embarrassed fashion '—about how they they'd fired the place and—and treated—the womenfolk, and were now stopping for a short rest and to eat before going back to their lord.'

Gisela asked sharply, 'Were they Mauger de Cotaine's men?'

Sigurd shook his head decisively. 'I wasn't near enough to recognise any device; anyway, they were all wrapped up against the cold, cloaked and hooded. I reckon they were all from the same company as—' His voice petered off as he remembered the last time routiers had struck and how talk of that would upset his mistress.

'They should be arrested,' Gisela raged, 'now, while they are unsuspecting. In that hut, sure of their own safety, they should be easy to take. . .'

'We're too few,' Edwin declared, 'and we're not suitably equipped for a fight. These men'll be armed to the teeth. They're desperate fellows, used to fighting off attackers, even experienced well-armed men.'

'More likely they're used to vulnerable victims,' Gisela snapped bitterly. 'Are we to let them off so simply?'

'One of us could ride fast to the castle, inform Sir Clement of marauding mercenaries so close to Allestone and perhaps he'd send out a small company in pursuit,' Algar suggested.

'Yes.' Gisela seized on that suggestion. 'Algar, you do that. I shall be quite safe with Edwin, Aldith and Sigurd and we can come on more slowly.'

Algar looked to his friend for guidance. He was reluctant to leave his lady since he had been sent out specifically to escort her wherever she went, but, as Edwin nodded, he made a hasty salute to her and set off immediately back along the track towards the main ride which led to the village and castle approach.

Edwin looked sardonically at Sigurd. 'And you, my friend, get rid of those rabbit carcases. You can't be seen in the village with those. We came out to warn you the head groom is after your blood as it is.'

Sigurd looked down at his prizes with real regret. Poaching these had taken all his skill and they were meant to be offered to Winfrith as proof of his devotion and willingness to risk his hide for her.

Rabbit warrens were the exclusive preserves of the knightly class, only recently introduced to this country from Normandy, and the small creatures were valued for their tender flesh and their fur when other fresh meat was out of season. Winfrith had declared her delight in such delicate fare and he was sorry that he must do as Edwin warned and bury these somewhere close, in the hope he might be able to retrieve them tomorrow.

Gisela waved to Sigurd impatiently. 'Never mind that now. I want you to take me back to the hut.'

'*What?*' Both Edwin and Aldith exploded the single word almost simultaneously.

Sigurd simply stood and stared at her, the two rabbit carcases still dangling from one hand.

Aldith, who had dismounted before Algar set off, hurried over to Gisela and clutched at her arm.

'You cannot mean that, my lady.'

'I do. I want to see for myself what device these creatures wear and in what direction they go. Edwin, you need not accompany me if you do not wish to do so and you, Aldith, must remain here to guide Sir Clement's company when they arrive. If these men leave the hut, it is essential for us to know where they are heading for the pursuit to successfully follow.'

Edwin blustered, white to the lips. 'My lady, such a course would be very dangerous indeed and in direct disobedience to the Baron's orders. I cannot allow you to do that.'

Gisela's mount sidled as she faced him squarely. 'And how do you propose to prevent me? Will you lay violent hands on me, Edwin? Do you think that would please your lord?'

If possible, the tinge of white beneath the normal pallor of Edwin's skin paled even more as he contemplated in one stark moment of panic what would happen to him if he dared behave as she challenged. His choices were all bad and doomed to disaster for himself. If he allowed his mistress to go into danger unescorted, he would have to face his lord's wrath; if he abandoned her, the Baron's fury might well be even worse.

Gisela saw his dilemma and her haughty tone softened. 'I have to go, Edwin. Those devils might well be the very ones responsible for the damage to my home and for my father's injuries. I have to bring them to justice if I can and, mark my words, I *will* go back alone if I have to.'

Edwin stared helplessly at Aldith, whose expression was as grim as his own. She turned back to Gisela but there was no help there and she shrugged uneasily.

Sigurd said unhappily, 'It were best if we go back on foot.'

Edwin dismounted and fastened his horse's bridle rein to a low branch, then came to assist Gisela down and did the same for her palfrey.

He said doubtfully, 'You must understand, my lady, that Sir Clement may not send a company. He may think discretion would be better in this matter while the Baron is away. His main responsibility is the defence of the castle.'

'I know,' Gisela said quietly. 'That is exactly why we must spy on these fellows now and discover what we can about their home stronghold.'

Aldith was clearly afraid, not only for her mistress but for her son. She took the carcases from him and nodded as he turned once to be sure of Gisela's determination, then set off again down the track in the lead.

Their progress was no slower than when mounted, since, before, they had had to go very slowly and watch out for pitfalls that might disable their mounts. Sigurd pulled back the low branches that overgrew the track for Gisela to proceed, and they had soon struck off the track into the undergrowth itself and came out before a slight rise from which they could observe the entrance to the hut itself.

For the moment they could see no movement, though the fire was still smoking and the stink of scorched flesh hung heavy on the air. There were sounds of loud laughter and voices in the hut, many speaking French in a stronger accent than Gisela had observed in her husband's speech. These routiers were mainly Normans then, not native men-at-arms from this region.

Gisela lay on the carpet of leaves, her head just below the top of the rise, Sigurd on her left, Edwin to her right. Beyond the hut she could see a wider track along which the routiers had obviously come, probably leading towards the Oakham road. Why had they not set off immediately for home ground? Had there been a pursuit? She doubted that.

Knowing the trail of devastation that been left at Brinkhurst, she thought there was unlikely to be anybody left at the doomed manor in a fit enough condition to instantly order such a move. No, these fellows had been so sure of their own immunity from arrest and punishment they had decided, as Sigurd had said, to find fresh meat for themselves before going further. Probably they were even now within the hut dividing up the spoils.

Her blood was running so hot she had to hold herself in tight control so as not to run forward and confront them. She gave a bitter inward laugh. She was not so foolhardy as that. No, if she could gain evidence against

Mauger de Cotaine from the presence of these men so
near Allestone Castle, surely she could force the sheriff
and her husband to act against the man and bring him to
justice.

Was it even possible that Mauger himself was one of
the raiding party and, even now, in the hut with his men?
Her excitement grew. She wriggled forward a little but
felt Edwin's restraining hand on her arm.

'Be very careful, my lady,' he whispered urgently
into her ear.

She realised instantly the common sense of his warning
and stayed where she was. Her eyes and ears strained
for any further sign of movement from the hut.

It seemed hours while they remained perfectly still,
their very breaths held pent against discovery, and Gisela
began to feel the chill from the damp ground beneath
her begin to permeate the stuff of her closely woven
garments. She was becoming so stiff she felt she would
be unable to move when that became possible at last.

Suddenly the warped door of the hut was thrust back
and a man came out. He began to kick at the still-
smouldering ashes of the fire the mercenaries had made.
She wondered that he was bothering to be so careful of
so broken down a property, then the thought came to her
that the hut might well have been used on other occasions,
even after the raid on Brinkhurst.

She felt sharp bile rise in her throat. Yes, the place
might well prove useful to these men in the future whenever they were in this neighbourhood on some marauding
venture and would need a secluded bolthole.

She could hear further sounds of movement then, as if
men were rising and stretching, gathering up possessions,
preparatory to moving on, and she strained forward again.
Both men, this time, kept tight hold on her arms.

One by one the routiers emerged and stood yawning
and laughing and gazing contentedly around them. There

appeared to be six of them and Gisela noted the red-headed rogue to whom they were turning for instructions. Gisela was almost sure now that this was the man who had led the raid on Brinkhurst and she burned to stand and accuse him but her escorts continued to restrain her and she dared not, at this point, make any sound.

For the first time it occurred to her that there was no sign of horses. The men could not be travelling on foot. Where had they left their mounts? Were they hidden in some well-known spot nearer to the Oakham road? If so, it was even more possible that they could be taken if they had some distance to go before retrieving their mounts. She ground her teeth in fury. Why hadn't Sir Clement sent men as she requested? Was it really too short a time for that to be possible? It had seemed so long while they had lain silently watching.

She felt totally impotent. If these men walked away now and disappeared among the trees and she dared not follow, there would be no advantage to her. No, she must summon up her courage to follow, whether or not her two escorts resisted her determination to emerge from cover.

The company drew into a single line and the red-headed leader took the rear, looking back as his men began to merge into the undergrowth to see if they were being observed, not, thought Gisela bitterly, that it would have disturbed him in the least. He would simply dispose of any innocent bystander who hindered his progress as a man would swat an irritating fly in summer.

When it seemed that the red-headed man would disappear with the others, her impatience knew no bounds. It could be assumed that the men would take the Oakham road, but she had ridden this part of the wood often with Kenrick and, though she was not so familiar with it as Sigurd, she knew well that there were several other tracks that could lead on to other roads to Empingham or Stamford. She had to be sure which route was followed.

She wrenched her arms free before her two surprised guards could prevent her, scrambled up and began to mount the rise and make for the track where the last man had disappeared from view. Behind her she could hear Edwin cursing softly and the blundering attempts made by the two stiffened bodies to follow her. She did not look back but, holding up her skirts, ran towards the entrance to the track.

The leaf mould and dead leaves beneath her soft leathern riding boots could not make so great a sound, she reasoned, but the mercenary captain must have had ears like a cat for he stopped suddenly and, turning, began to move purposefully back in her direction.

He stood stock-still, thumbs thrust into his sword belt at sight of the girl hurtling towards him.

'Well, well,' he boomed good-humouredly, 'here, *mes amis*, come and see what Lady Luck has brought us— something even more worthy than those hags we found in that manor.'

He spoke in clear Norman French, without the foreign intonation of his companions, and Gisela thought he was probably from these parts and more often spoke English rather than the Norman French he was using now to alert his comrades.

She gave a startled cry and turned to run back towards her two escorts, but her foot caught in the hem of her gown and the man was on her before she could rise from the stumble and begin to run again. She heard his great belly laugh as a brawny arm seized her shoulder and turned her back to face him, uncaring that her jarred ankle was now giving pain. She felt herself drawn inexorably towards the man's hard, stocky frame.

She could smell his foul breath on her cheek as she saw his wide grin, which split his bearded mouth, and, in stark shock at his nearness, she glimpsed his rotting front teeth. Gisela fought desperately, but was numbly conscious of the fact that it was quite hopeless.

What aid could Edwin and Sigurd give her if they did come to her aid? They would be helpless to free her. It would doubtless be better for them to stay within cover and give a good account of what had happened when they returned to Allestone or when a rescuing company arrived too late.

She gritted her teeth and was determined to fight the fellow with tooth and claw like an animal. If she was fortunate, he would become so infuriated that he would deal her such a buffet that it would land her unconscious and she would know little more of her terrible fate.

He was laughing and she sensed, rather than saw, some of his fellows return to join him and rejoice in his good fortune to find such a prize fall so simply into his hands. Despite her determination to fight to the finish, she was almost fainting when she thought she heard the thunder of approaching hooves along the track behind them.

That could not be. No one would ride at such a pace in so difficult a terrain. The rider would risk both his own neck and his horse's. She struggled through failing vision to make sense of it.

There was a shout of command, then a challenge, and the man who held her released her so suddenly that she fell to the ground and lay there gasping. He had held her finally by the throat for some of the time in an effort to control her struggles and she had been choking; now she could only lie and fight for breath.

Dimly she was aware of running feet and the arrival of more horsemen, riding more cautiously this time. At last she looked up wonderingly and encountered Baron Alain's furious dark eyes staring down at her beneath the shadow of his conical helmet and noseguard.

Chapter Seven

For one moment Gisela was too amazed to do anything but stand awkwardly and stare back at her husband. He had dismounted, come to her side and now seized her arm in one mail-gauntleted hand so that she was able to steady herself against his body. She could feel the hard cold steel of his mail and she laid her forehead against his shoulder and let out one little choked cry. She was temporarily oblivious of all that was going on around her.

She had believed herself doomed to die—and horribly—and here was salvation so unexpectedly in the presence of her own lord. Her breath was still coming raggedly, then she forced herself to lift her head and begin to breathe more slowly.

He bent and gave her shoulder a little shake.

'What in the Holy Name of God are you doing out here?'

She gazed about somewhat stupefied, for signs of her assailant, but saw only a small troop of the Baron's men gathering in a half-circle to protect her.

She tried to thrust herself free of Baron Alain's hold, but he continued to grip her tightly, his gauntlet digging mercilessly into the soft flesh of her upper arm just below the shoulder.

His voice came again in an infuriated hiss. 'Tell me.

155

What were you doing here? Have you so little concern for your own safety and, incidentally, for my commands? Did I not warn you not to venture far from the castle without suitable escort and permission?'

She ignored the question and peered round for sight of the men she had been so steadfastly pursuing.

'Why are you wasting time asking foolish questions?' she demanded. 'Get after those men. They will escape us even now. I am certain I recognised that red-headed fellow as one who was present at the Brinkhurst attack.'

His voice was rock-hard. 'I am not interested in the fate of such rabble, only in the safety of my lady wife. Answer me, damn you, who was so crassly foolish as to let you ride here?'

She exerted all her strength and wrenched free from him, swinging round to face him, breast heaving and blue eyes snapping with cold fire.

'I command you to ride after those routiers, take prisoners, force a confession from one of them. That is all that matters to me.'

He surveyed her coldly. 'The man who held you turned and ran as I rode into sight. He will have gone to ground by now. By God's Holy Wounds, he might have killed you.'

'But he did not,' she ground out, her temper rising by the moment. 'Why do you think I risked myself to follow him? I want him taken and questioned and Mauger de Cotaine arraigned for the villain he is.'

'I dare say you do,' he said suavely, 'but there are other considerations of more importance. By the blessing of the Virgin you are safe. My prime concern is to return you to the castle and see if you are hurt and require Joshua's attentions.'

She stamped her foot, causing acute pain to her injured ankle. 'I am well enough. Leave me, sir, and get after those men. It is your duty to lead a hue-and-cry posse after disturbers of the King's peace. They are laden with booty taken from yet another stricken manor.'

He turned to his sergeant, who was questioning Edwin. Another man was bending low in the saddle and held Sigurd's arm in a harsh grip.

'Send one of your men to see if he can track those fellows,' the Baron barked. 'The rest of you return with me to Allestone.' His brooding gaze fixed on Edwin. 'I'll question you later.' Then, to the man who was holding Sigurd prisoner, 'See that fellow is held in the gatehouse guardroom until I can deal with him. Secure my lady's mount. She rides with me.'

'I can ride——' Gisela began but he cut her off and, sweeping her up into his arms, carried her to where his destrier was restlessly pawing the ground and laid her across his saddle bow, then effortlessly sprang into the saddle behind. While keeping a firm grip on Gisela with one hand, he used the other to gather up the reins and turned his mount skilfully in the narrow way, calling for his men to fall in behind to ride back towards Allestone.

In vain Gisela protested that she was safe and uninjured and perfectly happy to remain in the clearing while her lord rode in pursuit of the mercenaries. Her objections were ignored and the Baron rode steadily onward as if he had not heard her.

Choking back her disappointment and anger that her quarry had escaped her, Gisela was forced to lean back submissively against her husband's body and allow him to return her to her home. They rode in sullen silence through the village until Allestone Castle came in sight and they passed beneath the gatehouse arch and into the bailey. Instantly grooms sprang to attend to their Baron's needs and one gently assisted his lady down.

Gisela made to run impatiently towards the keep steps, but her ankle almost gave way beneath her and she gave a sharp cry of pain. She could not believe that her husband would have wantonly ignored her pleas for assistance in arresting those men and did not know whether it was pain or absolute fury that brought tears to her eyes.

Without a word Alain de Treville lifted her once more into his arms and strode across the bailey, up the keep steps, through the hall and up the tower steps beyond to their chamber. Here he laid her carefully down upon the bed and stepped back.

'Do not stir,' he commanded. 'I will send Joshua to you. Your maid is already in the hall.'

'My lord,' she called him back as he reached the doorway. He stopped and turned. She saw his eyebrows raised in part amazement that she should question his order and part irritation.

'What is it?'

'Why did you not ride after those men?'

'I told you. They are of little or no importance to me. Your safety was my only consideration.'

'But mine was to pursue and punish them.'

The hard line of his mouth did not relax. He continued to regard her haughtily.

She deliberately changed her tactics. 'Can I have been mistaken in the mettle of the man I married? Were you afraid, my lord?'

She heard his one short intake of breath, then he came hurriedly back to the bed. He lifted his hand as if to strike her and she thrust up her chin defiantly as if to receive the blow. His hand fell back to his side and she saw his Adam's apple move as he swallowed back his anger.

'We will talk of this later, when both of us are in a more receptive state,' he said coldly. 'I found Algar riding through the village as if all the devils in hell were close on his heels and, when stopped and questioned, he told me of your idiotic notion to pursue those routiers. I could do nothing but ride after you. Have you any idea what peril you were in? Do you think those scum would have spared you, even knowing who you are?

'You are my wife and you will obey me and no one else. I do not answer to you, madam, neither will I stoop to explain my reasons or to excuse myself of such an insulting charge. You will do as I say, wait for Aldith and Joshua and we will talk further when I am in the right mood to discuss this. It may well be that the matter will be broached no more. Do you understand me?'

She drew back from him across the width of their bed. Her intense blue eyes, brimming with tears of helpless fury, met his obsidian dark ones. She made as if to speak, then thought better of it and nodded dumbly. He looked down at the length of her tautly angry, youthful form, then turned and stalked from the chamber.

Joshua ben Suleiman arrived very soon after, bearing his small chest of medicaments. He examined Gisela's ankle very gently under Aldith's baneful glare. Aldith considered that her own nursing skills were sufficient to treat her lady and was somewhat jealous of the Jewish physician's standing in the household.

'There appears to be no broken bone,' the old man said quietly. 'The limb is merely sprained and badly bruised. You should rest it for a day perhaps, my lady, and all should be well.'

He applied a soothing compound that Gisela, from her own herbal lore, thought to be comprised mainly of witch hazel but to which was added some other exotic-scented balm she could not identify. Almost immediately the pain diminished and she thanked the physician, who bowed in his courtly Eastern manner and went off to report to his lord.

Gisela sank back upon the bed and gnawed her underlip. She was still raging inwardly at what she considered Alain's perfidious behaviour. How could he have allowed those marauding devils to escape him? Guiltily she recognised that her accusation of cowardice was totally unfounded, yet why had he not before ridden out against Mauger de Cotaine, whom all in the county knew to be the master of these men?

Quite apart from her own need for vengeance, there were other innocent, vulnerable people who would suffer in the future if these depredations continued unchecked. If King Stephen had placed her husband in a position of trust here at Allestone, surely it was his duty, as she had reminded him, to assist the shire reeve in apprehending those responsible for these outrages.

She poured out the cause of her dissension with her husband to Aldith's usually sympathetic ears but, this time, found her maid less responsive.

Gisela checked and leaned down towards Aldith, who was frowning abstractedly and, clearly, had not listened to half of what her mistress had said.

'What is it, Aldith? Do you think I was unwise to tax my husband with dereliction of duty?' She did not add that her most telling insult was even more ill advised. Aldith must not know of that.

Her former nurse regarded her doubtfully. 'I imagine the Baron is most concerned for the defence of the castle,' she said bluntly. 'Naturally he would not consider a minor raid on some small nearby manor as grounds for an attack upon a neighbour.' She paused and then added succinctly, 'I think, since you ask, my lady, that it would be wiser not to anger your lord husband unnecessarily.'

Gisela was about to retort that she did not consider the need to prod Alain de Treville into action against these lawless routiers unnecessary when she sensed Aldith's very real alarm.

'You are very worried—about Sigurd?'

Aldith turned a pale, frightened face to her lady. 'He

is held in the guardroom. It will be discovered that he went to the wood to poach after being warned. I am afraid. . .'

Gisela caught her breath in a little gasp. She had been so incensed against Alain that she had had no thoughts for the men whom she had inveigled into helping her. The two men-at-arms would decidedly come under the Baron's intense displeasure, possibly Sir Clement too, for the seneschal had not taken great care to enquire too closely into her reason for leaving the castle, yet, surely, she had given a good enough excuse and Sir Clement should be exempted from blame.

But Sigurd and Edwin had led her into the wood despite their avowed fears for her safety and she knew they would doubtless be severely punished. Aldith's hoarsely expressed fear earlier which had led them in search of the boy, 'He could lose his hand,' hit her forcefully and she quailed at the knowledge that she could be responsible if the worst were to happen.

Had she not insisted on the boy acting as guide, he would not have been discovered by his lord in a questionable position and Sigurd would not now be languishing in the guardroom in fear of the consequences of his 'feckless but understandable' misdemeanour, performed only in the desire to please his light of love. It hit her squarely too that, by her own actions, she had placed herself in a postion where it would be extremely difficult for her to plead with Lord Alain to be merciful.

She said, with a confidence she did not entirely feel, 'I will speak with my lord about Sigurd the very first opportunity I have. I am sure he will be pardoned, Aldith.'

Aldith's tortured countenance, as she faced her mistress before leaving the chamber with the bowl of water and towels used for bathing by Joshua ben Suleiman, was anything but optimistic.

Gisela lay back against the pillows and tried to understand Lord Alain's behaviour. Sir Clement had told her that he had refused to ride out to de Cotaine's manor shortly after the attack on Brinkhurst. The terrible thought occurred to her, hastily dismissed, that the two men could be in league with each other.

Men previously considered honourable before now had behaved so disgracefully during the long years of this anarchy in the pursuit of personal gain. No, that could never be. It was not to be thought of. Alain de Treville was true to his oath of fealty. She knew that instinctively. Then why was he so reluctant to deal with this man who terrorised the neighbourhood?

She would have to face her husband soon and be more conciliatory, if only for Sigurd and Edwin's sake. Surely Algar had naught to fear. He had gone immediately for assistance and could not be faulted for that.

There was a sudden scrabble of paws upon the stair and Hereward hurtled on to the bed, throwing Gisela backwards against the pillows, licking her frantically. Laughingly, she tried to thrust him off as Huon burst into her chamber, red-faced and anxious. He caught the excitable and ecstatic dog by the collar and pulled him free of Gisela's helpless form.

'My lady, I am so sorry. He got free of his leash and flew up the tower stair before I could prevent him and—and,' he said breathlessly, 'Lord Alain said he was not to be allowed to get to you, for you are hurt.'

'No, Huon, it is nothing.' Gisela sat up on the bed, still laughing. 'I am glad to see Hereward, indeed I am. I have wrenched my ankle, that is all. I will not allow your lord to censure you. I know how determined this naughty dog is.'

She reached out and ruffled Hereward's soft fur and gently pulled his ears while he stuck out a rough pink tongue and panted in delight, his round brown eyes regarding her adoringly.

She had no opportunity to enquire after Sigurd's fate as she had promised Aldith. She found her sprained ankle more painful than she had thought when she attempted to put weight on it and was unable to descend the tower steps into the hall for supper.

She sent her apologies to Lord Alain by Aldith but he did not come near her and sent merely a terse message that he was sorry she was still indisposed and ordered supper to be served to her within their chamber. Nor did he join her in their bed that night.

She was left to lie wakeful, regretting her impulsive accusations and longing for him. His discovery of her presence near Kenrick's tomb had already put a barrier between them and this rift had now been deepened by their later altercation in the wood.

The interpretation he had placed upon her desire to see the routiers taken and hanged must surely be that she passionately desired vengeance for the loss of Kenrick. Soberly she considered this in the darkened chamber. Yes, that could not be denied. Nevertheless, if she were to live in some degree of harmony with her husband, the rift must be bridged.

She had flung at him the greatest insult a woman could give to a man of honour. She punched her pillow, now wet with tears, in helpless frustration and vowed that tomorrow she would rise early before he had a chance to ride out into the village and make her apologies.

Later, she would do her utmost to convince him that the acts committed by his men and the young serf were due to her determination, which they had dared not disobey since any attempt to do so would have left her in peril. Surely then he would hold his hand and not punish any of the three too severely.

She and she alone deserved punishment. A shiver went through her body as she thought that any other man might well have asserted his right of chastisement and thrashed her had he been so provoked. Alain de Treville had been about to strike her, he had been very close to doing so, yet he had held back.

Unfortunately she was prevented from confronting her husband as her father, now much improved, paid a very early visit to her chamber. She was still not fully dressed and Aldith wrapped her in a bedrobe before admitting Sir Walter and, at Gisela's nod, left the chamber afterwards.

He came straight to the point. 'I hear there has been some quarrel between you and your lord.'

She gestured for her father to seat himself. 'What have you heard?' she asked cautiously.

'I heard that you deliberately placed yourself in danger and that Lord Alain took you to task for it,' he said grimly. 'It is all over the castle that Lord Alain's lady has deliberately disobeyed him. Daughter, you must know this has placed Lord Alain in a humiliating position—and before his own men, too.

'While I understand this marriage is no love match, I expected that you would play your part and be a good wife to de Treville. He has a right to expect loyalty and obedience from you.'

She did not attempt to excuse herself. She sank down on the bed beside him, clutching her furred robe close around her, her eyes searching the ground at her feet, unable to meet his gaze.

'Did you know why I disobeyed him?'

'I understand you went off hawking or some such nonsense in Allestone wood.'

'No,' she said in a low voice, 'I went in search of young Sigurd who has been poaching and has already been warned off but—' she took a hard breath '—while we were there we found signs that routiers had holed up in an abandoned charcoal burner's hut.

'I persuaded my escort to follow, hoping they might be apprehended and punished. It was clear they had been on another raid and I wanted—' She broke off, tears raining down her cheeks, and he reached out and took her hand.

'I see. Vengeance can sometimes turn out to be a very cold dish indeed, daughter.'

'Yes. You do not know the worst of it. Lord Alain refused to ride after those men and—and I accused him of cowardice.' There, it was out and she winced inwardly at the ugly sound of the word.

'Not before his men, I hope.' Sir Walter was clearly deeply shocked.

'No,' she murmured, 'it was here, in my chamber. We were alone.' She paused. 'I regret that, for—for I believe it to be untrue but,' she added in a little rush, 'Father, I cannot understand his reluctance to hound these men to their destruction. Everyone in the county believes Mauger de Cotaine to be guilty, but my husband will not take any hand in bringing him to justice.'

Sir Walter was silent, his brow furrowed. 'He must have his own good reasons,' he said at last, 'though I confess this puzzles me too, but—' and here he reached up and, putting out one finger, tilted up her chin and forced her to face him '—whatever the reason, you cannot allow it to damage your relationship with your husband. He has done well by us. He has talked with me frankly and I know he does not expect too much of you.

'It seems now that your primary desire is to press him into a retributive attack upon de Cotaine? Do you not think *I* have dwelt on this matter? How do you think it has been for me—lying for days too helpless to take any action in reprisal? The man has to be brought to justice, Gisela, and will be, and I pray I may take an active part in bringing him before the King's court, but you cannot allow this desire to goad you into ruining your life with Alain de Treville.

'I had thought—after your first night together that—in time—you and he—would come to a mutual regard for each other that would develop into something resembling the love your mother and I shared. Make something of this marriage, Gisela. I want happiness for you now, more than I want justice against de Cotaine, more than I want anything.'

She drew away from him shakily. 'I know I was wrong to taunt him so and—and I know such a wound can fester if not soon healed. Father, I am not sure if I can heal it, but I promise I will try and—and I have to try and save the three who helped me from punishment, especially Sigurd, for he is in greatest peril—for Aldith's sake.'

By the time Gisela had dressed and descended to the hall she found that Lord Alain had indeed left the castle. Sir Clement, who was finishing breakfast, looked at her a little reproachfully. Gisela was about to explain to him why she had told him somewhat less than the truth yesterday, then thought better of it. There was nothing she could say that would excuse her conduct.

She encountered Huon in the bailey when she went in search of Hereward.

'The dog followed Lord Alain, my lady. He rode into the village.'

'Had he business there? Do you know why he has gone this morning?'

'No, my lady, but it was being said by some of the men-at-arms that he has gone to question one of his serfs.'

Gisela's heart jumped. Had Alain gone to bully Winfrith into telling him the truth about Sigurd's illegal proceedings in Allestone wood? If so, the boy could be in very grave peril of losing his hand, or worse, his life. The girl would probably be sufficiently in awe of her lord to be unable to conceal anything from him.

Huon was waiting to be dismissed.

Gisela said, 'Is the boy, Sigurd, still in the guardroom?'

'I think that is so, my lady.'

'And Edwin and Algar?'

The boy looked puzzled. 'I saw Algar ride out with Lord Alain, my lady. I have not seen Edwin this morning.'

Gisela drew a relieved breath. So far none of her pressed companions had come to harm. She went to the bower, recently prepared for her use behind the hall, where she found Sir Clement's buxom and friendly wife, Lady Rohese, sorting silks and embroidery wools. It appeared to Gisela that Sir Clement had not reported his lady's strange behaviour to his wife for Gisela was greeted cheerily and without rancour.

They sat amiably discussing the colours needed for a new hanging then, as Aldith appeared in the doorway looking drawn and haggard, Gisela requested that Lady Rohese go to the kitchen for her and discuss today's dinner with the castle cook. Lady Rohese was delighted. She had been afraid that that her position in the castle would be usurped by Lord Alain's wife and was relieved to find Gisela grateful for her advice and help in matters of household management.

Gisela hastily told Aldith all she knew of Sigurd. 'He is still in the guardroom but, as yet, unharmed, I am sure. I have had no chance to speak with Lord Alain on his behalf yet. He has gone to the village. I am somewhat concerned that he might have frightened young Winfrith into informing him about other misdeeds, particularly the constant raids upon the rabbit warren. I do not know the girl, but I am sure she will be very fearful if hauled before her lord.'

Aldith nodded, her expression not lightening one whit.

'Do not worry, Aldith,' Gisela consoled her. 'I will make it my business to confront Lord Alain the moment he returns to the castle.'

Aldith was about to take up a gauze veil she had been hemming the day before when both women were startled to hear sounds of arrival. The castle dogs barked, horses whinnied; the sound of hooves on cobbles and the chink of armour and accoutrements told them armed men were entering the bailey.

'Go to the keep steps and discover if that is my lord returning,' Gisela ordered. 'If so, I must see to my appearance. I must look my best when pleading for Sigurd. That might help the situation.'

Aldith went at a run and Gisela took a small copper mirror from the hanging purse at her belt and scrutinised her appearance critically. She straightened her veil and noticed, with satisfaction, that her golden hair was braided neatly and becomingly beneath it. She still looked pale but there was little sign of puffiness about her eyes after last night's bout of weeping.

She had been gratified to find, after Joshua's treatment, that her injured ankle pained her very little this morning but wondered if a slight limp when greeting her lord might make him more sympathetic to her pleading.

Aldith returned very quickly and unduly excited.

'It is a visitor requesting to see Lord Alain urgently and he is still away from the castle. He announces himself as Sir Rainald de Tourel. He has but three men as escort, but all are armed and dusty as if they might have set out very early indeed this morning and ridden hard for Allestone.'

Gisela turned, somewhat perplexed. She had not expected quite so soon to be required to act as sole chatelaine to her husband's castle and to perform the courtly tasks of greeting.

'Send Huon to conduct Sir Rainald to the hall at once,' she said a little breathlessly.

The man who came through the screen doors into the hall proper where Gisela had hastened to meet him was thick set though quite young—scarcely older, at Gisela's guess, than Lord Alain himself. He was clad in mail and still coiffed, which he pushed back as he entered the hall, revealing a crop of thick, closely cut brown hair. He strode to greet her, followed by his escort of armed men who remained in attendance politely near the screens.

She saw, with a faint pang, that his good-humoured countenance and pleasant features, though his skin was weathered to a leathery brown, probably by prolonged campaigning out of doors, reminded her somewhat of Kenrick. He had none of Lord Alain's tall elegance and grace of movement, nor had he that stern aloofness of manner which proclaimed her husband as lord of his desmesne, but it was evident that this man was a soldier used to authority, for all his ease of manner.

He stooped to kiss her outstretched hand. 'My lady, Huon informs me that my friend has married at last and I am delighted to be received by so lovely a lady.'

Gisela's lips twitched despite her resolve to greet this knight with the due courtesy and coolness his rank deserved.

'I am sorry, Sir Rainald, to inform you that my husband is away from the castle on business on the desmesne, but I expect him back very shortly. I hope your business is not so urgent that you will be unable to accept our hospitality for a while, at least.'

His smile broadened as he came, invited by her gesture, to warm himself by the hearth fire, unclipping the clasp of his brown frieze mantle as he did so

'I shall be privileged to accept for at least one night, my lady, if it will not put you to too great an inconvenience at this festive season. Yes, I have urgent business to discuss with Lord Alain but not so desperate that it cannot wait until after dinner.'

Baron Alain de Treville rode into his own bailey two hours later to find strange horses being rubbed down in his stable. On enquiry, he discovered that his visitor was his old campaign companion, Sir Rainald de Tourel.

He had been kept in the village longer than he had intended, examining with his reeve some repairs needed to two of the cottages, the roofs having suffered considerable damage in a high wind last week. He had also had brought before him the girl, Winfrith, whom his reeve had informed him had been keeping company with Sigurd.

The girl had been at first clearly alarmed by the summons and stood awkwardly in the dirt of the road, staring up somewhat fearfully at his restless mount, as he had sat in the saddle above her. However, despite her awed respect for him, he had got little out of her.

Her father, a brawny fellow, who was not easily bullied into hard work on the desmesne land or on his own strips, for that matter, had attempted to force his way to his daughter's side and bluster in her defence, but had been held back by one of his men—not Algar, Lord Alain had noted grimly.

Winfrith had held her ground. She was a tall willowy girl, scarce more than fifteen, Alain had thought, with grey eyes, a mop of curly light brown hair and striking, bold features. Already her youthful, taut breasts pressed hard against the rough homespun of her tunic. Unlike her father, she had gone to some trouble to keep her person reasonably clean and tidy and, once over her initial shyness in Alain's presence, had answered his sharply put questions with some degree of confidence.

Wryly, Alain had thought he could not blame young Sigurd for his attraction to the wench and willingness to put himself in danger so as to shine in her eyes. Not only was she pretty, but showed signs of making some fellow a capable and bedworthy mate before long. He had recognised a native shrewdness in her answers and at length had dismissed her with a warning to keep clear of trouble. She had tossed back her luxuriant curls and had cast him a beguiling smile as she had sauntered off to join her father, who had pulled her roughly through the door of their cottage.

Lord Alain had smiled somewhat grimly. No, he could not rely on Winfrith condemning Sigurd out of her pretty, pouting mouth. He must go by his own instincts when questioning the lad.

Now he hastened up the keep steps, anxious to see his friend, only to be informed that Sir Rainald was being assisted to bathe by the ladies of the castle, Gisela and Rohese. Without stopping to cast off his hooded mantle, Alain pushed open the door of the small first-floor tower chamber used as a bath house and strode in.

Outside he had been greeted by the sounds of merriment; now he stood, one hand on the latch, regarding his erstwhile companion seated in the tall tub, up to his neck in hot water brought up from below in steaming pails by two sweating kitchen lads with Lady Rohese energetically rubbing his brawny back with some of their finest soft soap, made last year in the castle brewhouse, and Gisela standing ready before the visitor, two large linen towels draped over her arm.

She was laughing out loud at the last sally de Tourel uttered and the man gave a great delighted chuckle at sight of his friend. 'Alain, you are a lucky dog, I find you married to one of the two loveliest ladies in all Christendom.'

Here he half-turned to the red-cheeked smiling Lady Rohese, who flushed even redder at the compliment, before de Tourel turned again to his friend's lady, his brown, twinkling eyes, like a robin's, alight with admiration. 'How do you manage to do it, I wonder, you who have always insisted that you have no winning ways with ladies?'

Lord Alain masked his own unreasonable annoyance at finding his lady engaged in what was only the normal customary assistance offered to a knightly guest and strode forward to clasp his friend's very wet hand tightly in his own.

'Welcome to Allestone, Rainald. I see you are already making yourself at home.'

Rainald de Tourel chuckled. 'You know you can always rely on me to do that. Being on campaign so much of my time, I take advantage of more luxurious accommodation every time it is offered.'

Lord Alain said a little curtly, 'I'm sure your attentions to Sir Rainald's back are completed now, Lady Rohese, and I—' he swung round to neatly snatch the towels from Gisela's hand '—I am here now to see to it that Sir Rainald has all the assistance he needs.'

Gisela opened her mouth to protest but caught the angry snap of those dark eyes and gave both men a little curtsy. She waited while Rohese, with a little girlish twitter, put down the bowl of soap and, wiping her hands on a frieze apron she had wrapped around her while attending the guest, joined her and they withdrew from the bathhouse.

At dinner Lord Alain sat, sombrely watching both ladies again fall under the spell of Rainald de Tourel's charm. He half-turned to Sir Clement but he, as usual, was occupying himself with the food on his trencher and appeared to be in no way put out by his lady's interest in the visitor.

De Tourel had come straight from the King's camp near Wallingford, which he was besieging. Affairs were taking their slow pace as was normal, particularly in so inclement a season. He made light of their discomfort under canvas and entertained the ladies by amusing tales of mistakes and misunderstandings amongst the King's commanders.

Once he turned to his host, with that amusing twinkle, which was part of his stock in trade, and related an incident that had happened long ago and concerned their combined siege to one of the late Queen Matilda's ladies. He, de Tourel, had come off worst in the affair, as it happened, having been discovered in the lady's bed-chamber by her irate husband, and soundly thrashed by that lord with the riding whip he had been carrying at the time.

Lord Alain, who had encouraged the affair—indeed, laid wagers on the outcome and been partly responsible for her betrayal of her husband—had, of course, got off entirely without blame.

Gisela turned a flushed, amused glance at her husband but found he was not amused by the story. The smile died on her lips and she showed embarrassment where, formerly, on the understanding that the lady in question had acted willingly in the whole sordid affair, she had laughed heartily with the others at high table at Sir Rainald's witty narration and ability to laugh at his own misfortune.

At the close of the meal while the trestles were being removed, Lord Alain suggested that they repair together to the small chamber where he dealt with manor business. Gisela rose and curtsied, then retired with Rohese and Aldith to her bower. Sir Walter, sensing that the business which had brought Sir Rainald to Allestone concerned him and Lord Alain alone, complained that his old wound was troubling him and took himself off to his chamber to rest.

Rainald de Tourel settled himself comfortably in the leather fald chair to face his friend. A charcoal brazier warmed the small chamber and, since he had placed

one of his own men-at-arms outside the leather-curtained
entrance, Rainald was assured that no one could overhear
their talk. His manner changed immediately and he
became the able soldier Lord Alain knew him to be.

'While, as I said, I am delighted to see you more
comfortably appointed here, I shall be able to report to
the King that you have already made strides, as he hoped,
in strengthening the defences of this castle.'

Alain inclined his chin in answer. 'Baron Godfrey had
unfortunately allowed things to slide but all is in order
now, though there are still matters which can be
improved. I shall begin strengthening the tower buttresses
and deepen the dry moat once the weather improves in
the spring.'

'And your report on the activities of Mauger de
Cotaine?'

Lord Alain shrugged apologetically. 'I am sure he has
been in touch with Henry FitzEmpress, despite his com-
mitment to King Stephen's cause, but, as yet, I have no
direct evidence.' He sipped from the wine goblet Huon
had placed at his elbow after filling a goblet for Sir
Rainald and withdrawing from the office.

'It has not been easy. De Cotaine has a company of
mercenaries, as you well know, at this castle of his near
Empingham and has recently acquired an even more dis-
reputable rabble of routiers—from the slums of Caen, I
imagine, from their accents. They have been amusing
and enriching themselves by raiding nearby manors, particularly the smaller ones whose defences are meagre.
My wife's manor, Brinkhurst, was attacked and damaged
only a couple of months ago.

'Feelings are running high in the county and I am
being pressed to take up arms against de Cotaine. As
you know, that would be fatal to our cause before we
are sure of the depths of the man's treason.' He gave a
regretful sigh. 'My lady, in particular, is most disturbed

by my seeming reluctance to bring the man to justice.'

Sir Rainald's eyebrows rose. 'I can understand that is causing you problems. You have fallen deeply in love. I can recognise that when I see it, my friend. Give it time.'

Rainald's brown eyes narrowed shrewdly. 'I saw admiration in her face too, perhaps more than that. Was it my over-sensitivity that discerned some measure of disagreement between you?' He frowned thoughtfully. 'Did I overplay my hand as the charming clown? I trust not.'

Lord Alain gave a wintry smile. 'You guessed at the truth. I am so deeply besotted that I am irritated by her attentions to any other man—even a dead one. A close neighbour was killed in that raid and I believe she was in love with the man. Perhaps there is more in her determination to see my refusal to accuse de Cotaine as an assessment of my apparent cowardice. She also requires me to be the instrument of her vengeance—and that rankles.'

De Tourel gave a low whistle of understanding.

'So you see,' Alain said with a slight grimace, 'I am caught in a trap and can only be released by the King's order.'

De Tourel pursed his lips. 'I may have the means of your salvation. The King sent me on rather a delicate mission, hence the reason for my riding with so few men-at-arms.'

Alain leaned forward eagerly. 'He has work for me? Does he need me at Wallingford? If so. . .'

'No, my friend. The siege goes on as ever. You know only too well how these affairs progress slowly, if at all. It may be we will lift the siege at any time. There have been suggestions that we try to lift the siege at Malmesbury, but no decisions have been made yet.' He paused and looked down into the lees in his wine goblet. 'The

King has been informed that you were once friendly with Henry Plantagenet.'

Lord Alain's expression grew grave. 'If the King doubts my loyalty. . .'

'No, nothing like that. Is it true you know the Empress Matilda's son well?'

'No, not well. I served with him briefly as a page and I met him again just once at the French Court when the King sent me on an embassy to King Louis.'

'Do you rate him highly—as a man—and commander?'

'Yes.' Alain spoke without hesitation. 'Though, of course, that is my opinion only. As I said, our acquaintance was short. I left service with him and went to serve in Robert of Beaumont's household.

'Henry struck me then as a boy who would be a good friend and a bad enemy, but one who considered justice highly, always an excellent trait in a ruler—and there was no trace of laziness in him, always on the move, restless, but with purpose. Of course, he may have changed—and now that he is wed to Eleanor of Aquitaine his ambitions will have no bounds, I would think.'

'The King believes that Henry will soon land on the south coast, probably at Poole or Wareham. We know he planned to set sail from Barfleur soon after Christmas.'

'Ah.'

Rainald de Tourel said very softly, 'The King would like you to try to meet with Henry again.'

De Treville's dark eyes widened perceptively. 'But that would be construed as treason.'

'By some, yes. The mission would not be without risk—from both sides. Henry would be unlikely to welcome you either. You could be arrested as a spy.'

'The King wishes me to treat with Henry FitzEmpress? Surely there are greater men than I to perform such a service.'

'Greater but less trustworthy. No, the King does not wish you to go to any such lengths. Indeed, without the consent of his Council, that would be outrageous indeed.'

'But Rainald, there have been so many attempts at truce. No side will give way. Matilda considers her claim unassailable and Stephen was the barons' choice. . .'

'The King is tired, Alain, and, I fear, unwell. He wants an end to all this—for the sake of the realm.'

Alain shrugged. 'Amen to that. So do we all—but how?'

De Tourel tapped meditatively upon the rim of his wine goblet with one finger. 'It has been suggested that if the King should die—Henry might be an admirable choice to succeed him.'

'But the King's sons, Eustace, in particular, would never agree to that.'

'Eustace, perhaps not—he is headstrong and unruly—but William might, if it is the King's will.'

'And is it?' Alain questioned bluntly.

De Tourel said quietly, 'Eustace is becoming more and more out of hand. The people fear his brutal excesses. Since the Queen died, Stephen is beginning to feel more and more at odds with his elder son—and doubtful about the final outcome.'

'But surely I am not to put such a consideration to Henry, even should I be allowed into his presence?'

'No, naturally, you could not dare go so far, but the King wishes to know your assessment of Henry's character now, and whether he would be acceptable to the people of England. God knows his father, Geoffrey, would never have been. If you could meet with him again, however briefly, and report to His Grace, we could have a better idea of how far to proceed with the possibility of such a proposed treaty in council.'

Alain sat back in his chair and stared bleakly at the glowing charcoal in its brazier.

'You wish me to go in secret?'

'Yes.'

'And should I be taken and arraigned for treason. . .?'

De Tourel smiled grimly. 'It would be for the King to do his best for you, but. . .'

'"But" is the operative word.'

'It is thought that Henry will meet with some of the defecting barons nearby, probably at Devizes.'

'Then the King fears many such defections?'

De Tourel sighed heavily. 'The war lags on and the land suffers. As we have said, many do not trust Eustace to succeed his father—and the Church is antagonistic towards Eustace for his ungodly behaviour. It is natural enough men should turn to a younger man they could hail as a saviour. The King needs to act soon—before he finds himself deserted by his ablest commanders.'

Alain was silent and sat for a while, turning his wine goblet and watching the blood-red liquid swirl in the dullish glow from the brazier.

He said at last, 'I would need to travel in disguise. This is not a role I am good at. Also I should need to ride hard and fast to reach the south before Henry leaves for an undesignated destination. I would need to take few men and in this winter weather—who knows how long we might be delayed?'

'Aye, I found it hard going in places riding here from Wallingford.'

Alain was thinking fast now. 'I could go as a wealthy merchant, anxious about these marauding raids in this district, fearful for my own property in Oakham. As you have already suggested, what more natural than men should seek out Henry as a possible future protector?'

'But once in his presence, should you be admitted, he would recognise you?'

'Oh, certainly. It would then be necessary for me to disclose, in part, at least, the true purpose for my arrival.'

'You would risk that?'

Alain shrugged. 'Henry is known to have a fierce temper. It is said to be the curse of the Plantagenets, inherited from the infamous witch blood of their legendary ancestress, Melisande.

'There is no doubt I could be summarily dispatched if I was thought to be a spy from the King's camp, but, as I have judged him previously, Henry is known to prize justice, and I believe he would listen to me patiently. I remember as a boy he was known to come to the rescue of younger lads bullied unmercifully. The mission is not without danger, but I have hope of success if once I can reach him.'

'What if you were to take a beautiful wife? Henry, I believe, is also known, like his father, to idolise lovely women?'

Alain's dark eyes snapped in sudden fury. 'You would have me endanger Gisela?'

'Not necessarily, you could take some other lass, but—' and Rainald de Tourel's white teeth gleamed in a knowing smile '—I do not think Lady Gisela would have aught to fear from Henry FitzEmpress, even should her husband forfeit his head.'

Again Alain sat for a while, gloomily silent. 'She is a fearless woman,' he said at last, 'and a fine horsewoman, unlikely to delay me on the ride; and God knows she is like to get up to the Devil's own business if I leave her here. De Burgh is unlikely to be able to curb her should she venture to once more ride out against de Cotaine.'

De Tourel said heavily, 'Alain, I would not willingly counsel you to do aught that would deliberately place your lady in jeopardy, but if she were to ride with you with only one attendant and few followers, it would serve to arouse less suspicion than a man riding alone. You could place her in safety in some inn when you reach the coast before proceeding on to Devizes.'

Alain stood up and stretched. 'I will go, of course,' he said decisively. 'The King has need of my services and I cannot, in honour, refuse, but you must leave to me how much, in the end, I feel the need to divulge to my wife. Is that understood?'

'Perfectly.' De Tourel smiled in answer.

'Then I will see you again at supper, and, Rainald, I would regard it a favour if you curbed your over-obvious charming manner tonight.' His smile faded, as he added more soberly, 'Afterwards, when I have thought further, I will decide what to do about the need for Gisela to accompany me.'

The two men were both on their feet now and regarding each other gravely.

De Tourel said, 'God guard you in this quest, Alain, and bring you safe back to Allestone, but know, all our hopes ride with you.'

Chapter Eight

Gisela was surprised when Alain entered their bed-chamber somewhat abruptly and earlier than she might have expected. Noting his grim expression, she called Huon, who was outside waiting attendance, to take charge of Hereward. The young page hurried in, snapped on Hereward's leash and, despite the pup's determination to jump up on Alain and lick his face, took him instantly outside the chamber.

Aldith, who was turning back the furred coverlet for her mistress, curtsied and followed the page, pulling to the door after her.

Lord Alain stood with his back against it, looking steadily at his wife. Gisela had donned a fur-lined bedgown for the night was cold. Her golden hair streamed below her waist and she stood hesitantly, one hand against her heart, as if she feared what might come of this meeting. It was the first time they had spoken alone together since she had accused him of arrant cowardice. She bit her lip, longing to break the deadlock, yet uncertain what to say.

In the end she said, a little awkwardly, 'I—I thought you would be closeted with our guest a little longer. Did he say if he was satisfied with our arrangements for his hospitality?'

Lord Alain said somewhat curtly, 'Considering what I saw in the bathhouse, he would be churlish to complain about the warmth of his welcome.'

She flushed hotly and fiddled nervously with the tasselled cord of her bedgown.

'I—I thought—it was explained to me that to assist a guest in the bathhouse was customary and expected of the lady of the manor. Lady Rohese was present and. . .'

'It *is* expected,' he replied shortly, 'it was just that you both seemed to be extra attentive, that is all, but there, Rainald has always had a way with women.'

'He *is* amusing,' Gisela said lamely. 'I know some of his stories may not have been in the best of taste, but. . .'

He waved away her excuse. 'No, it is nothing. There was no impropriety. Perhaps I would not have been so touchy had not I seen in your eyes a recognition of his likeness to Kenrick of Arcote.'

Her blue eyes widened in shock.

'So my feelings for Kenrick still rankle with you?'

He was unfastening his swordbelt, his shoulder turned on her, but he swung round instantly.

'Yes, it rankles, especially when I find you mourning him so keenly at the tomb only days ago.'

'I explained that. I. . .'

'Do you deny you love him still?' He was staring at her, his eyes hostile, his stance rigid, both feet planted determinedly upon the floor.

'I cannot deny I still have deep feelings for Kenrick. I always will have. He was my childhood companion. I thought him the love of my life, but. . .'

'But?'

She was very close to tears and turned away from him, one hand agitatedly moving, as if she would ward him off, though, in truth, he made no move to touch her.

She said, piteously, 'He cannot come between us now.'

'He can lie a cold ghost within our marriage bed,' he said harshly.

'If you believe that. . .'

'I *do* believe it, since, it seems, you are determined to make me the instrument of your vengeance. Your one desire is to avenge your lover's death.'

She swung round on him then, advanced, then began to strike impotent blows upon his unyielding chest.

'He was never my lover. You should know that only too well, my lord. You took my maidenhood, you and no other.'

He caught her hands in his own and forcibly halted their attack upon his person.

'Your body is mine, but your heart is still his. Confess it.'

'Confess?' She lifted vivid blue eyes to him, now drowned in angry and hurt tears. 'What do you want me to confess? You are my husband. I have not betrayed, and will never betray, your trust.'

'Aye, I'm prepared to believe that since the man is dead and there can be no temptation.'

She stood docilely in his arms. 'Yes, he is dead,' she said dully, 'and I regret that. I feel partly reponsible since I begged him to come back to Brinkhurst with me to plead with my father and to offer for me in order to save me from an unhappy marriage.'

'Ah.' The single word was an angry assertion of his previous conviction.

'My father pressed me to the match. You know that,' she flamed at him. 'I had no choice.'

'And will have no chance to break your vows. I'll see to that.'

She wrenched herself away from him then. 'Very well, play the tyrant in your own household. Keep me confined. Beat me if you will. You have that right.'

'When have I ever mistreated you?'

'You are threatening me now.'

'I make no threats, simply remind you that you are mine and I will hold you.'

Angry spots of vivid colour showed in her cheeks.

'As you said, a moment ago, my body is yours—but,' she added defiantly, 'my will is my own and my opinions.'

'That I am a coward? You made that very plain.' The words were grated out through gritted teeth and she saw his dark, opaque eyes light up with a sudden flame of rank fury.

Her momentary fear was so intense that she cowered back from him. 'I——I should not have said that. . .'

'But you continue to think it.'

'No,' she whispered, dry-mouthed. 'I was out of my mind with temper at your interference in the wood and since——have regretted those hastily uttered words. I know there is not one cowardly bone in your body.'

He gave a short, harsh laugh. 'There are cowardly impulses in all of us, lady, believe me.'

She was silent, waiting for him to make the next move in this frightening exchange.

He said, curtly, 'I have my own reasons for holding my hand over this matter of bringing Mauger de Cotaine to justice. For the moment he must be allowed to continue his depredations in the county unchecked. I like it no more than you do, but it has to be so.'

'I am sure I could have had proof of his involvement today. I saw their leader. I know he was one of the raiding party at Brinkhurst. If he could have been followed, I am certain he and the other routiers would have finished up at Offen——'

'I believe you, but, as I said, you must trust me in this.'

She let her shoulders rise and fall in a little gesture of utter helplessness.

'I am concerned about Edwin, Algar——and Sigurd,'

she murmured in a little hoarse whisper. 'I am afraid you
will punish them harshly, yet they were only trying to
help me. I am responsible for what happened.'

'You appear to constantly hold that tyrannical opinion
of me firmly fixed in your head,' he said coldly.

'I—' She hesitated. 'I know it. I tend to fear the worst
of you and—and have no real evidence to show any
undue severity towards your men on your part, yet—'

'You fear me.' He strode suddenly forward and took
her by the shoulders. 'Do not deny it.'

She trembled in his grasp and he forced up her chin
with one finger so that she was looking directly into his
eyes. 'Why?'

'You have—a reputation for strict discipline, my lord.'

'Yes,' he said softly, 'and with good reason.' His voice
was hoarse now with desire. 'I have the urge to compel
my wife to love me—and, perhaps, that might prove my
downfall.'

He was holding her so close now that she could smell
the clean fragrance of his skin, the faint muskiness of
his masculinity. She was afraid of his anger since she
had given him just cause to punish her.

She had disobeyed him, accused him of cowardice—
that most terrible attack upon his manhood and knightly
honour—and, in these last few hours, she had deliberately provoked his rising fury by appearing to be
bewitched by the flattering attentions of his friend.

She found herself suddenly lifted off her feet and held
against his heart, as his mouth closed demandingly on
hers so hard that, for moments, she was unable to breathe
and the sound of her own quickened heartbeats pounded
unnaturally in her ears.

She clung to him desperately. She had missed him so
dreadfully since that day in the church near Kenrick's
tomb, had longed for the feel of him beside her in bed,
the sensations his skilful hands wrought upon her own

taut, expectant body. She knew now that she loved him and none other.

They had warred since the first moment they had clashed near Aldith's assart cottage. He had teased her, resisted her demands, yet, in the end, he had tempered his judgements and given in to her pleading for his mercy, rescued her from a dreadful death in the raid on Brinkhurst, wooed her in the marriage bed and finally dominated her, not by harsh usage, but by the skilled and gentle knowledge of the arts of love.

Now she wanted only to surrender, to beg his forgiveness, to heal the widening breach she saw yawning threateningly between them—hear him declare his love for her.

He had carried her to the bed and laid her down upon it, kneeling up upon one knee beside her, his face pressed close to her now.

'Perhaps, my heart,' he said softly, 'I can teach you to love me if I cannot compel. Sweet Virgin,' he muttered on what almost sounded like a sob, 'do you not know how close I was to losing you out there in the wood, how near you were to being defiled and murdered by that red-bearded piece of slime? I love you, Gisela of Allestone, aren't you aware of that yet? Can you not understand that I cannot bear to have you so much as glance at another man, not even to mourn a dead one?'

She arched towards him and, for a while, there were no more words between them.

He had undressed quickly and hungrily pushed down her bedgown from her ivory shoulders. Then he ran his hands through the glory of her loosened fair hair.

If she had feared he would take her in anger she was soon reassured, for he deliberately curbed his desire, holding her close, nuzzling the soft flesh of her shoulder, pressing his lips to the proud stem of her throat. She sensed almost a desperation within him and, after his possession of her, which carried her to the heights of ecstasy, she lay back, replete, her own wild desires satisfied, and ran her hand lovingly over his strong arms and the hard rib cage.

'My lord,' she said quietly, 'you must understand that my feelings for Kenrick of Arcote were idealistic, the romantic longings of a child growing into womanhood. Who knows if they could ever have materialised into the mature love of a woman for her man? He is gone and I shall always think kindly of him but I am true wife now—and—and—' her whisper was tearful '—you have aroused me to delights I could not have imagined.'

He was very still and she thought he might well have slipped off into slumber and not heard her tearful avowal of love. She leaned down to look at him and his lips curved into a smile, half-content, half-triumphant.

'Then you do love me, Gisela of Allestone, just a little?'

She half turned away, nervous now of betraying herself too much. 'I am your wife. It is my duty to. . .'

'Do you love me? Tell me?'

'Yes,' she said at last in a little hiccoughing gasp. 'Yes, Alain de Treville, I truly love you.'

He drew her down again and kissed her so fiercely she thought she would die, bereft of breath and the aching, sweet pain emanating from the throbbing rapture of their combined passion.

They drew apart and she swallowed uncertainly, unwilling to break the pleasure of the moment by referring to the bone of contention between them, yet she owed Aldith an attempt to win some mercy for Sigurd. Surely Alain would listen to her now and grant her plea—yet she knew this was not the time. Something was disturbing him. She had sensed it earlier, as if he despaired of losing her even now. She waited in an agony of apprehension for him to broach what was on his mind.

At last he broke silence. 'I have to leave Allestone tomorrow.'

She closed her eyes in sudden dread. What she had feared was coming to pass. She said tremulously, 'Has Sir Rainald summoned you to the King's assistance? I thought that might be the purpose of his visit.'

'In a way.' He hesitated and turned to look into her troubled eyes. 'I need to travel south with only a small escort—in fact, my business there must be kept a secret for the time being.'

'Will you be in danger?' She reached out to touch his chest, her fingers curling in the dark hair there, in her sudden agitation.

'I do not anticipate any trouble,' he said lightly, but he was not looking at her now and she thought he was not as confident as he seemed. 'I shall take Edwin and Sigurd. That,' he added grimly, 'should keep them both out of trouble for a while at least. They can make themselves useful and be under my constant supervision.'

'Sigurd?' she said worriedly. 'He is no trained soldier. Should you not have a more stalwart companion at your back?'

He gave a little grim bark of a laugh. 'I do not intend either of them should fight. No man these days goes without an escort, however small, but my purpose is not military.'

'Then you go to reconnoitre—for the King?' Her voice was troubled. 'Could you not be taken by one of the opposing armies as a spy travelling in their midst?'

She was so close she could see one mobile eyebrow rise at her suggestion.

'I could, but by travelling with so small an escort, I pose no threat, nor am I likely to be attacked by any routier band, since a man so obviously unarmed and ill prepared for combat could hardly be wealthy enough to make the raid worthwhile.'

Her fingers clenched so tightly upon the hair on his chest that he gave an involuntary little gasp and she released her grip instantly.

'This mission is vital to the King's cause?'

'It could prove invaluable,' he replied cautiously.

'But why you?' she pressed. 'There must be many others at Wallingford who could go, and nearer the south country—Sir Rainald himself. . .'

'He would not prove suitable, nor would those other knights in the King's train. He knows that only I could be trusted to accomplish this mission and, of course, I cannot refuse him.'

She went cold as she thought how, only hours ago, she had challenged his courage; now, instinctively, she knew he was going from her into very real peril and she felt helpless to prevent it, yet desperate to try anything that might keep him safe.

'You will go in disguise?'

'Hardly.' He laughed. 'Nothing so dramatic. I shall travel in merchant garb. There are many such on the road going about their various businesses. Simple men cannot barricade themselves upon their property, despite their very real fears of venturing forth. The wars have gone on much too long for that. They would all be ruined.'

Her brain raced as she visualised the difficulties of such a journey. He might not face direct challenges, but he would be subject to insult and taunts most likely. This proud, honourable, stern man was not one to stomach such easily.

She said hesitantly, 'It might arouse less comment if a merchant was travelling with—his wife.'

One arm round her waist tightened and she pushed herself up in the bed to look down at him. 'Alain, let me go with you? Give me the chance to redeem my hard treatment of you. I had no right to impugn your honour and now I see how wicked and foolish I was. I will be obedient and circumspect, I swear it. I owe you recompense for the deadly insult I threw at you. Let me wipe it out by my presence at your side when you have need of me.'

She expected a hasty denial, but he lay quiet for a few moments then said slowly, 'I confess the idea has occurred to me—especially as, despite your assurances, I am concerned to leave you here unprotected. De Burgh is no match for your determination should you decide to flout my orders and I know it. I feel in my bones you might well be safer with me—but. . .'

'I can ride well and. . .'

'I know all that. If you promise to be guided by my instructions I will take you, with Aldith in attendance, part way. After I leave you safely installed at some nunnery or an inn, I can manage alone, for the greater part of the journey through the ranks of both armies will be done, but I must be sure of your compliance.'

'I swear it.' Softly she breathed, 'You will let Sigurd keep his hands—afterwards?'

'If he keeps them from thieving my rabbits in future,' Alain growled and she leaned down to kiss him heartily.

'Aldith will find me suitable clothing,' she said confidently. 'We shall not delay you, be very sure of that.'

Grimly he tried to convince himself that he was doing the right thing. She would not delay him. He had seen evidence of her spirit and determination. In this winter weather there would be discomforts along the way, but he knew well Gisela would not complain but—he ground his teeth in anguished concern. Wherever he left her, even with Aldith and the boy, Sigurd, who both adored her, she could be threatened by any rogue who thought her easy prey.

In these days no one was safe when not immured behind the solid walls of a castle like Allestone. He would pray that his secret mission would come to a fruitful conclusion for the sake of all those simple folk who wanted to go about their daily business in peace. The risk he took, even with Gisela's most precious life, was surely worth that.

They set off early next day; in fact, Gisela was surprised by the speed with which preparations were made. She had very little time to talk with her father and knew he was extremely curious as to Lord Alain's reason for leaving Allestone at this time of year and, most of all, his decision to take Gisela with him.

Gisela knew she could not explain to him that Lord Alain's mission was for the King and secret, and had to lamely agree with Lord Alain's brusque explanation that the King needed him to conclude some important business he was unwilling to entrust to another knight.

Reluctantly Sir Walter took leave of his daughter. His only consolation, as he told her, was that he was considerably improved, thanks to the unceasing care of the Jewish physician, and would be leaving for Brinkhurst very shortly. Gisela embraced him tearfully, then hastened back to her chamber after breakfast to examine the clothes Aldith had procured for her.

It seemed it was not necessary for her to dress very differently. Her own sober, dark-coloured warm clothing would suit her role as a merchant's wife admirably and she would wear a plain hooded frieze cloak over all. When she descended to the hall again, it was to find Lord Alain clad similarly in dark chausses and a dark brown fustian tunic. Both of them forbore to wear any jewellery and Lord Alain's cloak pin was a simple affair of beaten copper.

Gisela wondered, fleetingly, if her husband was wearing mail beneath his concealing tunic. No weapons were in evidence, but she did not doubt he carried a sword and dagger within his saddle bag. The cloak he carried over his arm, like hers, was of grey homespun. Gisela knew she would miss the warm fur lining of the mantles she usually wore in this inclement weather.

It was decided that Algar, too, should accompany the party, since Sigurd could not ride even the most docile of mounts. Gisela could not help thinking that it might have been better to leave the boy behind, but, doubtless, Lord Alain had his own reasons for insisting he be one of the small escort.

Gisela mounted her own palfrey, its fine caparisons removed, while Lord Alain chose a sturdy hack rather than his fiery-tempered destrier. Aldith was mounted pillion behind Edwin while Algar carried Sigurd. Aldith was clad, like her mistress, plainly and well wrapped against the cold, while all the men wore hooded frieze cloaks over homespun chausses and leather jerkins. No one wore distinguishing badges.

Edwin led a sumpter laden with two panniers containing, Gisela supposed, sample goods Lord Alain was pretending to market in the towns they would pass through. On questioning Alain, she discovered that was, indeed, the case and were examples of good woollen cloth he had hurriedly sent for from one of the most prominent Oakham merchants.

When he had lifted her into the saddle, he asked only one question. 'You are sure you wish to do this?'

'Yes, of course I am.'

'Your father is not best pleased. Thank God he has no real inkling of just how dangerous this journey could prove to be, but he fears your palfrey might break a leg on some icy patch and throw you.'

She nodded. 'I had to be evasive and I think he understood something of what you intend, though you told him little.'

'I have provided him with a small garrison of thoroughly experienced men to defend Brinkhurst. You do not need to be worried for his safety while we are away.'

'Thank you,' she breathed softly. 'Do our men of the escort know anything of what we intend?'

He frowned, his dark, level brows rising imperiously. 'My men-at-arms learn not to question my orders. As for Sigurd, he is thankful enough to be free of the guardhouse again.' He smiled a trifle grimly. 'I need him with his mother to guard you carefully while I might have need of my two trained men. I trust only those two who have known you from childhood to have your total welfare at heart.'

Her answering smile was a trifle wan. 'I do not think I could manage without Aldith. In all events, I do not believe she would allow me to go without her—not without considerable protest, which would not be advisable—and Sigurd is more capable of defending himself than you think, though he is no experienced fighting man.'

He inclined his chin, well satisfied.

When off the main roads they travelled fast, or as fast as the terrain and the double burden of pillioned passengers would allow, but on the main highways they had to appear the humble merchant, wife and servants they purported to be.

Lord Alain headed for Leicester Town, then struck westwards towards Warwick and the old Roman Fosse Way, which would eventually lead through the Cotswold Hills towards Chipping Norton, Cirencester, Chippenham and finally their destination of Devizes.

'We will have to make a detour around the King's siege camp at Wallingford,' Lord Alain informed Gisela, 'and, possibly, we shall have to avoid opposing armies on the march. There will be men moving to try to raise the sieges of both Wallingford and Malmesbury, so it will not be easy.'

The weather was bad, but not so appalling as they might have expected. Gisela was amazed to find so many travellers on the road, expecting that most people would have kept to their hearth fires this frosty January, but many, it seemed, had business to occupy them and they saw soldiers, merchants like themselves and even monks and clerics on the road.

It was icy cold but not too wet, neither was there snow to delay them, but the hard-rutted roads were treacherous with ice and the going, in places, was slow and laborious.

They stayed wherever Lord Alain felt it safe to do so and where he deemed they would be unlikely to be questioned too closely about their business. In the abbeys which offered hospitality Gisela slept with Aldith, and in the one or two flea-ridden inns where sometimes they were forced to stay she was able to sleep again with her husband, and on those occasions she was able to reveal her passionate need for his love making. She controlled, fiercely, her own growing fears for his safety and showed herself only as the loyal, strong-minded companion he so needed her to be.

However bad things were—and often she was so bone-wearied when they reached their night stop she was ready to cry with exhaustion—she gritted her teeth, determined to make no complaint. Aldith, grimly, did the same, and following her gaze towards Sigurd, Gisela knew the woman was uttering silent thanks to the Virgin that the lad had not been left hanging from a rope's end at Allestone.

At Cirencester, Lord Alain heard the news he had been eagerly awaiting. The landlord of the inn proved a vociferous gossip and informed him that the young son of the Empress Matilda had landed in England on January the twenty-sixth at Wareham.

'It's being said he had thirty-six ships and over a hundred knights as well as some thousands of foot soldiers.' The landlord, who had joined Lord Alain in a pot of ale, wiped his mouth and went on.

'There'll be some as'll welcome him, doubtless, the way things have been round here for these last years. The King has tried to keep order, right enough, God bless him, but he's never managed it. Some of us never know if'n we'll rise from our beds in the morning, can't sleep well of nights, even 'ere so far West. This young sprig of Anjou might be able to sort out the mess. At least that's what folks 'ave been saying.

'Funny,' he mused, 'I 'eard from some chapman who passed through, it's being told in Wareham that when Henry landed and went to church to offer thanks to God for safe passage, the choir was singing, "Behold he comes, the Lord our Governor, and in his hand is right royal power and might." Kind of a prophecy, don't you think? This chapman quoted it word for word and it stuck in me memory.'

Lord Alain nodded absently, but inwardly his thoughts were seething with various conjectures. The man had not said how many of Stephen's commanders and barons had defected to meet Henry FitzEmpress. That he would have to discover when he reached Devizes.

Gisela noted that, once on the way south from Cirencester, they saw many more armed bands of soldiers. Lord Alain took great pains to avoid them whenever possible, but when they were stopped on the road by a mailed and helmeted sergeant leading a band of twenty men west towards Malmesbury, he agreed to open up his panniers on the sumpter to show his wares so they might proceed without further challenge.

Gisela, whose palfrey had been edged by Edwin very close to her husband's mount, saw that Lord Alain's lips were pressed tight together and she guessed his lordly nature was infuriated by this need to bow to the small authority of this boorish and bullying sergeant. She expected an explosion of fury, but the Baron kept his temper well in check and she was able to breathe more freely once they were out of sight of the laughing, jeering band.

Devizes, she saw at once, was packed with armed men, all apparently under the firm control of their lords. This surprised her; she had seen anarchy very close amongst the men she had glimpsed on the road. The situation at Devizes was very different and she realised that here there was a gathering of some of the kingdom's most prominent and powerful barons.

Lord Alain's eyes were everywhere and, once again, both his men closed in on their mistress, guarding her from the possibility of insult or attack. Since the men here were more disciplined, Gisela thought that unlikely. She had been more afraid of the small roving bands than she was of these larger, controlled companies, but she was alarmed for Lord Alain's safety.

Here, apparently, was the evidence of trained bands in revolt against their King, as she was informed by the talk around them that the young Angevin Duke Henry was installed within the castle and with him many of King Stephen's trusted barons.

They managed to obtain accommodation at an inn on the outskirts of the market town by luck, since a knight with his small escort had only hours before moved out, and Lord Alain took occupation of a fetid and small room at the rear of the property to house Gisela and Aldith. He and the men were to fend for themselves in the inn's even more insalubrious outbuildings.

Aldith hastened out to try to find water for her mistress's toilet and Lord Alain faced Gisela warily across the dingy little chamber.

He looked round distastefully. 'I am loath to leave you

here but you will have Algar and Sigurd to attend you and Aldith while I go about my business. I shall give explicit orders that one or the other must stay outside your door both day and night.'

Gisela was weary but even more disturbed by this news. 'You intend to be away possibly tonight? I don't understand. Surely you can discover what is needful without risking yourself during the hours of darkness? A merchant wandering about at night will arouse suspicion.

'This town is full of the Empress Matilda's supporters, and many who appear to have defected from their loyalty to the King. Now you have seen the devices of those men who are here to support Count Henry, you have enough information to stay one night and allow us to depart for home very soon.'

He turned from her and she could not see his features well in the poor light that filtered into the chamber from the one dirty oxhorn window the chamber boasted.

'I need to go to the castle,' he said at last. 'I—might be detained there some time. If that is the case, I shall try to send Edwin back with a message and he will have instructions to take you from Devizes immediately and make all speed for home.'

She gave a great gasp. 'My lord, you cannot risk yourself there. I heard talk of some of the barons and earls in attendance as we passed through the town. I heard mention of the Earl of Chester. He may have seen you formerly in the King's train. You could be recognised and taken. . .'

'I know that, that is the very reason why you must leave immediately if I send you word.'

She came very close to him and reached out timidly to take his hand. 'Haven't you proved your loyalty and—and your courage by venturing so far? You cannot fail to pass at the castle unnoticed.'

He sat down on the truckle bed heavily. 'I do not

intend to pass unnoticed. I shall join the many petitioners who call hour by hour to press their grievances about the present state of the kingdom upon Henry FitzEmpress and plead for his help to remedy the situation.'

She went white to the lips. 'But why? I do not understand.' Her blue eyes widened in doubt. 'Alain, you do not intend—you, of all people—who have benefited so much from the King's bounty—you will not act the traitor and offer your allegiance to Henry, the son of your King's mortal enemy?'

This was worse than her suspicions of cowardice. She could not believe it. Alain could not turn his back so blatantly on honour. The thought was not to be borne.

He said coldly, 'So, again, you choose to think the worst of me.'

'No,' she cried brokenly, 'I do not—please, my lord, tell me it is untrue, that you did not use my presence to help you through the lines in order to betray your liege lord.'

He rose, shrugging in that characteristic way she knew well. 'If that is your belief. . .'

Tears spiked her lovely lashes as she lifted her gaze to his, reaching out with one hand to detain him while she searched his features intently for the truth of this matter.

She let her hand drop at last and said very softly. 'No, I do not believe you capable of such an act of foul treachery. There is more to this than you will tell me— and more danger than you will reveal to me. I am your wife, Alain, I have the right to know. Can you not trust me?'

He sighed and pushed her gently down upon the bed. 'Then listen well, my heart. The King has entrusted me with a mission to Henry. I cannot give you the details, but suffice it to say it is with the King's blessing that I come here on this most secret business.'

'You will go into the presence of Henry?'

'If I can be admitted, yes.'

'Then if Chester is present or Salisbury you could be identified. . .'

'Yes, but in all events my greatest danger lies in being recognised by Henry himself. You see, we were well known to each other as boys, pages. I need to talk with him in private and my hope is that, seeing me, he will grant me an audience well away from his advisers.' He grimaced, 'On the other hand, I know Henry too well. He could explode into the most foul temper and order my immediate arrest on a charge of spying.'

'Then why reveal yourself to him?'

'I must, my heart. I am instructed to have secret discussion with him, as I have already said.'

She was growing more desperate by the moment. 'Then—if—if you are taken—the King would surely ransom you. . .'

He frowned. 'The King will deny any knowledge of my mission—he must—at this stage.'

Her heart was beating violently. 'How—how will you get in to see him?'

'I told you. I hear that many wealthy and, yes, poorer merchants are presenting themselves to beg him to help them end this war. They are being ruined, preyed on by mercenary bands. I do not have to explain the horror of those events to you. I shall join the other petitioners, hoping to catch his attention and be granted an opportunity to talk with him.

'Henry has an innate sense of justice. He genuinely will sympathise with these people. I believe that—but—' he gave a little grim smile '—I also know that he cannot bear to be thwarted.'

She was silent, considering, then she said, 'I have heard that he—he likes women. Is that true?'

'Like his father, Geoffrey, he is said to admire lovely women, yes.'

'Then if this merchant was to be accompanied by his wife—who added her pleas to his—surely it would attract a more sympathetic response, wouldn't you say?'

It was his turn now to remain silent, staring back at her, his dark brows drawing together doubtfully. 'I cannot—*will* not allow you to do that.'

'Yet you say this mission for the King is of the utmost importance.'

He hesitated. 'It is,' he said at last, very deliberately.

'And, as you said at Allestone, you can protect me best when I am at your side.'

His lips curved into a sudden smile and he shook his head almost in disbelief at her determined effrontery.

She waited, a little breathless, for his decision, then he said very slowly, 'If my remembrance of Henry is accurate, I cannot believe he would blame you for aught. Whatever my circumstance, he would release you, I'm sure, yet. . .'

'So it is determined,' she said, firmly cutting across any further doubts he might harbour.

Aldith had managed to brush off most of the dust and expunge the travel stains from Gisela's cloak. Underneath the hood, Gisela wore a fine linen veil and fillet, so, feeling more presentable, she walked with Lord Alain through the prosperous little market town towards the imposing castle on its high constructed earthworks.

Beside it was the almost-completed church of St John, its tower rising to so considerable a height it almost rivalled the castle battlements. They were accompanied by Edwin, Algar remaining at the inn with Aldith and Sigurd.

As they passed beneath the well-guarded gatehouse and passed over the planked bridge that crossed the deep defensive ditch, Gisela stole a nervous glance at her husband. They were surrounded by a press of people anxious to get into the main hall. Most were influential townsfolk, by their dress, but Gisela believed that some, by the stained state of their appearance and weary demeanour, had travelled far as she and Alain had done.

Apparently the young Count of Anjou had ordered the rabble of visitors to be admitted; though they were all watched carefully by grim faced men-at-arms from beneath the jutting noseguards of their conical helmets, no one was challenged. Lord Alain's horses had been left at the inn under Algar's care and he and Gisela found themselves pushed and jostled as they attempted to cross the bailey and force their way with the others into the castle's great hall.

Despite the intense cold outside, the hall was warm. The closeness of bodies exuding the combined stinks of wet wool and sweat made Gisela feel suddenly faint. Lord Alain placed a steadying hand beneath her arm as she was almost thrown off her feet by a portly man behind her.

The noise was intense, literally a hundred voices all jabbering at the same time. People pushed towards the dais at the far end of the hall beneath which a perspiring clerk sat at a small trestle table, trying to list the names of those seeking an audience with Count Henry.

Gisela saw that many of the petitioners were monks and there were several nuns. Grimly she faced the fact that many abbeys and nunneries had been raided in these unruly sacrilegious times and their treasures looted.

There was a sudden harsh command over the din and gradually the people vociferously demanding the attention of the clerk fell silent. All eyes turned towards an arras behind the dais that was lifted aside to allow the entrance of a small group of men. Lord Alain's grasp on Gisela's arm tightened warningly.

Three men stepped through and took their places at the high table. All wore civilian dress; one, a big black-avised

man, resplendent in scarlet tunic embellished with gold
thread embroidery and another, slighter, more elegant
figure in green over a golden brown, longer undertunic,
but Gisela, glancing at Alain, saw that his attention was
fixed upon the third who took his seat between them.

This, then, must be Henry Plantagenet, son of the
Empress Matilda—only surviving child of the late King
Henry—and Geoffrey, Count of Anjou, who styled him-
self the rightful heir to England and the dukedom of
Normandy.

She was a little disappointed by her first impression
of him. He was much smaller, though sturdily built and
well muscled, than either of his two attendant barons,
and plainly, almost soberly dressed in a fine wool tunic
of dark brown under a fur-lined mantle.

He wore no distinguishing chain of office or golden
fillet and his red-brown hair gleamed beneath the heavy
iron candlelabra bearing six wax candles that reared over
the dais, for the afternoon was already waning and the
poor light filtering through the unglazed lancet windows
and the dense smoke billowing from the central hearth
and collecting under the lantern trap were combining to
add to the intense gloom within the shadowed place.

She had heard that his father, Geoffrey, had been a
handsome man, but Henry undoubtedly was not. Gisela
thought that, even though he was still in his early twenties, his bright hair was already slightly receding at the
high, intelligent brow. He would run to fat later in life,
she concluded, but she also considered, by the restless
movement of his body in the chair, that for the present
that heaviness would be kept back by constant activity.

As she found herself pushed nearer by the press
behind, she saw that his features were square cut, the nose
large and dominant and the mouth wide and generous. It
was the eyes that saved the face from being thought
nondescript. They were piercingly bright, beneath heavy

sandy brows, and were now surveying the company with intense interest. She could not determine their colour—possibly blue grey—but they were alight with intelligence.

The mouth was curving now into a confident smile and it was clear that this was no boring dutiful audience but a sincere attempt to gauge the feelings of those present. Yes, she decided, he might not have the comeliness of his famed sire, but he would be, she was sure, intensely attractive to women.

She was pushed close to Alain by the movement of the crowd and saw that he was regarding her very intently. Momentarily she was angered. Was he always to suspect her natural interest in each man she met as threatening their relationship? Then, almost immediately, she experienced a strong emotional surge running right through her body as she realised the intensity of his new-found love for her.

They had no opportunity for a while to get any nearer to the dais, for, one by one, men were summoned up to the high table to place their petitions before the youthful Count.

Alain whispered in her ear, 'The dark, heavily built man is the Earl of Chester, the other, Robert, Earl of Gloucester, the late King Henry's illegitimate son and Count Henry's uncle. He has supported the Empress, his half-sister, for almost the entire length of this campaign.'

'Is he a good soldier?' she whispered back.

'The very best, a formidable enemy. Fortunately I am not acquainted with him, but Chester has seen me once or twice in King Stephen's company.'

She swallowed hard and glanced nervously around her. The very air of this place, thick with the stink of food served earlier, unwashed bodies and smoke spoke to her of Alain's very real peril.

She could not hear what was said, but the young Count

appeared to be gracious to those who pressed him for support. She could see that men were leaving the hall more satisfied than when they had arrived.

She wondered how they could have such confidence in this man when the war was not over and showed little sign of ever being concluded. She knew he had come once before to England but had been defeated by his own youthful inexperience and forced to return to Anjou, but he was older now and it was clear that he was winning the backing of many of the King's former commanders.

There was a little stir near the door and men were pushed away to form a space for a newcomer with several men-at-arms as escort. These, differing from the mix of townsfolk and merchants around them, were wearing mail beneath their cloaks and sported serviceable broadswords and daggers.

Alain glanced hastily their way and put out a protective arm to draw his wife closer to him. Their leader was tall and, as he pushed back his hood, Gisela saw his mop of curling dark hair. For one moment he half-turned in her direction and she gave a great gasp of recognition.

Too late for Alain to restrain her, she thrust aside his arm and moved slightly forward, her lips parting in the total shock of seeing the newcomer in this company.

A page was announcing him as he bent the knee before the three seated at the high table.

'Baron Mauger de Cotaine of Offen, bringing urgent news for you from Malmesbury, my lords.'

The escorting men-at-arms ranged themselves behind their lord, instinctively protecting him from any jostling that might come from others impatient to put their complaints before Count Henry.

Gloucester welcomed the man, rising to greet him. 'You are welcome, my lord. Count Henry is well aware of the many services you have done him and is glad to see you, at last, here in person.'

By the sheer fury of her desperation Gisela launched herself forward and the crowd, astounded by her determination, gave ground until she found herself standing almost beside her most hated foe. Even the men of de Cotaine's escort were taken by surprise and unable to prevent her.

She stood before Count Henry, her breast rising and falling agitatedly as she turned and pointed an accusing finger at de Cotaine. Every other thought in her head— her husband's danger, the reason for their presence here—had been cast out by the sight of this handsome, smiling devil.

'My lord,' she appealed to Count Henry, 'I demand justice. This man is a monster of depravity, well known to be so in eastern England. He surrounds himself with the scum of England and France, routiers who live on his bounty, who, no doubt, pay him a considerable sum from the spoils they take by preying on their hapless neighbours. His devils attacked my home, half-destroyed it and nearly killed my father.

'I have sworn to take vengeance upon him, my lord, and I appeal to you, for I know you have true justice at heart, to grant me this and arrest and try this man for his many crimes against those you profess to be your subjects.'

There was instant commotion within the hall. Two men of de Cotaine's escort tried to seize Gisela to prevent any further outbursts, but Count Henry half-rose in his chair and caused them to desist by the commanding movement of one upheld hand.

Gisela was panting and trembling but her fury was draining all fear from her. She continued to hold her ground while the Earl of Chester bawled for silence as pandemonium broke out amongst the townsfolk in the lower hall. Gisela felt a touch on her arm and turned, half-stung in surprise, to find Lord Alain at her side.

Angry tears blinded her to the sight of his shocked features, pale with anger as great as her own.

Mauger de Cotaine was protesting his innocence, but could hardly be heard above the excited commotion. The Earl of Gloucester banged down the base of the heavy salt cellar upon the table and added his voice to Chester's to call for quiet.

'My lords, good people, all of you, allow us to investigate the reason for this disturbance. Stand back, please, do no harm to the lady. This matter will be dealt with, I assure you, and then we will proceed with the business for which this meeting was called.'

It was some considerable time before peace was partially restored. De Cotaine's men resumed their efforts to seize and silence Gisela but were restrained by Alain and men in Gloucester's livery and both Gisela and Alain found themselves surrounded and virtual prisoners. Struggling in Alain's grasp, she realised, too late, what this stupidly impulsive action had cost them both.

She turned, her blue eyes swimming with tears, appealing to him frantically for understanding. He remained impassively silent, and she was not sure whether that was because he thought it impossible to be heard over the general noise or whether he was too angry with her to find suitable words.

De Cotaine spat out at last, his genial smiling face, for once, dark with anger, 'The woman is raving. I do not know what she is talking about.'

He shrugged and spread his two hands in a deprecating gesture. 'My lords, I know nothing of any of this. I can only suppose this poor wench is suffering from delusions.'

'I was Gisela of Brinkhurst,' she retorted, 'and you know my family well. All in our county of Rutland know this fiend by reputation and yet still he walks abroad unchallenged.'

The Earl of Chester's black eyes were now unblinkingly fixed upon Alain. He put into the argument.

'This woman is now married to Baron Alain de Treville,' he announced, 'one of King Stephen's ablest commanders and now master of Allestone Castle. Here, I believe, is the man himself and I ask myself why he is in your presence, disguised, if I am any judge, an undoubted spy in our midst.'

Gisela gave an instinctive cry of alarm. 'My lords, that is not so. He. . .'

The Earl of Gloucester made a gesture of command to his men.

'Let us deal with this matter privately, my lord,' he said, turning respectfully towards his nephew. 'There can be nothing to be gained by ironing out these quarrels in open court.'

Count Henry was staring from this lovely, wild-eyed young woman to the handsome, jeering countenance of the man she accused. He gave a little start as his uncle looked to him for guidance.

'Indeed, yes,' he said quietly. 'I suggest that the lady be conveyed to the ladies' bower above, where we can interview her later and—' his sandy lashes half-veiled his sharp eyes as he looked at Alain '—as to the man, let him be well guarded, in the gatehouse.'

Gisela was weeping now as men separated her from Alain. Despite his frantic struggles to reach her, he was yanked away roughly towards the outer door.

'No, no,' she pleaded brokenly. 'My husband has meant no harm to any here. You must listen. . .'

Soothingly the Earl of Gloucester addressed her. 'All shall be considered, my lady. Do not be afraid. In the meantime, Baron Mauger shall also be kept under guard, I promise you. He must, in fairness, however, be granted an opportunity to refute your grave accusations of misuse of his office.'

The ladies' bower of Devizes Castle was not occupied, so Gisela was unsure whether the present seneschal was married or if that lady had taken refuge in some other fortress. She found herself handed into the care of a toothless old crone who was not communicative, but provided her charge with water for washing and a platter of broken meats and fine manchet bread as well as a flagon of good wine.

Gisela pushed away the food but was grateful for the wine, which poured welcomingly down her parched throat and seemed to give her strength. She sank down on a cushioned window-seat and gazed bleakly at the courtyard below, which still teemed with petitioners either leaving or striving to pass through the guarded door. She could see no sign of her husband with his guards and turned her gaze to the grim gatehouse beyond.

Her heart was pounding wildly as she understood at last what she had done. She had doomed Alain. He had been recognised, arrested as a spy through her foolishness, her wild unreasoning desire to obtain vengeance for Kenrick's death.

Had she remained silent, Alain might well have obtained an audience with the Count, succeeded in his mission and possibly had opportunity to place the case against Mauger de Cotaine squarely before Henry of Anjou. Now it would be unlikely that he would be allowed to see his former companion again. He would be judged guilty of spying and hanged out of hand.

She broke down then, despite the presence of the old woman, and sobbed out her despair. She choked on her disgust for her lack of simple discretion. She, alone, had brought him to disaster. Even should she obtain justice from Count Henry against Mauger de Cotaine's contemptuous treatment of her and hers, it could never compensate her for the loss of Alain de Treville.

What could she say in his defence if she were questioned? Alain had impressed on her the knowledge that his mission was secret. Even she, Gisela, did not fully understand the possible consequences of it. She must not betray him, but she must, in all conscience, try to impress upon her interrogator, whoever he might be, that Alain meant no harm to Henry FitzEmpress's cause.

In actual fact, it proved to be Henry himself who came some hours later into the bower. He was unaccompanied and gestured to her dragon guardian to be seated some way off where they would be unlikely to be overheard.

Gisela struggled to her feet and curtsied. Gently Henry took her arm and helped her to seat herself again.

'I trust someone has brought you food and seen to your comfort, Lady Gisela,' he enquired courteously.

She nodded uncertainly and searched his face for signs of sympathy for her distress. They were there, but it was soon clear that Henry FitzEmpress took nothing for granted, certainly nothing he had heard from others, without very careful consideration. He stood in front of her, thumbs pushed into his ornamental sword belt, and regarded her steadily but sternly.

'Now tell me exactly what happened at your manor and the nature of evidence you have against Mauger de Cotaine,' he demanded.

Gisela took a hard breath and, looking back at him, as steadily, quietly told her story. He listened without comment, occasionally tugging at one ear-lobe as she thought he might often do when concentrating hard on some information.

She stopped at last in a sudden rush as she had come to the point when she had recognised de Cotaine in this castle, uncertain how she should proceed without further incriminating Alain.

He moved away, restlessly pacing the rush-strewn floor of the bower, and then came back to her.

'You say de Cotaine is known for his crimes by most
honourable men within the county, including the shire
reeve, but de Cotaine is too powerful for any to act
against him?'

'Yes, my lord, I truly believe that,' she answered
quietly.

'And you, later, recognised the captain of the band
that attacked your manor?'

'Yes, my lord.'

'But you have no real evidence that this man is a
servant of Sir Mauger's?'

She hesitated. 'No, my lord, that is true, but I am
certain he is. There have been other occasions when
manors have been attacked and their owners had proof,
but dared not either accuse Sir Mauger in the shire reeve's
court or attack Offen Castle.'

Henry gave a little decisive nod.

'Are you aware that this man, de Cotaine, has been of
some service to me?'

'I heard it said in the hall, my lord. It seems that he
is a traitor to his King also,' she added bitterly.

The sandy lashes swept back and she found his pierc-
ing eyes hard upon her.

'Yet I am sure you will assure me that your husband
is not, yet he appears disguised in our stronghold. Do
you not agree that a charge of spying could well be
levelled against him and proven?'

'Yes,' she said softly, 'but if you yourself question
my husband, my lord, I am convinced he can assure you
of his good faith, though circumstances appear to be
against him.'

He smiled then and, for the first time, she realised that
this plain, stocky young man had indeed great charm;
despite her own fear, she managed to smile back.

'I promise you I shall do that,' he said as he came
towards her and took her hand. 'I think the best thing

now is for me to summon your servants from the inn
you speak of. You should have a guard to convey you
there. This town is full of undesirables, soldiery in particular, some of it undisciplined.'

He gave her his sunniest smile once again. 'You tell
me you have a man waiting within the bailey. Tell me
what he is wearing and he shall be sent to the inn with
a message.'

She complied, describing Edwin as accurately as
she could.

'But my husband?' she ventured to recall the Count
as he made for the door.

He turned back to face her. 'I have promised that he
shall have justice at my hands as Mauger de Cotaine
will—in time. I know he will want you to be safely far
from this place and so your servants should take you
immediately home.' He held up a hand in remonstration
as he saw she was about to argue. 'You have already
done all that you can for him. His one desire will be to
have you safe. You will obey my instructions and give
no trouble to your escort?'

She shook her head weakly, tears starting to her eyes
again. She had no idea how lovely she looked and did
not note how Henry FitzEmpress's heart, so easily moved
by beauty, was softened by her obvious distress.

He turned once more, one hand on the door latch.
'Trust me, Lady Gisela, to have your interests at heart.'

Then he was gone and she was left once more to her
own doubts and terrible fears for Alain.

Chapter Nine

Alain de Treville kicked the door of the tiny guard chamber in which he was confined in a final act of furious frustration. Outside, in the room designated for the comfort of the guards during relief periods, he could hear their bawdy banter, the banging down of heavy-bottomed flagons on the table and bursts of raucous laughter. No one took the slightest notice of his bellows to bring him before one of the barons within the castle and at once.

He had been pulled roughly from Gisela's side, frog-marched to the door, across the courtyard and thrust unceremoniously into this inner guardroom. As yet he had not been manacled though he could see in the dim light which filtered in through a grating far up on the outer wall that there were stanchions and chains ending in manacles habitually in use to further ensure prisoners could not escape.

There was one rough-hewn stool and a pail, plus a bundle of soiled straw that had served the last prisoner as bedding. Lord Alain wrinkled his nose at the sour stink of it and thanked God and the Saints the pail, at least, had been emptied.

He had banged at the door for hours and the darkness and chill of the place was deepening. He sank down upon the stool at last, exhausted by the efforts to summon attention and by the emotional agony which, once he was quiet, surged through him.

Sweet Virgin, where was Gisela? The instruction he'd heard to convey her to the ladies' bower had not been reassuring. He did not know if she would be there in the care of the castle's chatelaine, but knowing Henry's reputation, and recalling his wife's distressed beauty, revealed in his last sight of her, he could not convince himself that she would remain inviolate.

He gave a great shuddering breath. What a fool he had been to bring her here. How could he have allowed himself to be persuaded against his better judgement? The very sight of her was sufficient to excite passions, especially in this town teeming with loosely disciplined soldiery.

He knew, only too well, that it was hard to keep men in check when actually on the march or on campaign, but when let loose in some town. . . He let out another agonised breath, unwilling to face the mental pictures his fears for Gisela summoned up.

What ill fate had brought Mauger de Cotaine to Devizes at this time? Yet Alain might well have expected it for he had suspected for a year or more that the man had been in traitorous communication with King Stephen's enemies. That had been the very reason why he had not agreed to ride against de Cotaine's stronghold, despite the temptation of his wife's angry taunts.

His job had been to keep an eye on de Cotaine and discover if he could find out more of what went on between Gloucester's force and de Cotaine. He could well believe that smiling devil had found it profitable indeed to seem to serve two masters.

An even more terrible fear smote him. What if de Cotaine, released from guard, was allowed access to Gisela? The man's hatred for the woman who had accused him must be tremendous. How simple it would be to strike at the unprotected wife of his neighbour!

No, he mustn't think like that. He would run mad. Henry, for all his faults and rages, would not allow a gentle girl like Gisela to become prey for an animal such as de Cotaine.

He forced himself to try to think logically about his own predicament. What would Gisela say of him if she were questioned? He knew she was brave, loyal and spirited, but in this place, surrounded by so many powerful men, she must be terrified. He smote an impotent fist against the rough stone of the wall as his fearful anger rose again threatening to choke him.

How long must he stay here? Dear God, would he be allowed a chance to explain his presence here in Devizes Castle in what amounted to a disguise? Grimly he faced facts. He doubted it. He was a spy and—as a spy—he would hang, probably at first light. He pulled the stool up against the wall and leaned back wearily.

It was almost pitch black in this cell now; he could scarce see his own hands and feet. There was nothing he could do but compose himself for an attempt at sleep, here, on the stool, not on that filthy straw. It was unlikely anyone would think it worthwhile to feed him and he was not hungry though it had been some time now since he last ate.

He let himself think of Gisela as she had been those nights she had lain in his arms and of her fortitude upon the journey. He had recently found himself filled with overwhelming jealousy that had threatened her growing affection for him.

He knew he loved her now beyond reason, yet he could not move a muscle to protect her and, once again, she could fall into the hands of that handsome, smiling predator. Agonisingly he recognised the probability that

his last sight of her would be standing there in the hall
outfacing them all.

He must have been asleep for some hours when he woke
suddenly, very confused to find a glaring light shining
in his eyes, and knew that a kick had made contact with
his shinbone. He started up with a growl to find a stocky
figure standing over him.

A genial voice purred, 'Now, now, Alain, no show of
temper. That wouldn't be wise. I'm sorry to rouse you
so unceremoniously from sleep, but I considered this was
the best time for you and I to have a private talk together.
It was your own lady who advised me.'

Alain stared blearily up into the smiling features of
Count Henry as he stood holding the flaring resin torch
high above them, scrutinising the face of his prisoner.

'My lord?' Alain stammered doubtfully.

'Just let me fix this torch in the bracket there and have
a stool brought for me to sit on. Neither of us can be
expected to sit on the floor in this filthy place.' The
Count sniffed distastefully as he regarded the dirty straw,
then slid the torch into the iron bracket upon the wall
behind Alain and bawled to someone just outside the
cell door.

'Roger, bring me a stool. Hurry up about it, man. The
night will be over before I see my bed at all at this rate.'

A heavy-set man still clad in mail, considering the
lateness of the hour, complied immediately with his
Count's order and hastened into the cell, carrying a
second joint stool which he dusted down carefully before
setting it down upon the ground. He, too, gazed round
the cell in disgust and looked enquiringly at his lord,
who waved him imperiously to the door.

'I shall be quite safe, man. The guards will have seen
to it that our prisoner here is not armed and, as you
know well enough, I am capable of defending myself,

though—' he smiled warmly at the dour-faced soldier who was looking down at him anxiously '—I am always gratified that you are rarely far from my back. And, Roger see to it that we are not overheard.'

The man glanced warningly towards Alain who was standing awkwardly, back against the wall, then nodded, bowed and stepped through the door. Alain heard the harsh sound of bolts being drawn to on the outside.

The Count seated himself, grimaced at the chill in the bare place and pulled his heavy furred mantle about him. He gestured to the stool opposite for Alain to sit down again.

'Now, I understand you wanted to see me. Here I am. It seems a long time since we served together and this meeting now is in unfortunate circumstances, but it will have to serve.' He looked up, grinning. 'Tell me why I shouldn't hang you out of hand, *mon cher ami.*'

Alain sank down as the commanding gesture was repeated and blinked somewhat owlishly at his companion. He had still not accustomed his eyes to the light and was confused at being woken so suddenly.

Count Henry continued cheerfully, 'I see you have not lost the art of getting to sleep in uncomfortable surroundings. Remember when we two shared sleeping accommodations stretched out on the cold stone floor outside our lord's chamber?'

Alain nodded and forced a grim smile. 'I do, my lord, and am gratified that you remember the occasions, too.'

'*Bon*, so tell me I have no reason to fear that you have now turned against me and came here to harm my cause. Your lady says I must believe that, despite the way things appear.' His sharp bright eyes turned upon the merchant's garb, now sadly dirtied and torn at the shoulder by the rough handling of the guards and contact with the floor when Alain had been first thrown into the cell.

Count Henry read instant alarm in Alain's face as again

he half-started from his stool. 'My wife, where is she? If someone has dared to harm her. . .'

'The Lady Gisela is perfectly safe. By now she should be asleep in her chamber at your inn and, tomorrow, on her way home to Allestone with her own men and six of my most trusted men-at-arms.' The count indicated the closed door. 'My captain, Roger de Miles, handpicked them for me. She will suffer no insult upon the road, believe me.'

Alain sank back again, visibly relieved. 'My lord, I thank you from the bottom of my heart. All these hours—' he drew a shuddering breath '—I have been fearing—' He passed a grimy hand across his eyes and looked up once more. 'I should never have brought her here, but. . .'

'Yes, now we come to it. I am at a complete loss to know just why you are here at all.' The mobile mouth quirked. 'In this damned campaign friend is often set against friend. That is the devil of it, but I know you owe your allegiance to Stephen and, frankly, cannot imagine you playing him false any more than I can believe you came here to do me harm.'

'I come at the request of my King, my lord.'

'Ah.' Henry leaned back on the stool and his smile faded as he regarded Alain now gravely. 'You come on embassy?'

'I have no direct authority, sir. If I do meet the fate you suggest, the King will make no complaint at my summary treatment at your hands. Indeed—' it was Alain's turn to give a grim smile '—no help could possibly reach me in time. I realised that only too well. That is why I made arrangements for Gisela to leave here if— if the worst happened.

'I brought her because the importance of my mission demanded that I take every opportunity presented to get into your presence. She lent similitude to my pretence of being a merchant upon my journey here and she herself was adamant about accompanying me.

'Her own servants adore her. I knew she would be safe with them, but. . .' he paused, a trifle shakily '. . .I could not have anticipated the presence of Baron Mauger de Cotaine of Offen here in Devizes and her reaction to the sight of him. She lost all sense of discretion, as you saw.'

'He *was* guilty of the attack upon her manor?' The question was sharply posed and Alain sighed.

'Aye, my lord, not personally, but, as she alleges, he has surrounded himself with scum who do his bidding.'

'And he takes the pickings.' The Count nodded. 'It is as I thought. The man is useful but—scum, as you say. You realise that, for the present, I must release him from confinement and allow him to continue in his work for us, but—'

His lips parted in a knowing smile, which was not reflected in the colourless grey eyes. 'He will be well watched. I will not have such men in my service. In the end he will be recompensed for his service, though maybe not in the manner he hopes.'

The two exchanged long looks and Alain made a little intake of breath, as if satisfied at last.

Count Henry continued to stare long and hard at his prisoner. 'Well, man, you come on the King's business. What business?'

Alain turned to avoid that stare for one moment, then turned back to face the Count.

'Nothing official must be implied. I think,' he said slowly, 'the King wished me to see you again to judge whether, in my view, you have changed.'

'For better or for worse?' The words were lightly uttered but Alain recognised the keenness of the question.

He smiled. 'I think he feared, my lord, you might have changed for the worst, but, after what I have seen both in the hall this afternoon and from that last observation of yours just moments ago, I am convinced there has been no change.'

'Not even for the better?' Henry said flippantly.

'In so short a time I could not know that, my lord, but we have both learned a deeper sense of responsibility, I trust.'

The Count nodded.

'In short, my lord, the King is ailing—and tiring. He would like to achieve a lasting truce but—' Alain shrugged.

'On what terms?'

Alain was disconcerted by the shrewdness and quickness of the question. He gave a slight gasp. His eyes were wary. 'Nothing must be said officially of what I—surmise.'

'You have my word and on my knightly honour.'

'It will be for greater lords than I to settle the terms of any proposed treaty, but—'

'But?'

'The King wishes to know your mind on the—possibility of a permanent peace based on the premise that—he would continue to reign until his death and—' Alain saw the frown gather upon the Count's brow and he continued '—on the understanding that you, my lord, would succeed him.'

If he had expected an immediate response he was disappointed. Henry was silent, pulling thoughtfully at his ear lobe. He said at last, 'And what, *mon ami*, would the King's sons have to say to such a proposal?'

'Eustace, I'm sure, would be outraged; but William could be appeased, I think, if suitable provisions were made for him.'

'But Eustace is the stumbling block.'

'Undoubtedly, but he is not popular amongst the common folk and he constantly antagonises the church and some of the more powerful barons. Many would not be averse to putting him aside in your favour if a permanent peace could be agreed.' He hesitated, then said quietly, 'And what think you, sir, would your lady mother have to say about laying aside what she considers *her* rightful claim?'

Henry shook his head. 'She is a determined lady but she, too, is tired. For years now she has pressed on me that her continued claim is to establish my right to succeed to the English throne.'

Alain shifted awkwardly upon his uncomfortable stool.

'As I understand it, my lord, the English council, which was called the Witan, decided the succession.'

Count Henry said haughtily, 'Can you deny my mother the Empress was King Henry's only legitimate surviving child? The barons swore allegiance to her before him.'

'I know that, sir, but a forced oath, even before a king, is not always accepted by Holy Church as binding. The succession to the English throne does not always go to the nearest heir. King William was not succeeded by his eldest son, Robert, and it must be remembered that it was the English Witan that chose King Harold to reign over them after the death of the sainted Edward, the confessor. King William succeeded only by right of conquest.'

Count Henry's smile grew even broader. 'Do you suggest I push on and emulate him?'

'You may be forced to do so, my lord, and it could take your lifetime.'

'Aye.'

'And, meanwhile, England suffers at the hands of men like Mauger de Cotaine.'

The grey eyes glittered strangely in the torchlight as Henry leaned back on his stool.

'Well, what word of me will you carry back to your King?'

Alain started, then said hastily, 'At present I am in no position to carry back any word, my lord.'

Again the Count's lips parted in a meaning smile.

'Indeed you are not, so—we must arrange for you to escape. Since this embassy is secret and binding on neither party I cannot allow news of it to leak out to any of my supporters—at present.'

Alain drew a relieved breath. 'And what do you wish me to convey to my King, my lord?'

'That I am willing to consider the proposal but, as I am sure, he must, too, receive true embassy as to the terms; following that, I must have sufficient time to consult with my advisers and, first and foremost, my lady mother.'

He rose and, sweeping his mantle clear of the soiled rushes, moved to the door. 'I will see to it that you are sent down some food. Roger de Miles will come to you before dawn and take you to the picket gate. I will leave it in his hands to arrange for your guards to be less than watchful. Roger de Miles is a most resourceful man. I take it you will ride first to Wallingford?'

Alain's thoughts flew to Gisela on the road for the Midlands. He frowned. 'Since you assure me my wife will be safe I should do that, my lord. It should not delay me for more than a day, two at most.'

The Count turned, one hand lifted to knock upon the door to summon his captain to open up for him. 'And what will you tell Stephen of my character, *mon ami*?'

Alain's smile was almost dazzling. 'That you are as true to your word and loyal to your friends, and as just, even to your enemies, as I remember, sir.'

'And should I become England's king, Alain?'

'In the course of time I shall be honoured to serve you, my lord.'

Count Henry inclined his chin slightly. 'As I shall be

to confirm you in your holdings. Go with God, Alain de
Treville and quickly, to your lady.'

Gisela watched numbly as Aldith hastily finished their
packing. She had not slept and when she had returned
to the inn, escorted by the six men Count Henry had
given her as escort, she had fallen into her former nurse's
arms and sobbed out her despair. Aldith had banged on
the chamber door, ordering Sigurd, who had watched in
silent misery, to go to the stables, stay with the men-at-
arms and see she and her lady were not disturbed.

'Come, sweeting,' she exhorted, using her endearment
for her when Gisela had been a babe in arms, 'tell me
where is Lord Alain and what is so terrible that you break
down like this?'

It had been impossible to reveal to Aldith the true
reason for their visit to Devizes Castle, but Gisela had
the feeling that in some obscure way Aldith had guessed
at the truth and when she had sobbed out her fears for
his safety, Aldith had listened in silence and hugged her
closer to her heart.

'My dear lady, if the Count assured you that he would
deal justly with Lord Alain, you must not fear.'

'But he gave no promise that his life would be spared.'

'But he has treated you well. You tell me that Lord
Alain knew the Count when they were boys. Friendships
like that never entirely disappear. He will do his best for
his friend.'

'But he is confined in a dungeon somewhere in the
gatehouse and—and—it cannot be denied that he was
spying on the Count's force.'

Over her charge's bent head Aldith's expression hardened and she compressed her lips. Before leaving for the
castle, Lord Alain had impressed on her that it might be
necessary to remove Gisela from Devizes at a
moment's notice.

'If you receive word from me by Edwin, you must not wait for me but go at once. Get your mistress back to Allestone. Edwin and Algar have had instructions from me that that is their prime task. They must think of nothing else but their mistress's safety.'

She had known then that he was going into danger; and when the plan changed and Gisela had accompanied him, her fears for her mistress had grown into the night hours. Only now, as she held Gisela in her arms, could she believe that there was hope for her—for Lord Alain she could have little, but of that she must not speak to Gisela.

She had insisted that Gisela lie on the bed and rest, but knew from the sound of her restless movement through the remains of the night until the grey spears of dawn light forced their way through the ill-fitting shutters that Gisela had not slept; neither had she.

Now she gave up any attempt to make Gisela eat, arranging with Sigurd to buy bread and cheese and cold bacon at the inn to carry with them.

Gisela could hear the men leading out the horses for the journey. She stood up and allowed Aldith to wrap her hooded cloak around her.

Through stiffened lips she murmured; 'Oh, Aldith, how can this be? Only days ago I discovered how deeply I love him and was able to tell him of it—and now—and now—he could hang this morning and our new-found happiness be shattered all too soon. Will he know and understand—and forgive my stupidity in betraying him like that?'

Aldith kissed her gently upon the brow. 'He will know you are safe and that will be all that matters to him, but things may not be as bad as you believe. You must keep hope within your heart, sweeting. Trust in the Count's good offices.'

'Aldith,' Gisela said on a little gasp, 'Count Henry

will let him know that I am safe, won't he?'

'I'm sure he will. Come now, my lady, it is time to go. Nothing can be served by endangering our own men.'

Gisela nodded and moved from the chamber down the rickety stair to the chill of the courtyard outside. It was a damp, misty morning. Everything was shrouded in greyness and wet as if the world itself was weeping with her own lost hopes.

Edwin hastened to her side to lift her into the saddle of her palfrey. His face looked strained in the grey half-light.

She caught at his hand. 'You didn't see him?'

He shook his head. 'No, my lady, one of the Count's men came and demanded I take him with those others to your inn. I had no choice. I had to leave him.'

He turned to watch as the Count's men were busy checking girths and making ready to mount. 'Once on the road I could possibly make off and ride back to Devizes.'

Her fingers tightened feverishly on his wrist. 'Edwin, will you go, find out what has happened to him, reach him if you can?'

He looked down at her thoughtfully. 'It will mean breaking my word to him. I swore I would extricate you from this tangle, but. . .'

'This is my command to you, Edwin. Go when you can and—' she gulped back a sob '—if things go badly— bring me word.'

Again he looked back at the small escort. 'Algar will ensure your safety and even Sigurd will fight like a wild thing to keep you safe, but. . .'

'I trust the Count's men, Edwin.'

'I wish to God I did,' he muttered through his teeth, but squeezed her hand then walked back to the older man in charge. She could hear him calling that he was doubtful about his mount's left forehoof.

'She was walking stiffly the day we arrived, then

seemed better, but I noticed her shying back just now when I bent to look. Her shoe doesn't appear to be loose but better if I don't carry the mistress's attendant pillion. Will one of your men do that? Then, if I have to drop behind and find a smith, you can keep up the pace and I can catch you up on the road.'

Gisela bit down on her bottom lip as she strove to hear the man's reply but it seemed that all was well as Aldith was mounted behind the leader himself and he rode to her side.

'Can we ride out now, my lady?'

'Yes, yes,' she murmured, 'let us start at once,' though the words were forced out. The one thing she wanted to do was to stay in Devizes and discover for herself Alain's fate, but she understood, from the last strained glance Edwin gave her, that her husband's one chance was to have Edwin's help if that could be managed.

If he could be freed, the last thing he needed was to worry about her presence in the town. No, she must obey the instructions he had given her before even leaving Allestone—that she must leave with his men if needful.

They left the town without being challenged. She had discovered that these men were of the Earl of Gloucester's force and no one here would dare to delay them. She looked back longingly as the town dissolved into the grey morning mist behind them and prayed that Alain would be safe.

They were all cold and miserable, but the men rode stolidly without complaint. Later, the mist began to lift and Gisela could see the still brown fields on either side of the road. She glanced back once and the sergeant informed her that both her maid and the young lad were mounted comfortably. She looked round anxiously for Edwin and Algar rode up to her side.

'Edwin has had to drop behind, my lady. One of his horse's shoes was loose. He's gone back to the town to find a smith. He'll catch up with us soon.'

She felt a surge of relief. At least that one plan had gone smoothly. Edwin would return to search out the truth about Alain. She dared not hope that the man's ingenuity might manage to aid an escape.

From then on she did not dare to enquire further for Edwin. When, by nightfall, it became clear that he was not going to rejoin the party Osbert Greetholm, their sergeant in charge, muttered an embarrassed assurance that nothing could have happened to the man and that he would doubtless find his way home in his own good time. If he suspected that Edwin had returned to Devizes, he made no comment.

He had his orders: to get Lady Gisela de Treville back to her home at Allestone; he could not now bother himself with one of her party who had decided to desert her. Privately, he thought the fellow might well have found himself some wench in Devizes but that was no business of his. The lady was well protected on the journey and the loss of one man could make little difference to his task.

The weather steadily improved over the next few days, though to Gisela, sunk in a torpor of emotional torment, it seemed as miserable as ever. Osbert took good care of her. As on the outward journey when she had travelled with Alain, Osbert studiously avoided contact with bands of soldiers on the road and took roundabout routes round castles known to be possibly under siege or belonging to opposing parties.

Her comfort was assured at the inns and abbeys where they sought accommodation and she made no complaint in spite of the long days in the saddle. As on that first morning in Devizes after Alain's arrest, she seemed numbed and neither discomfort nor delay appeared to affect her. Aldith's concern deepened, for her mistress hardly spoke to her, not even when they were alone together in their chamber at night. Only once did she voice her concern for Edwin.

'He went back to Devizes,' she told Aldith, 'to seek word of my lord. Since he has not come after us, we must assume either that he, too, was arrested, trying to find an entry into the castle, or that he had bad news and was afraid of bringing it to me.'

'I doubt he would do that,' Aldith comforted her stoutly. 'Possibly he knows Lord Alain is still held in his prison and is trying to figure out some way of helping him escape or it could be that he has encountered some slight mishap on the road. His mount might actually have become lame, which would delay him.'

Gisela tried to make herself believe both those possibilities but there was ice round her heart and, as they pushed on back along the old Roman Fosse Way towards Lutterworth and the town of Leicester, she dreaded to take back to Allestone ill tidings of the loss of its lord.

She determined first to visit her father at Brinkhurst; it was when they were only six miles short of their destination that Osbert Greetholm had the first intimation that his task of protecting the lady might be less simple than he thought. One of his men reported that he had glimpsed a blur of light within the forest trees behind them along the track and that he had seen it several times throughout the day.

'I reckon it could be the sun catching metal, either mail or weaponry,' he announced. 'Didn't take much notice at first, sergeant, but it 'pears to be a keeping up with us. I reckon as 'ow we're being followed, though why?' He pushed up his conical helmet and scratched his carroty hair. 'I can't say. You'd think they'd take us in ambush if they meant business. O' course, don't know

'ow many as they be. We could be too big a force
for 'em.'

Osbert reined in for a moment. He'd ridden back to
talk to his companion when the fellow had signalled to
him, not wishing to call him forward and so alarm Lady
Gisela who would overhear what was said. Now he
turned and, shading his eyes against the weak rays of the
dying sun, peered back along the track.

'You say you've seen the glint of metal several times.
When did you first see it?'

Again the younger man scratched his head. ''Bout just
after we stopped for dinner, I reckon, sergeant. I was just
packing away the remains in my saddle bag when the
light glinted in me eyes. Didn't think much of it then,
but I've just seen it again for the third time, maybe the
fourth.'

Osbert Greetholm looked forward to where Gisela had
reined in her mount and was clearly impatient to proceed.
It was the first time throughout the journey she had shown
signs of animation. *Now she's near her destination, she
wants to greet her father*, he thought, *like an old horse
that scents the nearness of the stable*.

He sighed. They were still some miles off the manor
of Brinkhurst and were they to be taken by surprise it
could be a hard fight, yet if their pursuers had meant to
attack they would surely have done so by now. His best
course was to quicken his pace and get Lady Gisela to
the safety of her father's manor.

He cursed inwardly her decision not to ride straight
for Allestone Castle. If they were to resist an attack,
Baron Alain de Treville's stronghold would offer far the
best promise of safety.

'Eric,' he instructed, 'take one of the men and hold
back. Watch to see how closely we are being followed.
Take cover. Try to see the badges of any men-at-arms.

Don't invite attack. Keep hidden and, when you can, ride on to Brinkhurst and report to me.'

'Aye, sergeant.'

Eric pulled his mount's head round and beckoned to the man who had ridden beside him throughout the journey. The two moved to the side of the track. Eric dismounted and the other man followed suit. Osbert Greetholm avoided Aldith's anxious stare and trotted his horse back to Gisela.

'More trouble,' he remarked sourly. 'Another horse appears to be casting a shoe. We'll ride on, my lady. My men know their way well enough. Meanwhile, I think we'll make all speed now. At this time of year the darkness falls early and we don't want to be caught in this forest district, do we? The territory is foreign to my men and we could have more mishaps in the dark on such uneven ground.'

Gisela was anxious now to confide in her father her fears for her husband. She failed to detect the note of alarm in her escort sergeant's voice and nodded absently as he urged her to quicken pace.

They cantered well before dusk under the gatehouse arch at Brinkhurst and Gisela held out her arms to her father, who had hastened down the manor house steps to lift her down. She was half-crying, half-laughing with relief at seeing him.

Sir Walter gazed round the small company for Alain de Treville but, recognising both fear and despair in his daughter's eyes, helped her hurriedly into the hall after welcoming her sergeant of escort and shouting for grooms to see to the accommodation of their guests.

Sir Walter made sure his daughter was comfortably seated before the hearth and provided with wine and refreshment before he pressed her to tell the reason for her sudden arrival and without Lord Alain.

His own expression revealed his alarm as she baldly told what had happened at Devizes Castle.

'If—if he had died there—' Gisela stammered out, 'surely Edwin would have joined us and—and told me. Tell me there is still hope, Father.'

'There, there, child.' He rubbed her chill hands comfortingly. 'Of course there is always hope. We should know within days if. . .'

He broke off enquiringly as Osbert Greetholm pushed his way through the screen doors without ceremony and hastened to the group by the fire.

'Lady Gisela,' he said bluntly, 'despite the late hour we should make for Allestone immediately. My man Eric reports that we were being followed on the last days of our journey by two men of Mauger de Cotaine's company. He recognised one of the fellows who was in attendance on Mauger de Cotaine at the castle. My captain, Roger de Miles, impressed upon me that you could be at risk from the activities of that man.

'Obviously, these two are only scurriers who will apprise him of your presence here but—' he looked round searchingly '—this is no place to be caught by a full detachment of de Cotaine's mercenaries. It's likely he has been released by Count Henry and will be following with only a token force. He will send to his own castle for reinforcements. We must get behind the defensive walls of Allestone.'

Sir Walter started up, cursing roundly, and Gisela blanched.

'He knows I am his enemy,' she said steadily. 'I spoke out against him to Count Henry. I did not think he would dare. . .'

'That devil would dare anything,' Sir Walter said hoarsely. 'Your sergeant is right. We must get you to Allestone without delay, aye, and our people must come after us. He fears you will witness against him if it comes to an enquiry and, God help us, he knows he could not win in such a case. He will move to silence you and me and if all else fails he will burn to take vengeance upon us both.'

Osbert Greetholm was already making for the door and bawling for a servant to tell his men to make ready fresh horses.

Gisela turned a terrified face to her father.

'If we desert Brinkhurst, it will be fired again.'

'Daughter,' he said through gritted teeth, 'homes can be rebuilt, lives never. De Cotaine must know now that this war cannot drag out much longer. He and his ilk will be finished when that happens. This is a final throw of the dice. If he takes you, he may think himself well requited.'

Alain de Treville emerged from the small picket gate in the gatehouse of Devizes Castle. Roger de Miles, Count Henry's trusted captain, had come just before dawn as Henry had promised and led Alain out of his dungeon cell. There were no guards in the outer room and at Alain's raised, questioning eyebrow, de Miles had simply laughed and drawn him on into the courtyard.

'All has been arranged. I saw to it myself that the men who should have been here were well chosen. I'll be instructed to deal out punishment for negligence.' He shrugged. 'They'll make themselves scarce for a while. Count Henry does not wish his uncle, Gloucester, to know he arranged for your escape—at least, not just yet. He informed you your lady is well escorted and on her way home?'

'Yes, but. . .'

'I handpicked the men of her escort too. She will be safe. Trust us.'

De Treville held out his hand to grip the other's. 'Thank you. For a while there I was beginning to feel the sensation of hempen rope tightening round my neck.'

De Miles laughed softly. 'You had every reason. The Count urges you to leave Devizes without delay. He could not be responsible for your safety if one of Gloucester's men sees and recognises you.'

'Understood.' De Treville put up the hood of his merchant's cloak, turned once more to acknowledge the other, then stepped briskly across the cobbles towards the town market-place.

He would have to leave Devizes on foot. It would not be wise to return to the inn where he had stayed with Gisela and he needed a horse. Fortunately, he had coin enough to purchase one immediately he got clear of the town. All his property had been snatched from him in the first search of his person following his arrest, but Roger de Miles had handed him a leather purse containing sufficient gold to ensure his needs would be met on the journey.

He swallowed a sigh as he faced the fact that, though de Miles and Count Henry had sworn Gisela was safe and would be conducted back to Allestone, his whole being yearned to abandon his mission and follow her as swiftly as possible, but he had sworn an oath of fealty to his King and his duty must firstly take him to Wallingford.

Here he would report his findings to Stephen and then beg for permission to return to his own castle. Once he had ensured the safety of Gisela he could then, if the King required service of him, return to join the King's force at the siege of Wallingford.

De Miles had told him succinctly when asked that de Cotaine had been released after a stormy interview with Count Henry and the Earl of Gloucester, at which he had sworn his innocence of all accusations.

'Gloucester was reluctant to believe ill of the man. He has proved himself too useful,' Henry's captain had growled. 'Count Henry was helpless to intervene. He thought it best to keep his own counsel at this stage. I cannot think you will have aught to fear from de Cotaine. He knows Allestone is well defended and I doubt he would dare to take reprisals.'

As he trudged through still-darkened streets, Alain was less convinced. He knew the man's ugly reputation far too well to believe that de Cotaine would tamely accept his humiliation at Gisela's hands before the full council of Gloucester's supporters without wishing to revenge himself. It would be well to see to Gisela's security before he returned permanently to the King's active service. Again he cursed the need which took him to Stephen's camp instead of riding directly to Allestone.

It took much longer than he had expected to find his way on the correct route north from the town. As the sun came up he gave a grunt of satisfaction—at least some warmth might begin to lift the heavy dank mist.

He should pass an inn soon or possibly a smithy where the smith might have a horse to sell to him, otherwise he might have to reach the next village or even a town before he could acquire one. At least a village would accommodate some carter or even a serf driving a cart who could be persuaded to take him on to a town.

Again he cursed inwardly at the need for these delays. He was fevered now with the desperate wish to reach Wallingford, discharge his mission and be on his way home.

He was so preoccupied with his own discomfort that he did not at first realise that the rider who was coming towards him at a gallop was rising in the saddle and waving to attract his attention.

When it seemed that the man might ride him down he stopped and stared as his man, Edwin, dismounted and, leading his mount, approached.

'My lord, praise to all the saints. I was even now on my way back to Devizes, fearing I might have to carry back the news that I had seen your corpse dangling from the battlements of Devizes Castle.'

His first bewilderment soon over, Alain seized his man by the shoulder and tightened his grip cruelly.

'Damn it, man, what are you doing returning to the town when your mistress, I'm told, is already on her way home? Why are you not with her as I commanded?'

Edwin showed no sign of fear but grimaced and stood docilely in the harsh grip.

'My lord, she commanded me to return and discover news of you. She begged me to try to get you free if I could. I hadn't the heart to tell her that was nigh impossible but I swore I would carry news back to her as soon as I could. I swear I was convinced that she was well protected. Algar would give his life to save her and so would that young fool, Sigurd. I'd not have left her else, however she had begged me to do so.'

Lord Alain grunted and released him. 'Well, as you see, I am free and unharmed. I appreciate your concern for your lord—' he bared his teeth in a sarcastic smile '—but I would have preferred you to have discharged your duty to your lady. However, now you are here, you can do me a service. Will that nag of yours carry both of us some distance until I can find a new mount?'

'Aye, my lord, he's sturdy enough, if not the fastest steed I've ever mounted.'

He waited while his lord mounted and reached down a hand to help him up behind.

'Right, let us find some horse coper and then ride for Wallingford with all speed.'

They were fortunate to acquire a horse in the next village and after that made better speed, but the following day it snowed and progress was slowed again. Lord Alain cursed steadily against his ill fortune, but he dared not risk their horses' legs on the icy roads by attempting to travel too fast. He determined to keep Edwin with him, at least for the present. The man could hardly reach Allestone now much before he himself could and he might need the man's services.

Though he still ached to know Gisela had arrived home safely, he was somewhat mollified by Edwin's further assurances. Edwin was experienced in the art of knowing men's worth and had apparently summed up the attitude of the escort sergeant to his charge.

They stayed within an inn stable that night. Lord Alain had hoped to push on further into the night, but could not exhaust their mounts; neither he nor Edwin would be in any state to continue without rest.

The snow was not heavy and slackened next day, but the roads were still icy and there was still need to go slowly.

Arriving at last at Wallingford, Alain was further dismayed to learn that King Stephen had left with his army to attempt to raise the siege of Malmesbury. Alain gritted his teeth so hard in his frustrated fury he might well have broken one, rested his horses, took refreshment and again set out, this time for Malmesbury.

The snow had stopped, but there seemed little chance of a thaw yet and the ground was still iron hard. Alain hoped that conditions were better further north so that Gisela's journey would not be so uncomfortable or hazardous. He blamed himself for agreeing to both Rainald de Tourel's suggestion and her pleas that he take her with him in the first place. She should have remained snug and safe at Allestone.

He pictured her beset by blizzards, benighted, too far from a welcoming abbey or inn, even lying near some roadside frozen to death. Though he laughed inwardly at his own fears soon after they had come, it was hollow laughter. He could not rid himself of continuing fears for his wife.

One fact, he told himself grimly: Mauger de Cotaine would have an equally difficult journey home and was unlikely to leave Offen Castle, his stronghold, when he once reached it. Surely Gisela would be safe from him.

Alain reached Malmesbury at last and, to his relief, was conducted immediately into King Stephen's presence, once he had announced his identity to the captain of the guard. Rainald de Tourel hastened to greet him and led him to a battle tent where the King had been recently conferring with some of his captains.

'We had the devil's own difficulty in getting the barons to agree amongst themselves,' he confided in Alain. 'The Avon was in heavy flood, swelled by the recent snowfalls and Robert Beaumont, Earl of Leicester, Derby and Arundel were against trying to cross but Eustace, ever headstrong, wished to make the attempt and advised his father to chance it, backed up by the earls of Oxford, Warwick, and Northampton. It seems as if we shall soon have a surrender.' He glanced, frowning, at Alain but did not press his friend to divulge any news of his mission, which was for the King's ears alone.

King Stephen welcomed Alain warmly. He was seated in a folding camp chair, a tall man, handsome and charming as ever, though Alain noted with some concern that the King appeared unduly exhausted and there were dark shadows under the kindly brown eyes and the streaks of grey in the brown curling hair and beard more pronounced than when Alain had last been in his presence.

He dismissed his captains courteously as he was ever wont to do and invited Alain to sit on a stool near him.

'You look as if you've ridden with the devil on your heels,' he said mildly. 'Rainald tells me you have recently wed and that your wife is both courageous and beautiful.

You must be very anxious to return to her side.'

Alain bowed his head in acknowledgement.

'Did you manage to get into Henry's presence?'

'Aye, my lord, and we talked for some time privately—in my cell,' Alain returned grimly.

The King's eyebrows arched interrogatively and Alain hastened to explain what had occurred at Devizes Castle and the nature of the conversation that had followed between Henry of Anjou and his prisoner.

'Yet you are here—free.'

'Count Henry arranged my escape, sire, else it would have gone very badly for me.'

'I can imagine.' Stephen leaned eagerly forward in his fald chair. 'Then, at least, your relationship with Count Henry did not suffer too great a reversal from this rather fraught encounter.'

'No, sire. I had opportunity to see that Count Henry was as patient to hear the truth of the matter and as anxious to mete out justice as I had expected and hoped he would be.'

'Yet I am led to understand that he has a fearsome temper.'

'Aye, sire, but I have observed, at least from our past association, that he is always in control.'

'Ah.' The King smiled broadly. 'Then you believe that if—in time—we send an embassy to propose a truce on the lines suggested by your talk he would consider the matter favourably?'

'I do, sire, but—' Alain shrugged '—those more experienced and wiser than I in the art of diplomacy will be better fitted to decide the truth of this matter.'

Stephen leaned back tiredly. 'I am not so sure of that, Alain. I am tired of the constant wrangling between my barons.'

He sat, eyes closed for a moment or two, considering, then he looked up and smiled again.

'I am deeply grateful, my old friend. You have done me excellent service and not without risk to yourself. Now I know you are anxious to leave Malmesbury. First take refreshment and I would suggest you rest the night in camp. You will be provided with fresh horses and supplies.'

Alain rose and bowed. He was aware of the kindly, wearied interest of the King as he left the tent to join Rainald de Tourel outside.

De Tourel grasped his friend's sleeve and drew him away to a larger tent from which issued the succulent smell of roasted meat and savoury pottage.

'Further problems,' he grumbled as he pushed Alain inside and seated him at a trestle, bawling for a trencher and ale to be brought. 'Eustace arrived from a survey of the terrain and demanded to be admitted at once to his father's presence. Fortunately for me, Leicester arrived on the scene and drew him away to make a report on the possibility of some mining procedure on the east side of the castle wall.'

Alain tucked into pottage and meat when it arrived on his trencher and drank deeply of good ale. 'Did you see to it that my man was fed and our horses attended?'

'Yes, of course, but you'll not get much further on those poor beasts. I'll see to it myself that fresh good horseflesh is provided for your journey. Now, how is the Lady Gisela?'

'I hope, well,' Alain growled, and proceeded to tell his friend of her encounter with Mauger de Cotaine at Devizes Castle.

Rainald whistled long and low. 'I have heard tales of the man,' he said thoughtfully, 'but I know the King has been slow to act and, as you know, we thought it best to allow him enough rope to hang himself.'

'The very reason why I did not ally myself with the knights of the shire who are constantly murmuring against him to the shire reeve.' He sighed. 'I shall be thankful to be on my way early tomorrow. I shall not rest until I am with Gisela again. My seneschal is reliable but not the most imaginative of commanders and Gisela can be rash, especially where de Cotaine is concerned.'

His expression darkened. 'She is entirely consumed with a desire for revenge. It comes between us,' he said softly and Rainald glanced at him sharply.

Alain gave a little harsh laugh. 'Yes, my friend, I too am consumed but with jealousy and for a dead man, a pathetic state of affairs, is it not? You were right, of course. You said when you came to Allestone that I had fallen deeply in love. I am besotted, Rainald.'

'I told you then you must be patient, my friend.'

'Yes, you did.' Alain gave a little embarrassed laugh so foreign to him that, again, Rainald looked at his friend oddly. 'Yet I was not. I taxed her that she was still in love with the man that very night you stayed with us. We quarrelled but, in the end, she surrendered to me. God, Rainald, I held her in my arms and she told me she loved me. I believed her then, yet at times—I doubt—I cannot believe myself worthy of her love.

'She is brave and beautiful and spirited. You should have seen her there, Rainald, in the castle hall at Devizes, facing them all out. I was so proud of her—' He caught his breath as he recalled the pain of that moment when the Count's men had dragged them apart. 'I was so terrified for her—Count Henry assured me she would be safe on the journey but I ache to reach her. I cannot rid myself of some dread fear that she could be in danger—or lost to me—'

Rainald said, 'You need to rest tonight. The weather is still not good and travelling is hard and exhausting. You could be benighted. You'll make better speed in the morning if you sleep here and rest your mount. A few hours can make little difference, surely.'

Alain rose reluctantly and stretched. 'If you can find me a place to sleep I'll retire early. I'd ride on tonight but I have to think of Edwin, too. I've pushed him hard over these last few days and the weather has been against us.'

'There's a folding camp cot in my tent.' Rainald rose too and the two men headed for the tent flap.

They were not destined to reach it, for it was dashed aside and a figure stumbled in, mired with slush from the road, exhausted to the point of collapse and peering myopically round, as if he suffered from snow blindness.

'I seek my lord de Treville,' he said hoarsely, 'they tell me he is in here.'

Alain had reached his side in moments and lowered him on to one of the fald stools.

'Algar,' he said sharply, 'stay still, man, or you'll not manage to get even your message out.' He reached out a hand imperatively to de Tourel. 'Wine, quickly, Rainald. This is one of my men from Allestone. Something is very gravely wrong there.'

Algar gulped at the wine, half-choked, then drained the cup and forced himself upright on the stool. His eyes were adjusting to the dimness of the shaded tent after the snow glare outside. He clutched at Lord Alain's sleeve.

'My lord, thank God I have found you. I rode to Wallingford and—' he could hardly find breath to continue '—they told me you had gone on here and—and—I thought my horse would founder. I've half-killed the poor beast. My lord—Mauger de Cotaine is about to attack Allestone.'

Alain started but made no comment as Rainald gave a dreadful gasp behind him. He waited impassively for Algar to continue, fearing to interrupt him and lose the gist of his news.

'We—we reached Brinkhurst safely,' Algar gasped out. 'Lady Gisela wished—wished to see her father but—one of Gloucester's men of our escort had thought he'd seen followers, armed followers, and Osbert Greetholm, the sergeant, sent him back to investigate. He came riding back in haste to say he believed there were two men from Offen Castle. He'd—he'd recognised one from the castle when Mauger had waited upon Count Henry.'

He paused again to regain his breath. 'Osbert feared the possibility of attack and urged that we all ride immediately for Allestone—though it was almost full dark then. Sir Walter agreed to accompany his daughter with most of his people and we set out.'

He looked bleakly across the tent, swallowing hard. 'Someone was needed to ride back and try to alert you and I knew the way. I could not wait to be sure whether our fears were well founded and there would be an attack, but as I left for the Leicester road I saw a company of Mauger's men heading towards Allestone.'

Alain signalled for one of the waiting servants to bring Algar food and more wine.

'Thank you,' he said quietly. 'You've done well. You are sure she is safe behind the walls of Allestone?'

'Aye, my lord, I'm sure she would make it in time, well within the castle, but as to safety—' The man gave a helpless shrug.

Alain gave a wolfish smile. 'We must pray Allestone's defences are strong enough to hold until I can get there.' He turned and looked briefly towards Rainald. 'Will the King grant me a detachment, do you think, to help raise the siege? You said a surrender was expected soon here. He should be able to spare the men.'

'I'll see to it at once.' Rainald moved towards the tent flap. 'If the King gives me leave, I'll take my own men and join you.'

Again Alain's lips curled in a cruel smile normally foreign to his nature. 'Good. This time,' he said quietly but with deadly assurance, 'I'll see to it that Gisela gets her revenge and we'll rid the world of this devil who preys upon the vulnerable and weak.' He turned to Algar. 'You must stay here a day at least, eat and rest. Catch up with us when you can.'

Rainald had already left on his vital errand.

Chapter Ten

Gisela consulted with Sir Clement, her father and Osbert Greetholm within the small room Lord Alain used as his office. She looked miserably down at the unrolled parchment that lay before her.

'So, Sir Clement, you think we might have difficulty feeding our garrison if this siege is to be prolonged?' she asked, her eyes searching the seneschal's face for some sign of comfort.

'My lady, we had ample provisions for our own garrison, as you know—you helped to oversee the storing—but now that we have so many extra mouths to feed that might prove problematical.' He tapped the roll on which he had numbered the amount of barrels of salted meat and meal they had left. 'We are well into winter and the Brinkhurst community as well as the villagers makes an added burden, also the small number of your escort men.'

He pursed his lips as Sir Walter frowned at him over the oaken table. 'Of course, the weather might worsen and Mauger could decide to withdraw. As yet, he has made no move to attack, simply drawn a circle of men around our castle, but he can get supplies from the cottages within the village. Most have chickens still running loose and foodstuffs they abandoned when they made for refuge within the castle.'

Osbert said gloomily, 'He is well aware that the Baron is absent since he witnessed his arrest at Devizes, and relies on your vulnerability. There are no signs of siege weapons being brought up yet—but,' he added morosely, 'Offen is not far. Within days he could bring up mangonels and rams.'

'But the walls of Allestone are strong enough to withstand such an attack, surely,' Sir Walter said mildly. 'As yet we have little to fear. In time the shire reeve will be aware of our plight and send reinforcements to raise Mauger's siege.'

No one agreed with him. Osbert looked steadily away and Sir Clement coughed uncomfortably. 'That is by no means certain, Sir Walter,' he said. 'The presence of Mauger's besiegers makes it impossible for news of our plight to reach the shire reeve at Oakham. Our greatest threat is eventual lack of supplies, as in any siege.

'This attack comes at an unusual time of year, though,' he added quickly. 'I know the King has been besieging both Wallingford and Malmesbury, but we had not expected such a provocative move from Mauger de Cotaine so early in the year—if at all.'

Gisela said worriedly, 'Are all our villeins and serfs within the castle? How many are at risk from these mercenaries?'

Sir Clement shrugged. 'Some did not make it in time. Many refused to leave their properties, particularly the older ones. You know these people. They value their few possessions more than their lives. It is almost impossible to convince some of them that they must abandon their homes and come to safety immediately the warning is given.'

Gisela recalled, with a little shiver, that nightmare ride through the darkened wood to Allestone. She knew, only too well, what was at stake; it had not been hard to convince the men from Brinkhurst that they must assemble their families and follow to the safety the castle offered. They had seen with their own eyes the terrible carnage Mauger's unscrupulous routiers could manage in a few short hours.

They had piled what they had on available waggons and the rest had taken what they could on their backs and hustled their womenfolk to Allestone. The inner bailey was now packed with men, women and children, all huddling together miserably against the cold under improvised canvas shelters.

The older women and younger children had been accommodated within the hall of the castle, but it was necessary for the men of Allestone garrison to have room to move when there was need. A constant guard was kept on the roof of the keep and the gatehouse and at strategic points along the outer bailey wall.

Gisela could see now her husband's foresight in clearing the forest land well back from the castle environs. Mauger's men, so far, had kept a discreet distance from the firing range of Allestone arrows and were ringed just within the outskirts of the greenwood, barring all routes to the surrounding strongholds which might have come to their assistance but, thanks to the Baron's strategy, well within view of the defenders of a possible advance attack.

She dismissed Sir Clement and Osbert Greetholm courteously and they hurried out of the office, grateful to return to their own duties. Gisela looked appealingly at her father.

'Our situation is very grave, isn't it? Sir Clement is efficient but he is no de Treville and I feel totally inadequate.' She brushed away a tear. 'And I am responsible. I forgot all discretion and accused Mauger openly, which has brought him down on us so vindictively. Had I not done so, Alain would have been with me here now.'

She got up from her chair and went to the unshuttered lancet, striving to control her growing panic. All these men and their dependants looked to her for instructions, even Sir Clement. She had to hold Allestone for Alain, she must—and yet what would happen if he never returned?

Edwin had not come back to her. Why? Common sense told her he might have been delayed on the road and now he would not be able to enter the castle, but the intruding fear that pierced her mind when she did not rigidly keep it to the task in hand insinuated that the news was so bad that Edwin dreaded bringing it to her.

Was Alain dead, his body hanging from the gibbet on Devizes Castle? No, her fingers drummed fiercely upon the stone sill of the lancet window. If Alain *were* lost to her, she would surely know it. She would feel the agony of it pierce her heart. No, she must not allow herself to despair. Count Henry would help him. Alain would return and she must hold Allestone for him.

Her father was speaking quietly, consolingly. 'You have done everything possible, had good advice from the soldiers. Osbert is experienced in siege warfare and Sir Clement is brave and competent, if a little too reliant on the views of others. Gisela, my heart has swollen to bursting point with pride in you. I know Lord Alain will be ardent in his praise. You have ordered the men calmly, without outward show of panic, though you must be feeling it inside.

'Joshua ben Suleiman is busy laying out a section of the hall for the reception of the wounded, with Aldith and some of the village wise women to help him. All able-bodied men have been assigned duties and the womenfolk are ready with oil to heat and water as well as all available missiles for the forceful reception of those men of Mauger's force who are adventurous enough to advance too close to our defensive walls.

'Our archers are well practised and skilful. All precautions have been taken. You can do nothing more but wait for Mauger's next move.'

'But if he *does* bring up battering rams and mangonels he could breach our walls.'

'To do that he must remove men from the siege circle and that could allow passage for help from Oakham and the surrounding manors.'

'We all know the local knights are too fearful to openly oppose Mauger.' She thrust aside her remembrance that she had once thrown such an accusation at Alain. 'In all events we do not know if news of our plight has reached the reeve. Algar rode straight for Wallingford to alert the King and Alain if—if—' She broke down then and turned from him again. 'If only I knew.'

'Edwin would have joined your escort if he had had such dire tidings, I'm sure. He went to Lord Alain's help. He may yet be being held at Devizes and Edwin is attempting a rescue.'

It was a forlorn hope and both of them knew it.

Sir Walter said hastily, 'At least we have hope that Algar will reach Wallingford and Sir Rainald de Tourel will send help if he can. He is Alain's friend, you say. He will persuade the King to send a force, surely.'

If one can be spared, she thought wearily.

Mauger de Cotaine, it seemed, was in no hurry to make his move. For three days Gisela waited, her heart growing progressively heavier, while her small garrison anxiously watched the circle of mercenaries about their business. So far Mauger's men appeared to be under tight control. There was no sign of the despicable behaviour Gisela had expected.

She had thought insults as well as arrows would be directed at the defenders as well as some evidence of depredations to the village nearby, but all she could see, when she made her morning and nightly visits to the roof of the keep to look over the battlements, were men tending camp fires, sharpening weapons and cooking and eating food.

She thought she caught a glimpse of Mauger de Cotaine himself only once. Just out of reach of arrow fire from Allestone a striped tent had been erected, very close to the spot where Aldith's cottage had been destroyed in the clearance. She saw the tall, swaggering figure of the traitor lord emerge from the tent and direct his gaze mockingly upwards to where she stood by her father's side. Behind him she glimpsed the red-headed ruffian whom she had encountered at Brinkhurst and in Allestone wood and from whose clutches Alain had saved her.

She moved back nervously for a second, remembering their encounter in the hall at Devizes Castle and thinking longingly of Alain, then, deliberately, she drew near to the battlements once more and stood proudly, fearlessly looking back at her enemy.

Her father, realising her peril, for she was in line of fire from the edge of the wood, insisted on her withdrawing to the trap and descending again to the castle hall. Aldith hastened forward as she saw how white her mistress's face was.

'I saw that devil,' Gisela said, through grated teeth. 'How dare he continue to defy the King's laws! Will no man dare to combat this evil force that is decimating our lands and tenants' lives here?'

Sir Walter shook his head sadly. 'He is known, like Lord Alain, to be the King's man, and no one has the authority.'

'He is a traitor to King Stephen,' Gisela declared hotly. 'I saw him in conference with the King's enemies at Devizes. He has served both the King and Henry FitzEmpress. I, myself, will witness against him in the

King's court if he can be brought to face the King's justice.'

The grave expressions of those about her told her that there was little hope that the nearby knights would join together to oppose the man. They feared for their women-folk and their manor houses.

At supper Gisela fed Hereward with titbits. She looked guiltily towards her father who shook his head, smiling. She knew all food must be conserved, but it was from her own ration that she fed her pet, and her father and Huon, as well as Aldith, were only too glad to sacrifice some of their own food for the young dog they all loved.

'Where is Sigurd tonight?' she questioned Huon. 'I do not think I have seen him today or, come to think of it, yesterday either.'

Huon looked guilty and hung his head and Gisela turned quickly to Aldith.

'Is he with the girl, Winfrith? I thought she was safe within the hall with the other women of the village.'

'She is.' Aldith glanced across the crowded hall below the dais and Gisela saw her nurse's eyes alight on the head of a curly-haired girl who was greedily cramming bread and goat's cheese into her mouth.

'So that is Winfrith?'

Aldith nodded.

'But I do not see Sigurd. Where is he, Aldith? Do you know?'

Aldith chewed her bottom lip uncertainly. 'He may be in the bailey,' she said evasively.

'When did you last see him?'

Again Aldith looked almost furtively away. 'I am not sure, my lady. Perhaps two days ago.'

'But why is he keeping from you? I don't understand.'

'Sigurd has his own ways of·coming and going.'

'You mean you think he isn't in the castle?' Gisela looked stunned.

'He did not tell me what he intended. I imagine he was wary of alarming me and, at the same time, doubtful about giving me false hope.'

'But if he isn't in the castle he could be in grave danger of. . . How could he get out when the portcullis is down and the drawbridge raised?'

Aldith shrugged. 'He always managed to get out before. I don't know, mistress, I thought it best never to enquire. What I didn't know I could not reveal if questioned, but if he *is* free of the castle he will take good care to avoid Mauger's men. He knows the woods like his own garden plot. If he has made good his escape and is clear, he will be in Oakham by now.'

Gisela's lips parted in wonder. 'Then he could reach the reeve and it is possible. . .'

'Aye, my lady,' Aldith said fiercely, 'we can but hope.'

Gisela was summoned urgently by Sir Clement de Burgh next morning to the roof of the keep. She had been conferring with Joshua ben Suleiman about the care of a sick child.

Gisela was afraid that if the illness was contagious it could affect every living soul within the castle, but the Jewish physician assured her that the baby was suffering from severe wind pains and he administered a soothing cordial which appeared to calm the screaming infant and reassure the almost-hysterical mother.

Huon had come with the seneschal's message and she saw that he was very white round the mouth. She deferred questioning him and hastened up the steep spiral steps, her heart in her mouth.

What if she should look from the battlements and see some confirmation of Alain's death, Edwin, captured by Mauger's men perhaps, with information that would turn her limbs to water and her heart to ice?

Sir Clement was waiting by the trap as she emerged.

He, too, she saw, wore a very grave expression indeed.

'My lady, Sir Mauger himself is below and, beside him, one of his men with a flag of truce. He demands to speak with you, and you, alone.' He looked to the battlements and turned back to her. 'I am convinced you will be safe enough to confer with the man.' His mouth twisted. 'I have made sure. I have my best archer trained on him.'

She nodded and tried to smile back. Her heart was pounding uncomfortably now as she approached the roof edge and looked down, the sturdy form of Sir Clement protectively behind her.

Below she could see a smaller circle of men had approached nearer to the bailey wall and, in front of them, within hailing distance, Mauger de Cotaine himself, fully mailed and helmeted. Beside him was a man carrying a lance to which was tied a rag of dirty white cloth.

De Cotaine cupped his hands to his mouth and called up to her.

'I see you there, my lady. I talk under a flag of truce and will make no move on the castle at present.'

She peered down uncertainly. The tall, floridly handsome form seemed to waver in the flickering cold sunlight behind him. He appeared supremely confident that he would be perfectly safe, as he had when he had breezed into the hall at Devizes. Gisela's hatred blazed into sudden flame and was so sharp she thought she would be physically sick at sight of him.

He called again. 'Can you hear me, Lady de Treville?'

'I hear you,' she replied tonelessly. Deliberately she kept herself icy calm lest she betray the anger and fear that was choking her.

'My quarrel, you will accept, is between you and me, no one else. Alain de Treville has never offered me either threat or insult. You, and you alone, are responsible for the humiliation I suffered in Devizes Castle.'

'What of it?' she demanded coldly.

'I say you lied, my lady, that you have no hard evidence of any perfidious act of mine.'

'You are a traitor, my lord,' she flashed back at him. 'Your very presence at Devizes Castle in the presence of Count Henry of Anjou is proof of that, when your fealty is sworn to King Stephen.'

He shrugged his huge shoulders dismissively. 'What of that? Many have changed sides in this war. Your husband was also present and his oaths of loyalty to King Stephen are well known.'

'What is it you wish to say to me?' she asked. Her legs were trembling as she leaned against the cold stone of the buttress for support.

'I want you, Lady de Treville, none other. Perhaps we can come to an understanding.' Even from this distance she saw his black-bearded lips part in a grin of derision. 'Who knows? I am prepared to withdraw without one blow to your husband's castle walls if you will walk from the gatehouse of your own will, alone.'

Gisela heard Sir Clement give a great gasp of horror behind her and, for a moment, she turned from her view of the greenwood to face him, her own lips parting in sheer shock.

Sir Clement put out a hand and touched hers consolingly.

'Defy the man, my lady. You have nothing to fear. We can keep you safe.' He moved forward and leaned over the battlements.

'You lack honour, Sir Mauger,' he shouted. 'How can you believe that we would consent to tamely surrender our lady into your hands?'

'I rely on the decision of your lady herself and believe that she is sufficiently spirited as to insist on obedience to her will should she so decide to surrender herself.'

'You must be mad, sir,' Gisela said contemptuously.

'Why should I do anything so rash? Allestone walls are strong. Should you do your worst, you can only dent them. In the meantime we can do you harm, Sir Mauger. You will lose many men in the attempt.'

'As will you, too, lady,' he said jovially, 'and I believe you are anxious to save lives rather than endanger them.'

Her tongue seemed cloven to the roof of her mouth so that she could not immediately answer. He was right. If by surrendering herself she could save Allestone for Alain, without loss of life, would not that be an honourable and logical thing to do?

Sir Clement was placing a firm hand upon her shoulder. 'Do not think of it, my lady. Every one of my men would be willing to lay down his life for you.'

Yes, she thought, but why should they? De Cotaine spoke true. His quarrel was with her alone. Her foolish desire for vengeance might well have cost Alain his life. How could she lose his castle too, if she could save it by one simple act of courage?

De Cotaine was speaking again, his voice even more confident.

'The walls of Allestone are indeed almost impregnable—almost, not quite. Your husband would tell you, my lady, that castle walls fall at last, either to direct attack or when the doors are opened because hunger forces the issue. I understand Lord Alain is unlikely to attack. I understand he was unfortunately detained in Devizes.' He gave a loud jeering laugh. 'However your men declare their allegiance to you now, there will be mutterings when the true pangs of hunger bite.'

She could believe that. Worse, they could run short of clean water. There was no well within the keep. Alain had been in the process of having another dug within the cellars and should the outer bailey fall. . .

De Cotaine resumed his harangue. 'Your walls are thick, as you say, but human flesh is frail, Lady de

Treville, and I believe you to be a humane woman. Will you save yourself at the expense of our hostages?'

Hostages? Gisela almost fainted at the horror of the suggestion. She staggered back against Sir Clement when she saw the tight little circle of men behind de Cotaine part and a little group of villagers were thrust forward towards the bailey wall. At a hasty count she thought there were a dozen, all old and frail, two holding tightly to the arms of children.

Bile rose in her throat again as de Cotaine seized one of the children by the shoulder, a girl of about eight years, and held her defenceless young body hard against him. She cried out as his cruel mailed fingers bit into the soft flesh of her shoulder and arm; the old woman who was trying to protect her struggled with one of de Cotaine's mercenaries, who dealt her a harsh buffet that sent her sprawling on the ice-rutted ground.

'I see you are aware of the situation.' De Cotaine's voice was hardly raised now but seemed to carry easily enough through the chill air. 'There are always some stupid ones who will not fly for shelter.' His tongue clucked in derisive mock sympathy. 'They have not eaten, Lady de Treville, since our siege began, and will not, while I wait for you to leave Allestone.

'Indeed,' his falsely jovial tone hardened as he added, 'I will leave you with this thought. Each morning when the sun is fully up, I will kill one of them, starting perhaps with this young one?'

'Sweet Merciful Virgin!' Gisela was almost limp now against Sir Clement's body. As if from a distance she could hear him shout his own replied horror and scorn for the villainy of the threatened proceedings and Mauger de Cotaine's loud jeering laughter.

'Come, my lady.' Sir Clement drew her gently from the battlements. 'There is nothing more to be said. Come to the safety of the hall.'

Alain de Treville rode into Oakham early on the third day after receiving the news of Gisela's peril. He and Rainald de Tourel had ridden through the night with just four men as escort, de Tourel's company following more slowly. The shire reeve at the castle was woken hurriedly and received Lord Alain still wearing his bedgown.

Alain made no apologies for disturbing him at such an early hour and demanded to know if the shire reeve was aware of events at Allestone.

The man nodded. He was a tall, spare individual whose long, angular features wore, permanently, an almost lugubrious expression but whose worth Alain knew well. He was sure that Geoffrey de Marchmont would do all he could to assist Gisela once he was in possession of the full facts.

'A young serf, Sigurd, I think he called himself, reached us yesterday. I have sent out summons to all nearby castles and manors and am hoping to receive news of impending support companies to arrive today.'

Alain sank down near the fire at the shire reeve's invitation. He looked near total exhaustion but satisfied by the shire reeve's response. He drained a tankard of small ale and indicated his companion.

'You will know the reputation of my friend, Sir Rainald de Tourel. He has provided me with a company of men who should reach us here by nightfall at the latest.'

The shire reeve had been instructing his servants to provide refreshment for his two guests. He came to join them now by the fire.

'I have men stationed in the woods near Allestone, guided by this serf of yours. Last night one returned with news that Mauger de Cotaine had taken hostages from the surrounding villages and had issued an ultimatum to your lady. My men could not catch precisely what was said but the gist was obvious. I can only hope that Lady de Treville does nothing rash before we can get help to her.' He frowned doubtfully. 'Of course, we cannot prevent de Cotaine disposing of his hostages in time.'

Alain said heavily, 'Knowing my wife's mettle, we cannot wait for that, Sir Geoffrey. If she thinks she can save those poor souls she will surrender herself, if not the castle. Can my man, Sigurd, be recalled? If he was able to get out of Allestone, which I find astounding, someone, presumably, can get in.'

De Tourel looked pleased as food was set before him. 'I take it you will go yourself, Alain, and leave me to command the company?'

'Of course.'

The shire reeve pursed his lips. 'Would it not be wiser for you to head the relieving force, my Lord de Treville? You know your own castle and its weaknessess and strengths better than any of us.'

'True, but not, it seems, as well as Sigurd does and, in the meantime, my wife could recklessly allow de Cotaine to lure her into his clutches from a misguided sense of duty—I say misguided for that devil will kill his hostages in any case.'

'He would dare to kill Lady de Treville?' the shire reeve expostulated.

'I believe he will. He hates her with an insatiable passion, holds her responsible for his inevitable disgrace and knows he has little to lose now and he has a score to settle,' Alain said grimly. He ground his teeth in helpless frustration. He was so near to Gisela now, yet too far away to prevent her from sacrificing herself. He thought of her fair beauty at the mercy of Mauger de Cotaine and choked on his own despairing fury. Somehow he had to reach his heart's love in time, yet how, with de Cotaine's men entirely surrounding his castle?

Sigurd was brought into the hall just before noon. He had obviously been running and his young face looked strained and tired, but lit up at sight of Lord Alain. He ran to the chair near the hearth and knelt down.

'My lord, thank God you are here. We feared. . .' He looked away hastily and Alain bent and pulled him to his feet.

'Your mistress was well and unharmed when you left the castle? I take it you *did* leave Allestone, or did you never enter with the others?'

'Oh, no, my lord, I went in. I needed to settle Winfrith and her father as well as my lady and my mother.'

'Ah.' Lord Alain leaned back in his chair. 'So you *do* know a way in?'

Sigurd looked alarmed and hesitated, then nodded his shaggy brown head.

'Aye, my lord. An old archer showed me a tunnel under the keep and outer bailey right under the south wall. He used to use it, as I did, to visit a girl. . .' His voice trailed off. 'He's too old and too weighty to manage it now. We thought it would have filled up over time, but I cleared some of the fallen soil, shored it up with some abandoned timber planking left by the builders and used it to go out sometimes. . .'

'Yes, so you can get back in, with me?'

Sigurd looked even more alarmed. 'I don't know, my lord. It wasn't easy to escape the vigilance of the besiegers and I'm used to the woods. They'll be even more watchful now that—' he swallowed hard '—Lord Mauger has issued his threat. . .' He looked doubtfully at Lord Alain. 'Even if we can reach the entrance to the tunnel safely, you are much bigger than me, my lord. I don't know if you could get through. The tunnel's very narrow. . .'

'I'll make it if you show me the way. You need not make the attempt again. That would be tempting fate.'

'Oh, no, my lord, if you go, I go. I need to reach my mother and—Winfrith.'

'Best wait for nightfall,' de Tourel growled.

'No, my lords,' Sigurd put in quickly. 'Lord Mauger determines to kill one of his hostages in sight of the castle defenders today. I reckon Lady Gisela will be so upset. . .'

'Then, man, we must go at once.' Alain drained his ale cup and pointed to the remaining food on the trestle. 'Eat and drink, Sigurd. Sir Geoffrey will not object. Wait for me here while I make some preparations.' He turned to de Tourel. 'Marchmont can give you details of the lie of the land. If you come through Allestone wood with an advance company, as quietly as possible, you can come on the besiegers from behind.

'I hope, by then, Marchmont's summons will have put iron into some of the local knights' backbones and they will supply you with fresh men as reinforcements. At last we have Stephen's authority to take this man and try him. That should be sufficient incentive to obtain their support. They've been complaining long enough about his activities. Now my one fear is for Gisela. She will not wait for help to reach her if she fears for the hostages.'

Sigurd tucked into the good food and it seemed only moments before Lord Alain was back, dressed for action in a villein's borrowed brown fustian tunic and hood over brown chausses. He had darkened his face with soot from the chimney.

Sigurd nodded his approval. He, too, was dressed similarly and his youthful face, habitually weathered by his outdoor life, was still brown after the late suns of autumn and unlikely to show up well against the brown earth floor and undergrowth of Allestone wood.

Alain paused only to clasp hands with Sir Geoffrey and Rainald, who assured him that he would make preparations for the attack on the besiegers while waiting for his men to join him.

'God go with you,' he murmured fervently. 'I shall pray that you reach your lady in time and that we can swiftly deal with this devil in human form.'

Lord Alain took Sigurd up behind him and rode his hack until they reached the outskirts of the wood; then he allowed the beast to wander free. One of the men would find the animal and return him either to Allestone Castle or Oakham.

Sigurd led him quickly through the overgrown tracks of the wood until he stopped some paces ahead with a warning gesture. Alain padded softly to his side and the boy whispered, 'I can hear men moving ahead of us, my lord. We must go very carefully now. Keep close behind me.'

Alain listened and detected sounds of booted feet moving restlessly as if someone on watch was stamping his feet to keep warm. Then he heard muttered voices and a bark of a laugh.

He bent close and whispered in Sigurd's ear, 'Are we close to the castle now? You've lost me in the depths of these cursed copses.'

'Aye, my lord. We are close to the cleared land now and you must keep low behind the brushwood. In a moment I'll be able to point out to you the entrance to the tunnel. It did run right into the greenwood till the ground was cleared near Christmastide, but it's still pretty well hidden by a bush that was left, for some reason— I think, at the time, it was hard to uproot. Lucky for us, as it happens, for it gives a bit of cover.

'I had to wait a while, till the men watching moved away, before I dared creep out, but that was nearly three days ago. Since Lord Mauger gave his threat to my lady, I reckon as 'ow 'is men'll not dare take their eyes off the castle walls.'

Alain was sure he was right. He grimaced as he thought what Mauger de Cotaine would do to any one of his men who allowed one of his prisoners to escape through negligence.

He gritted his teeth and fingered his dagger thrust through his serviceable leather belt. He had concealed another weapon in his boot top, but even so armed it would not be easy to tackle two or three sentries, especially as warning to others would be instantly shouted. He could not rely on Sigurd to take on an experienced fighting man, would rather not have endangered the boy at all had there not been dire need.

Sigurd was crawling forward, head well down, towards a small rise in the ground ahead of them. Alain dropped to his knees and joined him. He almost gave a gasp of shock as he realised how very near they were to two of Mauger de Cotaine's men-at-arms. Alain could have reached out and almost touched the man nearest to him on the leg.

Sigurd scrambled back apace and Alain followed. They put their heads very close together.

'My lord, did you note that bush, about a hundred paces to your right?'

'Aye.'

'The entrance to the tunnel is on the far side, hidden by some piled brushwood. It can be approached from this side of the wood, but to reach the bush you'll still have to cross about fifty paces of almost open ground.'

Alain considered. On the face of it the distance was not great, but the two watchful sentries were very near and he would have to spend some time clearing the brushwood and examining the tunnel entrance.

Sigurd said hurriedly, 'I can lure the men away, my lord, or at least one, if you can deal with the other.'

Alain turned to him, frowning. What the boy proposed was dangerous to him in the extreme and yet, for Gisela's sake, he dared not wait to consider any other plan. He needed to get inside the castle before de Cotaine arrived to issue his challenge to her, for Alain knew, with a sinking heart, that she would allow herself to become the man's victim in order to save the hostages.

He said, huskily, 'Sigurd, you understand the risk?'

'Aye, my lord. I owe Lady Gisela and you much. My mother would urge me to do this, I know.'

Alain nodded. 'Very well, and God go with you.'

The boy waited no longer to half-rise and scramble some yards away, then, deliberately, he clumsily stumbled over a felled tree trunk and let out a yell. Already Alain had his dagger in his hand and made for the rise.

The first man let out an oath and turned in the direction of the cry. The other muttered something and stared round cautiously. The first guard gestured to his companion to stay on watch and made for the direction of the cry.

Alain could hear him stepping warily through the undergrowth. He thanked the saints the man gave no warning to others of the company nearby. Clearly his intention was to take the newcomer by surprise and haul his prisoner triumphantly before his lord. The second man continued to remain where he was, his eyes narrowed to survey the terrain, alert to the possibility of the nearness of another intruder.

Alain crept up behind him with the silence and agility of a wild, hunting cat and sprang. Before the guard could utter one word or gasp of warning, his throat was cut neatly and he collapsed perfectly silently into the arms of his attacker.

Alain laid him down carefully, half-rose from his knees, looked about him, then set off instantly for the bush and the hidden tunnel entrance. In the distance he could hear blundering feet heading well away from him and hoarse grunts. So far the first sentry was too occupied in his pursuit of Sigurd to give a warning and was totally unaware still of the death of his companion.

Alain spent some moments searching the ground behind the bush. The opening was well hidden; at last his sharp eyes saw that some of the fallen branches had been laid more carefully than by accident.

He dropped to his knees again and began hurriedly to pull away the covering. The entrance yawned before him and his heart misgave him. It seemed merely to be an enlarged burrow of some animal, scarcely wider than one of his own rabbit warrens. The boy had been right to be dubious. Could he possibly crawl through such a narrow place?

He hesitated and his bowels turned to water. All his life he had experienced a dread of confined places, had baulked at entering caves near his own village with his brothers, even dreaded being sent to dungeons to deal with prisoners.

His flesh crawled. Any other danger he would have faced willingly for Gisela, but the fear of being trapped in this dank, dark burrow was deeply unnerving, yet it would have been useless to send in Sigurd. The boy would have been completely unable to persuade Gisela against her determined course of action. He had to make the attempt.

The entrance was not such a tight squeeze as he had first thought. He managed to wriggle in and began the crawl. Someone, he thought, perhaps the man who had revealed the secret of the place to Sigurd, had partially shored up the roof with wattle and daub. Later, as soil began to fall, Sigurd had reinforced the roof with heavy branches, which further impeded the traveller.

The light from the entrance permeated the place for some yards and Alain was able to proceed, but with difficulty. Once, well within the tunnel proper, he felt as if the earth wall above was closing round him and the earthy, dank stink of the place began to affect him as if it were the interior of a prepared grave. He crawled steadily, for there was no room to even crouch, and some of the way he had to lie on his belly and pull himself along by his arms, finding just enough room to move onward, but in total darkness and without any sound from outside.

If he was once caught tight he would surely die here, buried beneath tons of soil, yet the air was not bad. It must be permeating in through holes to the surface, possibly made by Sigurd on his several illegal excursions. Alain told himself that his feeling of breathlessness was merely fear and pushed on.

At one point he found himself stuck and he froze in helpless panic, then realised that his belt had caught on one of the supports and was holding him back. He managed to reach behind and release it, which gave him sufficient purchase to continue. Several times soil fell, half-choking him. Greyish light was beginning to filter in from somewhere and he muttered a swift prayer of gratitude to the Virgin.

Outside, sounds were still utterly excluded and he could not tell how far he had to go, when suddenly the light deepened. He gave a triumphant grunt of satisfaction as he scrambled determinedly forward and pushed at lightly piled soil and straw, which had been pulled over to conceal the castle entrance from inside the tunnel. He lay still, panting, his outstretched hands within distance now of his goal.

He made the final push upwards to free himself and found he was in an angle of the inner bailey wall near the keep. He half-lay for a moment, his back propped against the chill stone, drawing in mouthfuls of cold air.

He was not at first discovered, for the men on watch had been drawn to the wall and stood on the wooden platform, backs to him, some peering across to the outer wall, others gazing upwards to where men on the keep battlements were gazing down on to the cleared land and the outskirts of the wood.

A trumpet sounded shrilly. Alain ground his teeth in fury as he surmised that Mauger de Cotaine was about to arrive before the castle and issue his threatened challenge to its chatelaine.

A man, hearing him dislodge a stone with his foot as he rose to his feet, turned sharply and saw the intruder. Instantly he drew his sword and advanced. Alain was acutely aware that he must be almost unrecognisable, in unfamilar garb, covered in soil and straw. He stood up and called imperiously, 'Hold there, man. I am your lord, Alain de Treville.'

The man halted, bewildered, as he was joined by two curious companions who turned to stare in hostility at the filthy stranger. One advanced, looked closely and gave a relieved shout. 'Praise the Virgin, lads, it is Lord Alain himself—'

Alain cut off the man's further expostulation and jabbed a finger towards the wall. 'De Cotaine?'

'Aye, my lord, come to. . .'

'I know why he's come,' Alain said harshly. 'Take me to your lady at once, man.'

Chapter Eleven

Gisela stood in her bower, facing a weeping Rohese and a stern-faced Aldith. She had dressed in her best, the gown she had worn for her marriage. When she walked through the gatehouse she was determined she would not present a picture of a terrified, shrinking girl but a mature woman, chatelaine of Allestone, going proudly to do her duty to protect her vulnerable tenants in the only way possible.

'Please,' she said gently, bending to raise up the tearful Rohese who had dropped on to her knees in a desperate attempt to plead with her friend, 'please, do not weep, Rohese. Let me go with a brave face. I know what I am doing does not please your husband, but, believe me, I can conceive of no other way to salve my conscience. Those women and children out there are my responsibility. Since Mauger de Cotaine demands only one sacrifice, mine, I must do as he demands.

'I was rash to accuse him so publicly. Had I not done so, he may have well thought twice before attacking Allestone and bringing this trouble upon our villages, so, you see, I am the one who must pay the price.'

'Aye,' said Aldith grimly, 'but are you sure you know the full price that devil is asking?'

'Yes.' The single word was forced out through gritted

265

teeth. Certainly she knew. Mauger de Cotaine would kill her, of that she was sure, but first—a shudder passed through her body, as she thought what might come first. Would he ravish her himself or—would he hand her over to his men? At all events it would end in her death, slow and painful. She faced Aldith determinedly and put out her hand. Her former nurse made an inarticulate sound like a sob and gathered her lady into her arms.

'Oh, my dear one. I promised your mother I would care for you always. . .'

'As did I.' Sir Walter's formidable tones came to them from the door. 'And by God, Sweet Jesus and the Holy Virgin, I will not allow you to do this. I'll lock you in your chamber first.'

He strode in and tore his daughter determinedly from Aldith's arms, shaking her. 'Do you hear me, girl, do you?'

'Father—' tears rained down helplessly now '—don't you know you are only making things worse for me. I am the mistress of Allestone. I will not allow you to make a prisoner of me.'

'No, but I will, and lash you to the bed before I'll allow you to take one more step nearer to that gatehouse.'

Gisela swung round, her eyes widening, the tears still raining down, her hands caught into fists by her sides, staring at the door, unable to believe the evidence of, first, her ears and then her eyes.

Sir Clement, who had accompanied her father to the bower to help remonstrate with his lady, had been pushed aside and a tall scarecrow clad in filthy, torn fustian clothes stood there, feet astride, chin jutting aggressively, stance, despite the inadequacies of his apparel, one of supreme lordship, not to be gainsaid.

'Alain?' Gisela mumured wonderingly, then tearfully, 'Alain, my love, is it really you?'

He strode in and she rushed to him, unmindful of the

full skirt of her gown, stumbling right into his arms. She was half-laughing and crying hysterically, her arms reaching up round his neck as if she could not bring him close enough to her. The two men stood and stared in utter bewilderment.

At last Gisela pushed herself a little from him and stared up into the beloved face she had thought never to see again.

'I cannot believe it,' she whispered brokenly. 'We thought—feared—'

'Aye, I know. I was forced to go first to Wallingford only to have to press on to Malmesbury. Since then I've been riding as if the devil were at my heels to get here.' He gave a little grim laugh. 'And now I am here, I find you preparing to do the most insane thing I could have ever conceived of. Stand clear of me, my sweet, I am filthy and have besmirched your fine gown already. . .'

'But—' She could hardly bring out the words for joyful tears. 'How—how did you get into the castle? We have been besieged for days and. . .'

'Sigurd knew of a tunnel, which explains my appearance.' He waved a hand as if to brush aside explanations. 'But I cannot wait to tell you. I must go change my clothes and don mail. I'll not face de Cotaine in this guise. No, do not argue with me, Gisela. In this I will be obeyed. Leave the business of the hostages to me.'

She clutched at his arm as if to detain him.

'He will kill one of them, Alain, even while we stay here talking, considering—'

'He will not, my heart. I am sure of that. He knows that if he does so before he is forced to it it will destroy his bargaining power, for he is counting on your passionate need to defend your own people. If just one dies you will recognise the full vindictiveness of his nature and may not trust him to keep his word over the others. No, if I judge him aright, he will hold his hand—for the moment. He does not want the death of some worthless peasant, he wants you.'

He turned to his seneschsal. 'Clement, can you get out there with Sir Walter and hold parley. Try to delay what de Cotaine has in mind. Promise that your lady is preparing herself in prayer in the chapel—anything to keep him occupied while I prepare myself to face him.'

'Aye, my lord.' Sir Clement turned briskly, thankful to have his lord returned to take full responsibility for what happened here—a brave man, Sir Clement, but not one who easily assumed leadership. He waited until the reluctant Sir Walter joined him.

Lord Alain said tersely, 'Do not concern yourself about Gisela, sir. She is mine and I will not surrender her, even if I have to do what I threatened, keep her penned and pinioned.'

Sir Walter nodded, satisfied, and went with the castle seneschal to do what Lord Alain commanded.

Alain waited only for a moment to draw her close once more, tilting up her chin and smiling down into her terrified little face.

'Trust me, my love. The shire reeve is even now bringing up reinforcements to relieve us and Rainald de Tourel waits in Oakham only for his men to join us and encircle the enemy. De Cotaine is caught in his own trap.' He bawled to Huon, who was even now racing up the spiral stair to wait on his master.

'Come, lad, help me arm and—' he thrust up a knee to ward off the joyful attentions of Hereward '—keep that damned hound away for a while at least.'

As he reached the door Aldith made an agonised plea. 'You said Sigurd guided you, my lord. Is—is he with you?'

He stopped momentarily in mid-stride towards the stair and turned back to her.

'I don't know how he fared, Aldith. He acted as decoy

for me, drew off the guard while I made it to the tunnel entrance. I can only pray. . .'

She bit down upon her lip, then gave a little rueful laugh. 'I know my son, my lord. If he was leading that guard astray, he'll lose him, right enough. Who knows Allestone wood like my Sigurd?'

Gisela longed to race after her husband. Even now she could hardly believe that he was back with her, safe and well. Then she wished to go to her father on the keep battlements and see what was happening to the hostages, but she found when she attempted to leave the bower that Alain had been as good as his word and left two stout men-at-arms to see that she did not leave. He was taking no chances with Gisela's safety.

She waited in an agony of suspense till he returned to her, mailed from head to foot and wearing his surcoat displaying the blue chevron of Allestone. She gave a little gasp of dismay. He had returned to her and was going immediately into danger again.

She clung to him desperately, feeling the deadly coldness of his mail through the woollen cloth of her gown. She had almost lost hope of seeing him again, indeed, her very resolve to walk out of Allestone into de Cotaine's hands had made her realise only too well what she was losing, yet here he was, so close to her, straining her tightly against his heart, and she knew this moment might well be the very last they spent together.

She forced herself not to plead with him to stay safe and hidden within the castle. She knew how he valued his knightly honour and she could not disgrace him now before his men. He felt her whole body trembling and bent to kiss her gently full upon the lips.

He took her hand. He was smiling, but his expression was grim. 'Come now, my lady. Let us greet Sir Mauger de Cotaine together.'

She felt her limbs would turn to water as she climbed

the keep steps behind him, Aldith bringing up the rear. When she had been helped through the trap onto the leads, he led her towards the battlements, nodding to two of his most experienced archers to stand behind her.

Sir Walter and Sir Clement were leaning down, engaged in shouted argument with the assembled host below. Lord Alain waved them back and, keeping Gisela slightly behind him, and yet in full view, moved forward and stood staring down at Mauger de Cotaine who had dismounted and stood defiantly, a drawn dagger in his hand, half-turned towards one of his men who held the thin body of a terrified girl child before him.

Lord Alain said clearly and contemptuously, 'This is the behaviour I would have expected of you, De Cotaine, the murder of yet more innocents. It is what you do best, make war on those who are too weak to defend themselves.'

De Cotaine turned back to the castle wall with a snarl of anger.

'De Treville? So they let you loose? I'd thought you dead and in Hades these days past.'

'Stoking up the fires for you?' Lord Alain scoffed.

De Cotaine stood, feet astride, in that insufferably insolent fashion Gisela had learned to recognise in the few short encounters she had had with him. He flung back his head and laughed, his black curls escaping from his mailed coif and blowing in the wind.

'Well, now you are home, my lord,' de Cotaine stressed the final words in mockery, 'and how do you think you will prevent me from killing every one of these before your lady's eyes? She will not enjoy that, the Lady Gisela.'

The mockery faded from the tone and the smile wavered. 'She has cost me my honour and possibly my life, if I fail to escape to France in time, yet Stephen is still too deeply engaged with his foe to come and take me himself and I still have time to enjoy my vengeance on the vindictive bitch who brought me to this.'

Lord Alain said calmly, 'How would any of that profit you, except to reveal you further as the villain you are, a disgrace to your knighthood? Even now the shire reeve is assembling the county knights against you. You cannot win and you cannot run, but I will spare you the humiliation of public trial.

'I challenge you to trial by combat, Mauger de Cotaine, deem you traitor to your King and a defiler of all that our knightly code holds sacred. Meet me here before your men below the castle walls and you may still be able to salvage some remnant of chivalry.'

'No, no.' Gisela flung off her father's arm as he moved to restrain her. 'No, Alain, do not soil your hands with this scum.'

Gently Alain pulled her clutching fingers from his mailed arm.

'It has to be this way, my heart. He has dared to threaten you. I challenge him now in the names of those he murdered that they might lie at rest and come no more between us.'

There had been mutterings from below and now there was an unnatural calm as if each man in de Cotaine's host was waiting in strained apprehension to hear their lord's reply.

Gisela stood staring intently into the unfathomable depths of her husband's dark eyes. He did not move, but remained smiling down at her until he made a little decisive movement of his chin. She gave a great sob and flung back her own head in answer. She knew now that it must be so.

She had accused him of cowardice and though she had taken it back, it lay between them—and only the spilling of blood could wipe it out. He was her knight, her champion, and she drew in her breath in a little sigh of acceptance.

Instinctively she knew that, if Alain were to kill Mauger de Cotaine, his men would no longer continue to menace Allestone. They would disperse, those who were not arrested by the shire reeve's men, and the lives of the innocent courageous defenders would be saved. If he were to die—she tasted salt blood in her mouth as she bit down savagely upon her nether lip. She would not think of that, not now when he had need of her courage to hearten him.

She reached up and kissed him full on his lips then, stepping back, tore her veil from her head and bound it tightly around his arm.

'Take my favour, my lord,' she said clearly, 'and may God give you the victory and defend the right.'

There came a second shrilling of trumpets. All eyes turned towards the main road leading to Allestone village and Gisela's hand stole out again to grasp Alain's.

'If I am not mistaken that is Geoffrey de Marchmont, shire reeve of Oakham, with his host to relieve our siege,' he said quietly and soon the encircling men about the castle began to stir and murmur amongst themselves as the steady tramp of mailed feet and the jingle of horses' accoutrements announced the arrival of a company of men.

Again the trumpet sounded and Gisela, straining her eyes towards the village, saw the first riders moving towards Allestone. From this distance she could not see the devices upon their pennants, but relief flooded through her as she realised that their salvation was near now. Allestone would be relieved.

Mauger de Cotaine let out an obscene oath and bawled to his sergeant to call his men to order, but it was soon very clear to the watchers that that would prove an impossible task for already the mercenaries were begin-

ning to panic. Those most in their lord's favour had
moved quickly to stand close and support him, but many
were already attempting to make good their escape into
the woods behind them yet, even as they tried, they found
themselves caught up from the rear by other men on foot
who had come through the woods in a surprise encircling
movement. Behind them Gisela saw more mounted
knights and recognised the gryphon device of Rainald
de Tourel.

Soon the relieving hosts had moved into position,
de Cotaine's men neatly trapped between their two
companies.

Geoffrey de Marchmont called up to Alain on the
keep leads.

'I trust we come in time, de Treville?'

'Well in time, my lord, thank the Virgin. Lady Gisela
is unharmed and the defenders safe.'

De Marchmont was dismounting and advanced to
where Mauger de Cotaine still stood, guarded by his
small group of remaining supporters.

The shire reeve's voice was authoritative as he said
crisply, 'Sir Mauger de Cotaine, Baron of Offen, I have
the King's authority to arrest you for treason and various
other specified crimes against the folk of this county.
It is useless for you to resist since our two companies
completely surround you. There is no escape.'

Lord Alain interposed, his voice carrying clearly. 'I
acknowledge your authority, lord sheriff, but I claim right
of combat against this man. I have challenged him to
mortal combat and was waiting for his reply when we
heard your trumpets. He has threatened my wife's safety
and injured her father and members of her household. I
demand he answer to me first to those personal charges
I hold against him.'

Rainald de Tourel had dismounted and conferred
briefly with the shire reeve.

He called to his friend, 'There is no further need for you to endanger yourself, Alain. The man will be charged and, please God, be found guilty in the King's court in Oakham.'

'Yet I insist on my knightly right of challenge.'

Again the two commanders conferred and Gisela whispered urgently, 'Alain, you have nothing to prove and everything to lose. Allow the shire reeve to decide this man's guilt or innocence.'

Gently he put her from him. 'I have everything to lose if I do not meet this man, my heart. Surely you must see that. Many in this county have wondered why I have held my hand against him. Now I must prove myself.'

The shire reeve was addressing de Cotaine. 'Do you accept this challenge, Sir Mauger?'

'Aye.' The answer was churlish. The handsome mercenary chief shrugged his broad shoulders. 'Let him come down now and face me before your men and mine and we shall see whom the gods favour.'

Gisela turned from the scene below to rest her head against her husband's shoulder. She felt sick and faint, yet she knew there was nothing she could do to prevent this bloodletting between her love and her bitterest enemy.

From the first she had wanted this, a goad to prod Alain de Treville into giving her revenge against the man who had killed Kenrick and attacked her beloved home. Now that they were to engage in mortal combat that desire for vengeance was as ashes in her mouth. She was shaking with fear and cold and Lord Alain called for Aldith to bring her warm fur-lined mantle.

He bent, tilted up her face with one finger upon her chin, and kissed her very gently. 'Stay here, my love, with your father and Sir Clement to guard you. Try not to fear for me.' He hesitated, then added softly, 'If aught should go wrong, Rainald de Tourel will take your case before the King and he will make provision for you.'

She reached out for him blindly as Aldith came to her side, but he pushed her very gently towards her attendant, nodded to Sir Walter and began to move towards the trapdoor that would lead him below. Once there, he walked out through the keep bailey and gatehouse to meet his foe before the assembled companies.

Gisela refused to go below and await the outcome in the great hall. She insisted on remaining on the keep leads in clear view of the coming battle. Her father saw to it that she was well wrapped against the cold and drew her to a slightly more sheltered place behind the crenellation. He forbore to argue with her. Numbly she remembered his comment made weeks ago: that vengeance was a dish best taken cold. Now the heat of her passionate thirst for vengeance was over, she did, indeed, feel deadly cold.

She watched Alain emerge with Huon in attendance from the gatehouse as the drawbridge was lowered, the entrance to the gatehouse guarded by men of de Tourel's company. He walked steadily into the ring formed by the shire reeve's men. De Cotaine's had withdrawn somewhat and stood surlily awaiting the outcome in trepidation. Whatever occurred now they could not hope to avoid punishment.

Gisela saw Alain remove his surcoat and hand it to Huon, who handed his lord his broadsword and a battle axe that Alain fitted carefully within his belt. Gisela recalled seeing Huon on several occasions over the last few days assiduously sharpening and oiling the blades of Alain's weapons in case of need and blessed the boy's optimism that his lord would return to him. Now Alain was well armed and prepared.

Her heart ached for him. He was near exhaustion surely, after riding so hard to her assistance and crawling through that vile tunnel to her rescue, yet he was going fearlessly into combat.

One of de Cotaine's men was acting as his squire and the mercenary chief was preparing himself, running a thumb down the blade of his sword and checking his mace, which hung from a leather strap from his sword belt.

They were to meet on foot, blade to blade. This was no chivalric tourney. Both men were aware of the fact that only one could emerge from this alive. Gisela drew a hard rasping breath and felt her father's comforting, steadying hand upon her shoulder.

The shire reeve was addressing the combatants. Gisela could not hear what was said but, all too soon, she saw his raised arm holding a small wooden baton and the two antagonists turned and faced each other, only a few feet between them. Rainald de Tourel stood close to the shire reeve, his eyes narrowed to watch the proceedings. Several of his own most experienced men had been detailed to ensure none of de Cotaine's men could interfere in their lord's favour.

Gisela had never seen men fight before. Tourneys had been declared ungodly by the church; though they often took place, she had never been taken to witness one. She had seen boys wrestle together on market days for prizes of pigs or coin, but that had been good-humoured and could end only in strained muscles or, at worst, broken bones.

Her whole body shuddered at the first heavy clang of sword on sword. She could not bear to look yet forced herself to do so. She could not fail Alain now through lack of the courage she had demanded in him.

To her, so far away upon the keep roof, it looked vaguely unreal. The two circled and lunged, withdrew and lunged again. Their movements looked clumsy as they swung the incredibly heavy weapons, she registered dully, as if she had expected something more polished and elegant.

Both were experienced fighters—she knew that instinctively. Whatever de Cotaine's faults, he did not lack courage, though he must have sensed that even if he should win, he would be later arrested. This mortal combat was a last defiant throw of the dice, a thirst for personal scores to be settled.

Alain's movements looked efficient enough. He did not display any show of weariness, at least not at first. The heavy clangs of the great swords continued to ring out and Gisela marvelled at the silence of the watchers. No one called out any insults or encouragments. Everyone, it seemed, was concentrated on the deadly nature of this business.

Once Gisela's heart came into her mouth as Alain was forced right back almost on to his knees, but he managed to recover and lunge back energetically at his opponent. She could hear, even from this distance, the harsh, wheezy breaths the two made now as stolidly they continued the fight, seemingly evenly matched and neither wishing to give ground.

She knew that Alain was deliberately reining in his own hot fury at this man he hated for threatening her and inwardly she prayed that that same careful deliberation would carry him to victory. Then, suddenly, there was a yell from one of the watchers as de Cotaine's sword flickered to the most vulnerable part of Alain's mail, that joint where the shoulders of the mailed coif met the body mail.

Lord Alain gave a great grunt; Gisela was certain he was severely wounded, then, before she could cry out her terrible fear, he made a sudden feint. De Cotaine staggered back, attempted to recover, then gave a gurgled scream as Lord Alain's blade stabbed mercilessly upwards and punctured his jugular, unprotected by the parting of his mail collar. He reared up, staggered again, pulled himself relentlessly upright and Gisela watched, horrified, as Alain stood back. The mercenary lord stood for moments, clawing at his throat, his own blade falling helplessly with a great clang to the ground, then he gave a final rasping, choking scream and toppled forward, face down, full upon Lord Alain's sword.

Gisela leaned down anxiously for sight of Alain. He had been sorely wounded, she knew. She saw him stagger and lean heavily upon Rainald de Tourel's shoulder, then men closed in round him and she could no longer discern his beloved form. Her father was urging her towards the roof trapdoor.

'Come below, Gisela. They will bring him to the Jewish physician. All is over. De Cotaine has paid for his crimes. The shire reeve will round up those mercenaries believed responsible for crimes within the county.'

She allowed herself to be persuaded, though her eyes yearned after the little knot of men helping her husband towards the drawbridge.

She almost flew down the steep spiral steps and to the curtained-off alcove Joshua ben Suleiman had had prepared for the reception of the wounded. He received Gisela courteously and made no attempt to bar her from the area.

Rainald de Tourel came into the hall with Alain leaning heavily upon him. Behind him, to the relief of both Gisela and Aldith, came Sigurd, appearing to have taken no harm. More than likely he had totally eluded his pursuer. The frightened villeins and serfs drew back, gazing worriedly at their wounded lord. Gisela hastened to her husband's side as he approached the alcove.

She saw with relief that he was grinning despite his obvious pain and the ominous spreading stain upon his mail.

'By all the saints, Joshua, I'm bleeding like a stuck

pig,' he grimaced as the physician helped him on to a low couch.

'Lie still, my lord, and let me see what damage you sustained.'

Gisela stood ready with a bowl of warm water and Aldith hastened up with torn linen for bandaging. Huon was anxiously bringing up the rear but Rainald gestured the boy away, as he and Joshua helped the injured man out of his mailed coat and cut open the oiled leather coat beneath.

Gisela almost cried aloud at sight of the ugly gash running from his collar bone on the right side almost to the navel. Alain made no outcry, but it was clear the action of ridding him of his garments had given a great deal of pain. Joshua bent to examine the wound. Rainald stood back, frowning, then he turned and gave Gisela what he hoped was a reassuring smile.

'He's taken worse than this often enough in the heat of battle,' he said on a falsely cheery note.

Joshua raised his head and waved to have the water and wine brought to clean the wound.

'It is a bad gash,' he pronounced, 'it is fortunate it has missed the vital organs, in particular the heart. A little nearer the left and—but we will not think of that. I see no fragments of leather or rust from the mail in the wound. It will heal when I have completed the stitching, but the blood loss is considerable. You will have to rest for some days, Lord Alain.'

Alain grinned back at him cheerfully. 'If that will keep me to my chamber with my lady, away from desmesne business for a while, I'll make no complaints,' he said and suffered the physician's ministrations with merely a grunt or two though Gisela guessed he was feeling exquisite pain.

A mixture of wine and water was brought for Alain

to drink and at last he was helped up the stair to his chamber.

Gisela busied herself plumping up the pillows of their bed, aware that she must not allow her terrible anxiety to show. He caught at her two hands as she smoothed the fur coverlet over him and made to withdraw slightly.

'I told you all would be well.'

'I wish I could have been as sure.'

'Kiss me, sweeting.' He drew her down hard upon his body and then gave a sharp whimper as the movement caused intense pain to run through him.

'You must not do that,' she remonstrated.

'I have been waiting days to do that, and now you say I must not?'

'Joshua ordered you to rest.'

'I will when you assure me that you love me.'

She stared down at him, her great blue eyes awash with tears. 'You know I love you. I told you so the last night we had together at Allestone and many times afterwards upon the journey.'

'Yet,' he said hoarsely, 'I doubted, feared that— Oh, God, Gisela, you are all in the world to me and I could so easily have lost you had I come but moments later than I did. My own crass jealousy blinded my eyes to the truth.

'Out there I thought only to avenge you, not only for what you suffered at Brinkhurst but for his loss, Kenrick of Arcote's, for, by the Holy Virgin, I believe he loved you and died trying to save you. I have no right to resent the youthful love you gave to him.'

She bent and kissed his eyes, his salt tears dampening her lips.

'I have told you, Alain de Treville, you are the only man to whom I have offered a woman's love and will always be.'

'You are satisfied?'

Her tears fell now fast and furious. 'Alain, you great oaf. Do you really believe that I wished you to endanger yourself?'

'I did, when we were first wed.'

'I was selfish and foolish. I know better now.'

He lay back against his pillows. There was a whiteness about his lips that caused her concern.

He said slowly, 'I love you with all my heart and soul, Gisela de Treville. I know I took you before you were ready, indeed, wondered if you could ever be ready to love me in return. It was wrong, but I could not resist the temptation.'

She put a gentle finger reprovingly upon his lips. 'I have suffered terribly since that moment at Devizes when I realised that by my fecklessness I could have caused your death I have loved no one else for many weeks now. When you are fully recovered, I will prove it to you.'

Yet it proved to be a full week before she was able to keep her promise. Alain ran a fever and felt much weaker than he had expected to. For one or two days Gisela lived in a ferment of fear as she saw Joshua ben Suleiman's pursed lips and furrowed brow, but finally Alain turned the corner and laughingly welcomed Hereward on to his bed, then banished him to draw his wife into his arms.

'So, my love, I am a fit man, and ready to receive your surrender.'

Despite his assurances she insisted upon their love-making being very gentle, for she knew he was holding in expressions of pain. She lay by his side and allowed him to caress her, knowing there would be time for their passion to flower, then grow into a warm glow that would be there for them throughout their lives together. Allestone was no longer a grim fortress, but a home enclosing herself and her husband in happiness through the still dark days of war ahead.

Three days before the Holy Season of Christmas of 1153, two days after Gisela's churching, Rainald de Tourel came to play his part of godfather to Alain's first son, who was to be his namesake. He was delighted to find Gisela in good health and spirits after a relatively easy childbirth.

He was able to impart the news for which they had been waiting. A final peace treaty declaring Henry Plantagenet, known as FitzEmpress, heir to the English throne had been signed at Winchester earlier that very month of December. Alain's mission had been successful after much bargaining by several embassies. The ailing King had given his consent gladly.

The war had dragged on for months and in July the only real obstacle had been overcome. Eustace, Stephen's heir, furious at the very suggestion of that truce and its terms, had stormed from his father's presence. Later they heard he had committed the most terrible sacrilege and pillaged the abbey in St Edmund's Bury.

Stephen, anxious to conciliate the shocked monks, had first captured Ipswich and hastened on to Bury to confront his errant son. It was at a feast there that Eustace had unaccountably choked upon a dish of eels and died horribly in the presence of his horrified father and his principal commanders. Rainald, who had witnessed the event, had declared sorrowfully that he was not sure whether the choking fit had brought on a stroke.

Men spoke in hushed tones of God's vengeance for Eustace's evil ways but, in all events, his death, in time, brought his sorrowing father, still mourning for his beloved Queen Matilda who had died in May the previous year, a measure of comfort that he could bring this dreadful civil war to its close.

'God comfort him,' Alain said piously. 'He has ever been a good lord to me and more kind and merciful to his enemies than many deserved.'

Looking down into the cradle of her sleeping son, Gisela echoed that prayer silently. The long days of civil war were over and, God willing, they could live here at Allestone in true happiness and peace.

Historical Romance™

Coming next month

A LORD FOR MISS LARKIN
Carola Dunn

Alison Larkin thought the most romantic thing in the world would be to have a lord falling at her feet and pledging eternal love.

With the arrival of her recently widowed and wealthy aunt, Alison's dream could become a reality. She was granted a Season and would be introduced to the *crème* of the ton.

How vexing that the first eligible gentleman she was to meet was a plain *Mr* Philip Trevelyan who had a way of making Alison forget that it was her dearest wish to marry a lord.

THE IMPOSSIBLE EARL
Sarah Westleigh

Having been reduced to working as a governess, Leonora was left her uncle's fortune and fine town house in Bath. But she also inherited Blaise, Earl of Kelsey! Her uncle had leased the ground floor to Blaise, where he ran a gentlemen's club.

Leonora's hopes for a respectable life in Society and the possibility of marriage would come to nought without a compromise, particularly when the Earl was so clearly *not* a candidate in the marriage mart.

MILLS & BOON®

Makes any time special™

MILLS & BOON®

Especially for you on
Mother's Day

Four fabulous new heart-warming romances
inside one attractive gift pack.

JUST FOR A NIGHT - Miranda Lee

A MAN WORTH WAITING FOR - Helen Brooks

TO DR CARTWRIGHT, A DAUGHTER
- Meredith Webber

BABY SWAP - Suzanne Carey

Special Offer—1 book FREE!
Retail price only £6.60

On sale February 1998

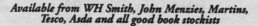

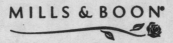

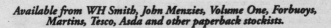

4 FREE

books and a surprise gift!

We would like to take this opportunity to thank you for reading this Mills & Boon® book by offering you the chance to take FOUR more specially selected titles from the Historical Romance™ series absolutely FREE! We're also making this offer to introduce you to the benefits of the Reader Service™—

* ★ FREE home delivery
* ★ FREE gifts and competitions
* ★ FREE monthly newsletter
* ★ Books available before they're in the shops
* ★ Exclusive Reader Service discounts

Accepting these FREE books and gift places you under no obligation to buy, you may cancel at any time, even after receiving your free shipment. Simply complete your details below and return the entire page to the address below. *You don't even need a stamp!*

YES! Please send me 4 free Historical Romance books and a surprise gift. I understand that unless you hear from me, I will receive 4 superb new titles every month for just £2.99 each, postage and packing free. I am under no obligation to purchase any books and may cancel my subscription at any time. The free books and gift will be mine to keep in any case.

H8XE

Ms/Mrs/Miss/Mr...................................Initials ....
BLOCK CAPITALS PLEASE

Surname ....

Address ....

....

....Postcode...................................

Send this whole page to:
THE READER SERVICE, FREEPOST, CROYDON, CR9 3WZ
(Eire readers please send coupon to: P.O. BOX 4546, DUBLIN 24.)

Offer not valid to current Reader Service subscribers to this series. We reserve the right to refuse an application and applicants must be aged 18 years or over. Only one application per household. Terms and prices subject to change without notice. Offer expires 31st July 1998. You may be mailed with offers from other reputable companies as a result of this application. If you would prefer not to receive such offers, please tick box. ☐
Mills & Boon® Historical Romance™ is a registered trademark of Harlequin Mills & Boon Ltd.